Alex Toxic & Nadya Lee

The DARK Healer

Have a nice game!
Alex Toxic

Nadya Lee

Book One

Magic Dome Books

The Dark Healer
Book #1
Copyright © Alex Toxic, Nadya Lee 2024
Cover Art © Natalia Radaeva from DrakArt studio 2024
Cover designer: Vladimir Manyukhin
English translation copyright © Dan Veksler 2024
Published by Magic Dome Books, 2024
ISBN: 978-80-7693-760-4

This book is entirely a work of fiction.
Any correlation with real people or events is
coincidental.

Table of Contents:

Chapter 01

CONSCIOUSNESS CAME BACK GRADUALLY, pouring like a thin stream into my mind, numb from its long slumber. Thoughts began to lazily churn in my head, and I slowly realized my rest was over. First, my heart started beating. Slowly, and with long pauses, it pushed my thickened blood through my vessels. Then, my lungs took in air, and my skin came to feel a chill. I opened my eyes, and saw... Not a damn thing! Total darkness. That's what I get for lying down for a 50-year nap. Why was nobody here to greet me? Where were my servants and subjects? And what about all the relatives feigning joy at seeing me?

I had left detailed step-by-step instructions, describing what to do, and in what order, to make my awakening as smooth and comfortable as possible. There should have been dim light, incense burning, and a string quartet playing right now, not this complete darkness. I guessed 50 years without my supervision had reflected badly on the discipline and responsiveness of the leaders of my clan. I'd have to see to that right away. I thought of my late grandfather, who was a kind of jaded optimist, and in this situation would have said something like, "At least they remembered to wake you."

As I lay in the darkness, becoming accustomed again to my body and checking how well I could control my muscles, I was surprised to notice that all I could hear around me was silence, and something like the sound of water, as though there was a stream nearby. But where would that have come from? Did this mean nobody had woken me? But then why did I awake? I would have to get to the bottom of this on my own.

I pushed on the lid of the sarcophagus. Despite my precautions, my body had lost mobility and strength. I had to strain to use the modicum of magic powers I had left. Strangest of all, I found them unacceptably depleted. It was to restore them that I had laid down in the first place — that's routine practice for a necromancer. After a 50-year recharge, I should be brimming.

But at least I didn't feel the abomination either, which meant my calculations had been correct, and my organism had digested and dissolved the enormous amount of foreign energy I had absorbed. That was great news, and I was sure the

Book One

Council of Princes would be delighted to hear it. In fact, on second thought, maybe I shouldn't just give them this precious knowledge for nothing.

In any case: I, Max Richter, the head of the most powerful clan on the planet, had awoken from my long slumber, and was ready to once again assume the responsibilities of chairing the Council of Princes. I grinned, thinking about how many of my former opponents would be unhappy at my return. Especially the Acting Chair, whoever that was — Their Excellency would have to relinquish their cushy seat, already warmed by their behind, at once, to me.

The lid of the sarcophagus only moved a little on my first try, so I pushed it again. With a deafening crash, it fell on the marble floor of the crypt, and probably shattered. But what worried me much more was the smell of dampness and rot that immediately hit me. How long had it been since someone had cleaned down here? I jumped down onto the slippery, muddy floor. Then, I felt around for a torch on the wall, and lit it. Luckily, that simple kind of magic didn't require much strength. But what I was seeing far surpassed all of my worst fears.

Practically nothing was left of the crypt in which I had descended into my slumber. Mud was slurping under my feet, and turned into a real sloshy mess closer to the walls. A crack had appeared in the crypt, and an underground stream was now seeping into it. That was the sound I had initially taken for a burbling brook.

In addition to the moisture, my once royally

appointed crypt now looked more like an abandoned cellar, with moss growing on the walls and tattered old webs in the corners, as though even the spiders had long ago forsaken this place. The decor, too, had long ago rotted or disappeared. I saw none of the things I had so carefully prepared for my awakening.

The most disappointing thing was that the plinths with the artifacts were gone — these would have enabled me to almost instantly recharge my energy to an acceptable level. That had been my backup plan. I was certain something had gone wrong. Either I had been betrayed by my own clan, or someone had taken advantage of my absence.

I took the torch from the wall and approached the sarcophagus again. I wanted to examine the runes that had kept me in my magic slumber. But, my meticulously crafted spells, which I had chiseled there myself, had been destroyed and replaced by chaotic signs and sigils belonging to a magic of a totally different level. Its objectives, too, were fundamentally different. My spell merely maintained the body in good condition, blocking the exit of abomination energy; whereas this new spell sought to imprison me here forever, and, just the opposite — drain all my energy. Sadly, it had worked quite well. Though it did fail to account for numerous factors, which I caught analyzing it. Amateurs! In fact, it was these errors in the new spell that had catalyzed my awakening.

Putting two and two together, I concluded that the crack in the crypt had resulted from an earthquake or explosion, which also shifted the position of my sarcophagus, along with the signs of the sealing spell. Thus, the energy from the outside world began to seep inside, and brought me back to consciousness. The malefactors were not gifted enough to completely overwhelm the effect of my own ritual, so it had continued to protect my body from decomposition. Still, this was a pretty unpleasant way to wake up.

Again, from somewhere deep inside my consciousness, I heard the voice of my grandfather: "At least you woke up."

I chased the voice away. That wasn't doing it for me. The guilty must get what's coming to them.

Now, it was time to get out of here. But what if there was an ambush outside? The things that had already happened hardly belied a friendly attitude. Someone wanted me to sleep forever, and my awakening definitely didn't fit into their plans. No, this wasn't the time to charge into the unknown — I needed to investigate the situation first. Besides, despite all my experience and powers, I was horribly weak. Their spell had drained me almost completely. My strength would come back in time, but for now caution was most advisable.

I walked around the crypt, carefully taking in everything, and trying to figure out if anything that remained could be used, until I arrived at the crack and noticed something in the mud, near the streaming water. I bent down and saw that it was a dead lizard that had died not long ago. It had probably been carried here by the current, and drowned. Poor thing. It would now be of service to me.

"Awake, my shadow scout," I commanded quietly, running my finger along its scaly skin. I'm not sure I would have been able to revive something bigger, but I had enough energy for a small lizard. Soon, it began to move its legs and stood up on the palm of my hand, awaiting instructions.

Right away, I sent it up above to gather information. Meanwhile, I looked around some more, and also examined myself. Unfortunately, I didn't have a mirror down here to better see what changes had taken place with my body in these fif... in these years.

I now seriously doubted I had slept the planned fifty years. With regret, I noticed that my magic suit, which was supposed to be preserved in brand new condition, had completely lost its magic. I was now dressed in tattered rags, and in some places the cloth was completely gone. It definitely wouldn't do to show myself in polite society looking like this.

"At least your private parts are covered," I again heard the voice of my grandfather — the one who had given me my own congenital optimism. This time, I agreed with the voice: indeed, my underwear was where it should be. Unlike regular magic spells, artifact cloth doesn't lose its qualities with time. Had I known, I would have ordered the whole suit to be made out of it.

But these were all trifling inconveniences. All I had to do was reach the castle. There was a new wardrobe waiting for me there, artifacts containing energy, and answers to, if not all, most of my questions.

Book One

The little lizard returned, and I immediately received the thought-image it was sending. 'Hm, seems like the coast is clear up there,' I thought. 'Just three not particularly gifted types walking around nearby with shovels.' Maybe they were my people? Maybe they'd been sent by the clan to dig me up after the earthquake. Only one way to find out.

*   *   *

"I told you there was nothing here," a young mustachioed grave robber named Barney huffed in exasperation. "This cemetery has been abandoned for hundreds of years already. Everything valuable is long gone, stolen by someone else."

"Quit your whining," angrily answered John, a big guy with puffed nostrils, who looked like a bull. "You never have any ideas. When we were discussing this, you shoved your tongue up your ass and agreed to everything, and now you're unhappy?"

"Exactly," confirmed the third grave robber — a bald, thin guy named Fred. "It's like this every time. You couldn't dig up a potato in a potato garden without us."

But Barney was no longer listening to them, as his gaze was now fixed on an ancient, abandoned crypt, from which a tall, thin man in torn rags had just emerged.

"Fellas, look!" he whispered to them.

The grave robbers both turned to look, but then Barney grumbled, "Oh, it's nothing — just a drug addict. Probably doesn't even have anything to steal."

"Let's go see," said Fred. "There's nothing else to do around here, anyway."

But, to their surprise, the stranger started moving toward them himself.

John hawked an impressive loogie, and called out, "Hey fuckface, who are you?" The man did not answer. He was staring at them with curiosity, disgust, and even a little pity. That facial expression really pissed them off.

"Answer the question, shithead," Barney joined in.

"Watch your tongue, worm," the man in rags calmly answered. "You are speaking to Prince Richter, leader of the great Clan of Necromancers." Though he spoke calmly, a chill immediately ran up all three grave robbers' spines. This stranger spoke like someone who was used to being in charge.

Their immediate reaction was to apologize. But, because they had always been rebellious, and not too bright, they did not listen to their intuition. On the contrary, John strutted forward threateningly, like a rooster. "What the fuck are you talking about necromancers, you fuckin' psycho. What are you on, huh?"

The stranger willfully raised his hand, palm facing out. The grave robbers almost gave a collective gasp when they saw a golden skull ring on his finger, with fiery ruby eyes. If the gold and stones were real, that ring was worth a fortune! And this prick was definitely not its owner. Aristocrats and rich people didn't hang around in places like this, especially not looking like this guy did. He must have stolen it somewhere around here!

John shot a brief glance at his buddies. He saw the same greed shining feverishly in their eyes that he felt himself. Without thinking any further, he raised his shovel, and yelled, "Let's get him, boys!"

* * *

That was not the reaction I had expected when I showed them the ring. They were supposed to prostrate themselves and beg for forgiveness, but instead they attacked me, which is a strange, albeit surefire, way to kill yourself. Even in the state I'm in, dispatching a gaggle of talentless losers is a cakewalk. All I had to do was step aside to avoid the blow of the shovel, and at the same time touch my palm to the attacker to suck out some of his life force. He didn't have much energy — frankly, it was trash — but it was enough to pump some strength into my muscles, so that I was able to take out the next shovel-wielding idiot with one good punch in the face. I got some of his energy, too.

While the first one was coming to, and the other one stood there dumbfounded, I grabbed him by the shoulder with one sudden motion, and literally sucked out the rest of his life force. I had forgotten how easy it was with the ungifted.

At that moment, the first one who attacked me — the most aggressive one, and part of whose life force I had already taken, regained consciousness. He tried to flee in horror, but I couldn't have him escaping and blabbing all over the place: my enemies may find out I'm back, but not yet strong, and that was something I could not allow. I picked up the shovel, and threw it after him like a javelin.

The shovel lobbed his head off, spraying blood and brains all over the gravestones in a radius of several yards. This guy was definitely not coming back to work.

I looked back at the other two, and chose the bald one. He was dark-skinned enough to last longer once we got back to a public place. Besides, I had already learned his name, and new servants answer best to their old names. It's like they still retain some of their old reflexes or something.

My new servant, Fred, was now slowly and painstakingly collecting trophies. I was going to assume I was at war, and in war, any small thing could make a huge difference.

The grave robbers were either poor, or unlucky. Their clothing was awkward — jackets made from some hard material, and pants from crude cloth — the kind they used to make sacs and sails from in my time.

I chose the largest clothes. They were still a little short, but I wasn't going to have to wear them for long. At least I would attract less attention in these.

Before putting them on, I dosed them with necrotic energy. They had never been as clean as they were after that, not even in the hands of the tailor who had sewn them. But still, I felt a little squeamish putting them on. Oh well, *à la guerre, comme à la guerre.*

Book One

From one of their shoulder bags, my servant produced a rectangular object that had a glowing picture on one side, with buttons underneath it. I wanted to know what it was, so I ordered him to give it to me. No sooner had I touched this object, when something vibrated and the picture instantly went dark. At the same time, I felt an iota of abomination enter my body. It was so small, I processed it automatically.

Interesting. I had thought there was no more abomination in the world, but it turned out all kinds of lowlifes were carrying around sparks from it. I would have to get to the bottom of this later. But for now...

"Fred," I said to the zombie. "Gather everything useful in your rucksack and follow me."

* * *

Twenty-three-year-old Olga Richter — a gifted aristocrat, albeit of the lowest status — was coming back from another call. No one in the city who came across the attractive, long-legged, dark-haired woman in the business suit could imagine the torment she was going through. Those who were of higher breeding, and stronger, despised those like her, and called them leeches behind their backs. They didn't scruple from taking advantage of their services, however. This time, Viscount de Merteilles from the Clan of Daggers had fallen into a coma after taking too much grace — an energy drug that enhances the powers of aristocrats. The "honor" of going on the call fell to

Olga.

It so happened that the "leeches" were the only ones who possessed the gift of sucking away excess foreign energy. However, they don't have their own source, so they couldn't use that energy by just dissolving it in themselves. The price they pay for this is the horrific pain they experience when their gift is battling with the foreign energy they've absorbed. Olga knew that tonight she would have to get blackout drunk, or the torture could drive her insane.

It could have been worse, though. The leeches were relatively alright, whereas the "garbage men," who have to clean the grace from various kinds of waste, themselves waste away much faster. And then there are "cleansers" — they don't live long at all.

But this was of little comfort to Olga. A cursed gift is just that — a curse. Its only use was that at least it enabled her to support herself and be considered an aristocrat among the commoners. But only among them. She would never be the equal of the real gifted. Her body rejected grace, which was extremely painful.

Olga sighed and stopped near her house, which she had inherited from some distant ancestors. It looked more like a service building, made out of huge gray stones. But the location was convenient, almost in the center of the city. Plus, it was large and spacious. It contained an office and an apartment, and Olga jokingly called it a loft. 'If life hands you lemons, make lemonade...' What a load of crap.

Book One

Cringing, she walked past the sign hanging at the entrance, reading in large letters: "Cheap energy suck," and a little lower, "No sex." The printers had purposely made the word "energy" too small to be visible, so the sign would attract attention. But it only attracted the attention of assholes, so she had to add the second part.

Olga was glad that the clients' village wasn't far and she hadn't had to even use the car. She was also glad she had stocked up on alcohol in advance. She entered the house feeling relieved, turned on the light, and lithely slipped off her high-heeled shoes.

Lifting her eyes, she saw a man she didn't know sitting in the guest chair. What fresh hell was this? Could she have forgotten to lock the door? Olga involuntarily froze as she studied her uninvited guest.

His clothes were cheap and worn, but something about him was magnetic. It could have been his aristocratic mein and the confidence that showed in every glance and every gesture.

In her work, Olga had dealt with people of wealth and power, but few of them could have compared to this strange man. Finally, Olga overpowered her ambient shock, and opened her mouth to ask him who he was and what he was doing here. But, before she could speak, she was stumped again by the visitor, who asked her three questions, each more surprising than the last:

"Who are you? Why are you living in my stable?! Where is my castle?!!!"

Chapter 02

FROM THE BEGINNING, my conversation with the young lady was difficult. I had to hand it to her, though: she was no scaredy cat. Nine out of ten people in her position would have had a fit, or fainted. This one was angry, but not afraid.

"I'm Olga Richter, I live here," she stated, taking that same glowing object out of her pocket, that I'd seen at the cemetery. "Get out of here or I'll call the police!"

"Call them?" I asked in surprise. "I don't see a bell here."

"What bell?" She seemed confused. "Are you being sarcastic?"

"I'm being logical," I replied. "And it's that same logic that tells me you're lying. I remember the name of every single one of the two hundred and seventeen members of the Richter clan. The only Olga I know is three hundred and two years old. And, unlike you, she's blonde and 5'2 in heels."

Olga's face registered aggravation, which was quickly replaced by an idiot smile, as though she was speaking to a child. "Don't worry about a thing," she murmured sweetly. "I won't call the police. Do you maybe remember the phone number of your doctor?"

There was no doubt she took me for a psycho.

She was handling herself pretty well. Worthy of a Richter. Her hair was disheveled, and her chest was heaving. And her clothing... I wouldn't even go so far as to call what she was wearing a skirt. It was astounding that a relative of mine could go around looking like that. Although, perhaps, that was expected in this epoch?

"I'm not insane," I explained to her. "Just call one of the clan elders. I need to speak to them right away."

By this time, I had realized that the world had changed much more than I could ever have imagined. It was hard to miss! On the way from the cemetery, I had seen self-driving carriages, not a horse anywhere in sight, and street lights that didn't look like they ran on either oil or magic. And the architecture was now more ugly and primitive.

But, judging by her last name, this young lady was apparently my relative. If she wasn't a con woman, that is. There must have been someone left from the clan who still remembered me.

One thing I couldn't understand was why she kept digging around in her little glowing box instead of responding to what I had just said. I came closer and looked into the box, but I didn't have a chance to see anything before she pulled away, and quickly said, "Don't you understand, there's no such thing as a Richter clan. You're confused."

"Nonsense," I replied in an imperturbable tone. "The Richters are the most powerful clan on the planet. No matter how much time has passed, nothing could have happened to them."

But she didn't give up trying to convince me otherwise. "I'm the only one left with this last name," she patiently explained. "And I never even lived in this city. I inherited this house from some distant relatives, but..."

I was tired of listening to this. Besides, the time was long overdue to ask a key question. "Olga, what year is this?"

"What year? Two thousand twenty-four, obviously."

Strangely, my question had astonished her so much that she dropped her glowing box from her hand, and a second later, fainted. Just moments ago, she had not seemed so impressionable. What was she so upset about? She wasn't the one whose nap had been prolonged by ten centuries! A thousand years! Twenty times longer than I had intended to sleep.

I knelt down and touched her, and immediately realized what was wrong with her. An enormous amount of abomination was spilling into her energy channels, burning her up from inside. It

Book One

was only her innate necromancer's gift that kept the poison in check.

Which meant she had not been lying when she said she bore my name. I even felt a surge of pride for how well she handled herself while in excruciating pain. I knew very well what that was like.

When foci of abomination began to spread through our world, no one knew how to handle them properly. At first, people were even happy about them — they were sources of free energy. But it quickly became clear that the only free lunch is from the dumpster, and that it can not only upset your stomach, but land you in an early grave.

The foci of abomination appeared here and there, in town and country alike, without any rhyme or reason. They tore through crowded cities, as well as through the middle of nowhere. They spread like ulcers, changing everything in their path that was living. The abomination affected both animals and plants, making them mutate very rapidly. When it appeared, the whole area was unrecognizable within hours. It affected people, too: after coming into contact with the abomination, they were no longer quite human.

Left unchecked, the foci would start to spread. The abomination squeezed out all the natural magic energy in our world. The more new foci appeared, the more they engendered new ones — their growth was exponential. The very fabric of existence was worn, torn in places. It was as though a cancer was eating the planet away.

the Dark healer

Magicians threw themselves headlong into combat with this new threat. They were able to resist the abomination longer than the ungifted could, but the side-effects were even more horrible. Not only did their bodies mutate, but also their energy systems. Like drug addicts, they could no longer live without the foreign energy, and they completely lost their true magic gift.

The side effects from an overdose were truly awful. Pain, fever, hallucinations, and a coma. But the rejection was even worse: they just became regular people. We necromancers were the only ones who were immune to the abomination. It's weird, but the foreign energy didn't see us as being alive. We could absorb and digest it. However, when one was only beginning to develop that gift, it was extraordinarily painful.

With all my experience, however, it didn't even cause any discomfort, it just tickled a little. That's why I took it upon myself to eliminate the last large node of abomination — in the Siberian Taiga. In the space of some decades, it had spread for hundreds of miles and transformed everything in its path.

I had several adepts helping me. They were in charge of my battle chimeras, who held back the local creatures. Meanwhile, I sucked up the foreign energy, right from the air. This took several days, until the abomination was all gone.

After doing that, I decided to take my little vacation. I thought the abomination had been destroyed, and the planet was safe. Surely I could rest for fifty years or so.

Book One

In the intervening years, the most powerful magic clan on the planet had been destroyed, and its last descendant was taking shelter in my old stable. How could this have happened? Why was there so much abomination in the world? I was absolutely certain that I had destroyed its last focus before going into my slumber.

It didn't seem like the kind of thing I could get to the bottom of in one day. I would have to get my bearings first.

I sucked the abomination out of Olga, but it would still be another several hours before she regained consciousness. Her body had been exhausted by the barbaric ritual. When she came to, I'd have to give her a stern talking to, and explain how to shore up her energy system to avoid fainting in front of guests. For now, I ordered Fred to carry her to bed in the bedroom on the second floor. Then, I picked up the glowing box she had dropped. The same thing that had happened at the cemetery, happened again: as soon as I touched the box, it vibrated, went dark, and sent an iota of abomination energy into me.

So, things that ran off of this force were now no longer rare or prohibited. That was very irresponsible, in my opinion. The abomination affected everything living, and now, even outside the foci, it was impossible to hide from.

In fact, I had noticed many new things on my way to the castle. That is, to the place where my castle used to be. The last millennium had definitely left its mark, and I would now have to learn many things from scratch.

I slowly paced around my old stable, surprised at how much you could fit in there with the horses gone. My horses were big — I had refined each one myself. One of them had eight legs. It couldn't move them too fast, but it could carry the weight you'd normally need ten horses for.

As I passed one of the doors, I heard a voice. Weren't we here alone? When I had arrived, I hadn't felt any living presence, other than Olga's, and I still didn't now.

The door was open a crack. The little lizard emerged from inside my sleeve, and dove into the room. It came back out just as quickly. There was no danger. I entered.

No danger, but there was an unpleasant surprise waiting for me: on the wall, there was a large panel, from which none other than Katharine Villon was broadcasting. She was a real bitch, always trying to interfere with me on the Council of Princes. And she was a nobody! Her clan was the weakest of all the Council member clans. And not because they had no magic potential, but because they didn't have the brains to use it right.

It was a shame Katharine had survived all these centuries, and apparently, had not ceased cultivating the image of the young and horny redhead witch, blinking like a fool and sighing languidly. In my time, only complete morons fell for her act. I guess there were still just as many of them now as there ever had been, since she was still putting on her show for them, shoving her double-D cleavage in people's faces. It seemed the top button on her blouse was strained to the point of tearing off, and revealing what little was left hidden. Her tits really were amazing, though. They were the only good thing the head of the Villon clan had. So, they're what I concentrated on as I tried to understand how this panel worked.

Katharine Villon was moving and speaking as though she were alive, but it didn't look like a holographic projection like the kind we used to use to communicate at great distances. Was this yet another new technology? It didn't seem like its purpose was communication, or else why would she be speaking to an empty room?

Just in case she could hear me, though, I grinningly asked, "Did you miss me, Katharine?" But nothing indicated that she could hear me. This must just be a recording of her. And what she was saying was complete claptrap! From what I understood, she was talking about some miraculous skin cream that would help preserve the youth of even the ungifted. She was lying, naturally. She owed her attractive face, which had not changed a tiny bit in a thousand years, exclusively to her innate gift, not to the potions of some alchemist.

Could it be that the Villon clan had fallen to the status of common peddlers? I had not expected this even from Katharine.

Oh well, to hell with them. I had a theory to test.

I approached the panel, and touched it with my hand. As before, it vibrated and turned off. So I was right: the new technologies really were using abomination as their energy source. Fantastic.

the Dark healer

Without Richters, the world had clearly lost its mind. It was time for me to find it again.

*   *   *

A warm ray of sunshine awoke Olga, and she stretched sweetly in bed. The ray had penetrated her curtains, and was softly caressing her face. It had been ages since she had woken up in such a good mood! She had had an excellent sleep, and what was even more astounding, was that nothing hurt. It was a real miracle! Yesterday's call had been a terribly difficult one.

Olga got up from the bed, noting that she hadn't even taken her clothes off. What wondrous elixir had she gotten drunk on last night that she felt so good the next morning?

The young woman furrowed her brow, and the face of last night's visitor arose before her eyes. But she shook her head, and the vision disappeared. It must have been a dream. Although, the man was quite handsome... What absurdity. It must have been the alcohol. Although, she had never hallucinated from it before. Her friends had told her she shouldn't work so much. Now, she was dreaming about men!

Olga was doing everything she could to convince herself that nothing had happened, but she kept growing increasingly anxious. Especially after she inhaled and smelled burning. Had she forgotten to turn off the stove? Or...

The young woman quickly traversed the room, but did not find her smartphone in any of the places she usually left it.

Damnit. Can't call the police or the fire department.

Well, she wasn't about to sit around, hoping everything would work itself out, either. Olga decisively went downstairs, not knowing what she feared seeing more: that the house was on fire, or the psycho from last night.

Strangely, however, the first person she saw was not him at all, but an unknown stocky, bald man with the face of a gangster, who was pale as chalk. He was standing at the stove, wearing her favorite apron with striped cats, and making pancakes. Paying absolutely no attention to the mistress of the house, he layed out a batch onto a big plate, then, in one smooth motion, ladled some more wet dough onto the sizzling pan.

In the kitchen, it smelled much better than upstairs: not like burning, but like freshly baked pancakes. But this did little to calm her. Olga almost suffocated from outrage.

"Get the hell out of here before I call the police!" she screamed, angry as a dog at the thought of having to throw away her favorite apron. She wasn't putting that on after this guy had worn it! And washing it wouldn't help.

But the man acted as though he hadn't noticed her at all. And his movements were very strange, like a wooden doll. She thought to herself, he was almost like a living corpse. The thought frightened her. That couldn't be, could it? Stupid. It's one thing to read or watch a horror movie about zombies. But everyone knows that kind of magic doesn't really exist! And if it did, the dead would not be stealing aprons and making pancakes.

"For the last time, leave before I make you! This is my house, and I have the right to protect my property!" Olga threatened, taking another frying pan down from its hook on the wall. For some reason, she also grabbed a ladle.

She began slowly but confidently approaching the strange man, but he didn't react at all, which really got her goat. Olga clenched her teeth, ready to dispatch this brazen uninvited guest once and for all. He'd had his chance to leave peacefully, and now he was going to get what was coming to him! With these thoughts, she raised the frying pan over his head.

Just as she was about to strike the pale stranger, she heard a now familiar voice: "Olga, don't! You'll break him." Max was standing in the doorway between the kitchen and the living room. That was what he'd said his name was, wasn't it?

"Break him?" she asked, startled.

Next to the guy in the apron, with the pancakes, last night's guest looked not so frightening. "Fred won't feel any pain, but you'll definitely ruin his looks. Better let him finish the pancakes, then we can have breakfast together."

"Fred?" Olga lowered the frying pan and took a step back in surprise. "So this is your servant?" But she quickly recovered herself and got in the stranger's face again. "What the hell are you doing in my house? Get your asses out of here, both of you!"

ℬook One

Max sighed. "Let's call things what they are. You have no house at all, it seems to me. This is a stable. A service facility for horses. And putting furniture in here doesn't change that."

His calm demeanor made Olga fairly livid. "Don't you dare say that! It's none of your business anyway! Stable or house, it's mine and belongs to me!"

Max gestured with his hand for her to calm down. "Olga, please relax. I'm not trying to hurt your feelings. Sit down at the table, there's a lot we need to talk about."

Immediately after saying that, he walked over and comfortably positioned himself on a kitchen chair. His gaze showed complete confidence that she was about to join him.

Olga had not stopped being angry, but weirdly, there was something in his voice that had an absolutely hypnotic effect on her. And he really didn't seem like a crazy person, even if last night she had been sure that he had escaped from an insane asylum.

Olga gave in and sat down at the table. "What's wrong with that man?" she asked, as she watched Fred obliviously laying out pancakes on plates. "Is he deaf and dumb?" His movements still appeared wooden and unnatural, and he was completely unfazed by the spectacle she had put on with the frying pan.

"No," answered Max, "Why should he be deaf and dumb?"

"Why is he behaving that way? Why does he look like that?"

"Like what?" the guest asked, lifting one brow. It was clear that he wasn't being difficult, but sincerely didn't understand her questions.

"Like... a zombie," Olga answered, not too confidently.

"A wraith, not a zombie," Max corrected her. Then, he launched into a mini-lecture.

"You don't know the difference? Zombies happen from accidental energy spillage, or are created accidentally by clumsy apprentices. Also, sometimes, they're created as disposable material, to save time. All the processes in their bodies continue, so they quickly go bad. Wraiths are a lot more practical, even though they require more professionalism to raise."

Meanwhile, Fred approached the table with two plates, and put them in front of his master and Olga. Under a strong impression from what she had just heard, Olga stared at him in horror.

Max's pleased voice brought her out of her stupor: "Bon appétit, Olga." He smiled at her, and started scarfing down his breakfast.

"So he's dead?" she asked, still trying to wrap her mind around what he had just told her.

"I wouldn't let a living servant in the kitchen!" said Max haughtily. "They sweat, their skin flakes, their hair falls out. It's so unhygienic! The best chefs are well-made wraiths, believe me!"

"So he's... it's true?.. How is it possible?.. A zombie." Olga whispered to herself.

Max reluctantly put down his pancake, looked at her in surprise, and asked, "Wait, are you not aware that you're a necromancer?"

"UHH, NO!" Olga said, both surprised and frightened. "What do you mean, a necromancer?!"

"Wait a second," I said, still unclear. "Then what do you consider yourself? What is your gift?"

"I'm a healer," said Olga.

I looked at the wraith, then at the lizard, then back at Fred. She was right in a sense... But no, I couldn't accept the idea that we Richters had suddenly become healers. I began to laugh out loud. "You can't be serious, right?" I said.

Olga stared at me in dismay, so I explained, "The Villons are healers. They can do anything they want with a human body. But definitely not you. Where did you get that nonsense?"

The young woman was absolutely livid. She

was so upset, she all but forgot what she had just found out — that necromancers existed. Though she shouldn't have been so surprised, because just the sight of Fred was evidence enough.

It turned out her abilities were based around absorbing abomination energy. What we had once considered a side effect of our gift was now considered the only ability it offered. And no wonder it was popular! All that toxic otherworldly energy was spilling out from literally everything. It was amazing that they hadn't all croaked already from living in such an unhealthy atmosphere.

"So what do you do, specifically?" I asked. I still couldn't wrap my mind around how she could consider herself a healer. I needed to understand.

Olga widened her eyes and looked at me as though I were a space alien, then she grabbed a pancake and, with a concentrated look, bit off half of it. After a while, she finally spoke: "So you don't even know about the epidemic?"

"What epidemic?"

"The Telford Epidemic. It was named after the place where patient zero lived."

This meant absolutely nothing to me, but I waited patiently for Olga to eat a couple more pancakes. For whatever reason, this conversation was making her hungry. Maybe she was nervous. She was already looking greedily at my plate. Noticing this, I pushed the plate closer to her. Let her eat, since she's so hungry.

Olga gratefully ate one more pancake, then continued:

"Basically, an infection appeared suddenly

and immediately spread throughout the world. The point of origin was never found. The symptoms were pretty much the same for all infected: a weakened immune system, and early aging. The body basically rejecting itself, refusing to function normally."

As Olga spoke and ate more pancakes, I kept listening to her story about what our thick-headed descendants had turned the world into. They had even made their devices run on abomination! No wonder everything living was mutating and dying off. This was exactly why the Council of Princes had prohibited the use of abomination a thousand years ago, and all its foci had been ordered cleared and destroyed. There were many who still wanted to use the free energy, but no one could stand up to my power and authority. Now, it was painfully clear that I had been right. Unfortunately.

Olga continued, "Only we healers can handle the surplus energy from which both the ungifted and aristocrats suffer equally." She stopped talking, and looked down guiltily at the empty plate.

"Fred, make a couple more batches for her," I ordered. Then, I carefully looked Olga up and down. How could so much food fit in such a skinny girl?

"That's alright," she protested, embarrassed. "I'm full."

I nodded to show I understood, but did not cancel the order. "You need the energy. So what about the epidemic?"

"That's pretty much it. There is still only one treatment, but it's mostly healers with a very weak gift who work with the ungifted, because the work is thankless…" Olga stopped, slightly embarrassed. "In terms of money, I mean. The people are very grateful. That's why I also volunteer, and see patients at a free clinic near here."

"What about your main work?" I asked.

"Well, to be totally honest, I'm stronger than most. And I have my own business. I see aristocrats."

"And how's business?" I snickered sadly. It was a shame what my descendant was forced to be doing to survive.

"I can't complain," Olga answered proudly.

"So that's why you came home last night overflowing with abomination?"

"Abomination? I don't understand. I did come back from a call, though, on which I saved one of my clients from a grace overdose."

I facepalmed so hard, I almost broke my forehead. That's what it was called now? Grace?! "You can't polish a turd, no matter what you call it," I said, shaking my head in disgust.

By this time, Fred had made a few more pancakes, and he put these down on the table. I could see the physical torture Olga was experiencing as she stoically resisted the temptation to eat more of them. Finally, she gave in and decisively grabbed a pancake. Having eaten it, as if by way of an apology, she explained, "It's been a hundred years since I've had a home-cooked meal, especially baked goods. It's so good." Then, she suddenly addressed the wraith: "Thank you, Fred."

"Unfortunately, he can't understand you," I

shook my head. "Right now he is only capable of following my orders."

"Oh, that's too bad," said Olga. "I'm... not used to this kind of thing," she added.

"That's alright, you'll learn fast," I reassured her. "By the way, if I put some more energy into Fred, he can become a lot more interesting than he is now." I kept the details of what I meant to myself for now, but any creature that's been brought back from the dead is primitive at first — on a kind of level one. The energy I had sucked out of Olga last night would be enough to raise Fred to a level two. Otherwise, he wouldn't have been able to even lift a frying pan. A level ten wraith can play the piano from memory, without even looking at sheet music. But for now, there was no reason to overwhelm her with these things. If I was going to teach Olga necromancy, I would have to start from the beginning.

But first, I needed to solve my own problems. My main weakness at this point was lack of energy. To pump my organism full of it by natural means, I would need to rest for another fifty years, which was clearly out of the question. The only other option was to absorb and digest abomination. This option was unpleasant, but much faster.

Suddenly, I had an epiphany. "Olga," I asked, "are you going to treat anybody today?"

"Of course not," she shot back immediately. "I have to rest after yesterday's procedures."

Weird. Had I not finished treating her? "Do you feel tired or sick?" I asked.

She stopped moving and stared into space for

a minute. Then she said, "Actually, just the opposite. I haven't felt better than I do right now in a long time. It's just that I always rest after calls..."

She furrowed her brow, and even bit her lip. I could tell by her face she was thinking hard. Then, she unexpectedly asked: "Did you treat me?!"

There was no point in hiding that I had, so I nodded. "Yes, I did," I said. "See, I, too, am, in a sense, a healer," I added, struggling to keep a straight face. "I've got a business proposition for you: you treat the addicts when they OD, and I'll treat you."

"For a percentage?" Olga asked immediately. Her gaze became contemplative, like she was turning the idea over in her mind.

"Yeah, for a percentage," I didn't argue. I didn't think she would understand if I just told her I needed the energy and that I was prepared to do this for free. She was liable to get scared and think I was nuts again.

"How much do you want?" she asked, squinting at me suspiciously.

"Seventy should do for now," I named an astronomical percentage and smiled wryly.

"Wow, that's a lot. What do you mean by 'for now'?"

"Think how many clients you'll be able to see if you don't have to take a day or two off after each one."

"That's true, but..." she gave her head a shake and started haggling like a regular street merchant. "I have a name, a reputation, and a brand. It's taken me years to grow my client base. They don't let just anyone treat aristocrats, you know. These are all valuable assets. I'll pay you 40%, but I can't go higher than that."

I found it amusing that when she had gone into negotiation mode, she also switched to business voice, like she was talking to a business partner. I guffawed. "You don't prize your organism very highly, do you? You realize it suffers damage from incorrect usage, yes?"

"What makes my usage incorrect?"

"I'll explain later," I dismissed her question. "The main point here is that no one else is going to offer you a deal like this."

"First, I would have to verify that you really are such a brilliant healer," Olga huffed. "Maybe it was just a coincidence that I felt so much better suddenly. I have to check at least one more time to be sure. And fine, I'll pay 45% for that test — if all goes as discussed, that is. Furthermore, I would like a notarized contract."

"Take it easy. One thing we definitely don't need is extra paperwork. I trust you, and you most likely won't want me to give my gift to another healer. You don't want me to get poached, now, do you?" I snickered. "To avoid that happening, let's settle at 50%."

Olga was haggling so hard, that I got some sadistic pleasure out of goading her further. I was growing more and more certain that she was my direct descendant. The Richters had always been famous for their neatness, precision, and fairness, and they never neglected to look after their own profits.

I guess what I had said had resonated with her, so she nodded in agreement. "Fifty then."

"And we'll go on a call tonight," I added.

"Wait, I'm totally confused. You seriously claim to have the same last name as me?"

"Would I jest about such things?"

"But..." she searched her mind for something to say in protest. "I don't even know what to call you."

"Your Grace, naturally. Don't they teach the youth anything these days?"

Olga looked at me skeptically. Outwardly, I looked like I was the same age as her, maybe a little older at most — twenty-five or twenty-seven. It wasn't registering with her that I had almost a millennium and a half on her. Before descending into my crypt, I had lived four hundred extremely eventful years. They were full of studies, research, and clan wars. Necromancers don't age, they look the age at which they feel most comfortable.

As for the 'Your Grace' part, I was joking, of course. I can't stand formality — it's usually a smokescreen for cowardice or treachery. I thoroughly enjoyed teasing my overly serious and assertive great-great-great-great... granddaughter.

"You don't think that'll sound too formal on patient calls?" Olga asked tactfully.

"I guess you're not into 'Grampa' either?"

Olga snorted, almost choking on a pancake. Then she said, "Actually, the idea of you being my relative is not bad. We have to explain who you are somehow."

"Alright, you can call me Uncle Max," I said.

"Shall we go then?"

"It's not that simple,..Max," she stuttered a little. "I have to arrange everything first. Which reminds me, have you seen my smartphone?"

I wasn't exactly in a rush to admit I had no idea what she was talking about, so I just shook my head no.

"Where could it be?" Olga wondered out loud, as she got up from the table. She started walking around the kitchen, carefully looking in every corner. Then, she saw that glowing box I had been examining the night before, on a small table. "Here it is!" she exclaimed happily, grabbing the box. Then, after pressing some buttons, she furrowed her brow. "That's weird," she said, "for some reason it won't turn on. Did the battery die again? I'll go get the charger from upstairs."

But, just as she was about to take her first step toward the bedroom, my lizard ran past her feet, which made her gasp and jump sideways. My shadow scout, as I had christened it, had risen to level two and could now patrol the area I had attached it to on its own, without need for commands from me. It had returned now to report the information it had gathered.

Once I received the thought-image from my little servant, I asked Olga, "Are you expecting someone?"

"No, but sometimes I get walk-ins. Why?"

"There are three men walking toward here right now."

"How do you..."

She didn't have a chance to finish her

question, as the doorbell rang. Olga gave me an even more suspicious look than before, but didn't ask me any questions. She only made one request: "Please stay in the kitchen. I'll open the door and talk to them. It's my house."

"No problem," I shrugged. I wasn't the least bit interested in boring conversations with clients, neighbors, visitors — whomever. Besides, my lizard could always watch them in case anything interesting happened.

And it did. No sooner had the guests said hello, than one of them announced in a grating and officious tone: "Olga Richter, we have an order for your eviction. You have one week to vacate the premises. The building will then be torn down."

* * *

Viscount Hugo Velasco loved his job almost as much as he hated brazen and ill-mannered young women. This category included everyone who had dared not to be fascinated by Hugo, and not to appreciate his subtle sense of humor, his intellect, and his status.

The Velascos were an ancient and renowned clan, and the fact that Hugo belonged to its most junior branch did nothing to dampen his inflamed sense of self-worth. His gift may not have been as strong as that of others. He may not have gone down the path of the "militants," who in turn considered him a boring pencil pusher. Even the way he looked — short, and always dressed to the nines — made them mock him. They hadn't the slightest idea of the power concentrated in the hands of this humble real estate inspector: the power to humiliate people. Every day. With impunity. He even got paid for it!

Most of his victims were from among the ungifted, but sometimes poor aristocrats who weren't able to pay their mortgage to the Velasco clan also fell prey to him. These were Hugo's favorite moments of all. Nobles would prostrate themselves before him, kiss his hands, and promise everything under the sun if only he would let them keep the roof over their heads. The very same young women who had yesterday turned up their noses at the sight of Hugo were now smiling seductively at him like hookers on a street corner. He disposed of people's lives — it was his to execute, or to pardon.

Hugo could have sent subordinate commoners to deliver the eviction notices, but he never missed an opportunity to deliver one himself. And now, the stars had aligned for Hugo. His spotlight moment had arrived. An eviction order for Olga Richter had appeared in the database.

Hugo knew this haughty, over-proud leech. He had once met her at a party at Baron Singer's house. He had offered her the honor of drinking a toast with him. So what if he was drunk at the time, and trying to grab her elbow? So what if she had gracefully laughed it off and walked away? Hugo was no fool, and he could tell when someone didn't respect him enough.

What a stupid tradition it was to consider leeches equal to aristocrats! But no matter, Hugo would put that scum in her place. He had even dressed up especially for the visit, and used his special occasion perfume. Why send a courier when that would mean you missed out on the sweet pleasure of watching the haughty Richter turned pathetic, writhing on the floor, begging him not to take away her house. As for how he would respond to her pleas, this he had not planned. It all depended on whether he liked the fear and obsequiousness he saw in Olga's eyes. And if the haughty bitch decided to resist, then she would be screwing herself over.

* * *

Olga stared at her visitors in befuddlement. One of them was an extremely smartly dressed aristocrat who looked vaguely familiar. He was wearing stylish, immaculately polished shoes and a starched suit, and his meaty fingers were decorated with precious rings.

He was accompanied by two others — apparently, bodyguards. They were frighteningly serious and gruff looking gentlemen. Real meatheads. They were also wearing suits, but these fit them very strangely: it seemed as though the jackets were about to burst on their puffed up muscular shoulders.

"You must have made some mistake," Olga answered the dandy. "I always pay my mortgage on time. I've never been late once. And I'm not the one who mortgaged the house, it was the previous owners."

"There's no mistake," the uninvited visitor gave a bitchy smile. "It no longer matters whether you pay or not."

"What does that mean?" Olga asked. "I'm absolutely solvent. This is illegal." She straightened herself up proudly. "And anyway, let me see your identification."

"Identification?!" the dandy demanded, taken aback. "Don't you recognize me? I am Hugo Velasco. What other identification do you need?" He concocted such an insulted facial expression, that Olga almost felt a little bad for not remembering him.

But that feeling quickly passed. "Yes, identification," she shot back. "And the eviction order, please." She stretched out her hand, but Hugo only became even more outraged than before.

"Don't you appreciate your position? The land you live on belongs to the Velasco clan!" he spat out, along with quite a lot of flying saliva. "I don't give a damn if you make your payments! No one will allow you to finish paying off your debt. You will have to move out immediately, and this ugly shack of yours will be torn down without delay."

It took Olga a moment to come up with a response as she stared at the guest in astonishment, and the thought shot through her head that maybe she'd had more than enough psychos visit her at home in the last twenty-four hours.

In fact, here came the first of them now. Olga heard steps behind her, and turning, she saw Max, who had walked out of the kitchen with a truly royal gait. He held a plate in his left hand, and a single fresh pancake in his right. Pointing it accusingly at Hugo, he pronounced, "How dare you call my stable a shack?!"

Chapter 04

THIS WAS INTERESTING! Since when did every manner of bottom-feeding bureaucrat have the right to trespass on the property of an ancient clan and wave silly papers around? In my time, aristocrats and commoners lived according to different codes of law from each other. The authorities, too, were different. For example, a mayor or governor could only get into the palace of a clan chieftain if they had an appointment, and they could only get an appointment if their presence was desired. Now, the gifted had degenerated to mere bureaucrats, the aristocracy had disintegrated. I couldn't believe what I was hearing, so I had to go see this spectacle for myself.

Naturally, my appearance immediately

shifted all the attention to me. Hugo even curtailed his tantrum in surprise. "Who the hell are you?" he spat out, involuntarily clenching his fists. He was really far too excitable for his job.

Olga threw me a pleading look. You didn't have to be a telepath to see that she still wanted me not to get involved. She had hoped to de-escalate the situation and solve the problem peacefully. "This is my relative, Uncle Max from Winfall. He's got nothing to do with this, he was just leaving. Isn't that right, uncle?"

She looked at me pleadingly again, hoping I would take her hint and go back to the kitchen. I took the hint, but I wasn't in a hurry to act on it. My life experience, of which I had several centuries more than Olga did, told me there was no peaceful way out of this interaction with Hugo Velasco. It wasn't for nothing that this aristocratic little brat had brought two cleaver-faced cutthroats with him to help. The visitors were very confident in their own strength. They were ungifted, too. But, judging by a typical tension in certain muscle groups, they were armed, and ready to use their weapons. It pays to know your anatomy. I wondered what they were packing. You couldn't even conceal an average dagger under coats like theirs.

"I'm staying," I said. "As for our uninvited guests, it would be better for them to leave."

Hugo was taken aback again, but quickly came back to himself and snidely slithered, "Is your uncle alright? Maybe you'd better explain to him who I am. I will not tolerate this disrespect!"

I sighed and took a step forward. "Disrespect?

$\mathcal{B}$ o o k $\mathcal{O}$ n e

No self-respecting nobleman would ever dream of appearing in the presence of another without an appointment."

"I am in the line of duty!" he shrieked, aggravated.

"All the more so then," I pressed on. "We could have been out." I couldn't believe I had to explain such simple things, as if he were a child. I continued, "And now, your surprise visit has interrupted our breakfast and ruined our good mood. I hope you will now have the decency to apologize and make yourself scarce. If you do that, I'll consider letting all three of you live."

Anticipating the catastrophe that was about to ensue, Olga shut her eyes tight. And she was right: the explosion followed immediately. The unhinged Velasco lit up like a match, and almost screamed, "That does it, Richter! Now you're in deep trouble. Your uncle has dared to threaten an official in the line of duty!"

It was fascinating, I couldn't stop staring at this little fool. It had been a long time since I'd seen such a naked display of emotion. Even the three grave robbers at the cemetery had carried themselves with more dignity than this hysterical little richie-rich, thinking he was being intimidating when really he was unable to even contain the spit in his own mouth.

"You'll not only lose your house, you'll go to jail, too!" he kept raging.

In all epochs, the youth has always been more interested in entertainment than in learning, but his ignorance was shocking. I was going to have to enlighten him.

"That won't stand up in any court," I said. "According to the edict published in 1106, an aristocrat has every right to defend themselves on their own land, including killing the trespasser."

Olga had recovered from her initial shock at my intervening. Now, she was looking not at Hugo, but at me, eyes wide open. Whereas before her gaze had been pleading with me to stop talking, now it belied hope. It seemed she had accepted what was happening, and decided to entrust the negotiations to me. The only thing she said in the end was to ask if that law really existed.

"Of course it does," I said, "I wrote it myself."

My descendant's education, too, left something to be desired. Of course, it was possible the law had changed in the intervening thousand years, but I bet a hundred to one that no one had bothered to cancel it. Knowing how the machinery of the state worked, and how aristocrats hang on to their privileges for dear life, the chance that I was wrong was so negligible that it wasn't even worth considering.

Meanwhile, Hugo had completely lost his composure. He cackled hysterically, then let loose another rasher of his ignorance. "You? Aristocrats?! Don't you mean lowlife leeches? You being considered noble is just a misunderstanding. A bone thrown to the dogs for your faithful service to us, the true gifted. As a member of the Velasco clan..."

I was sick of listening to him. It was clear he didn't have the brains to leave while he still could, and his idiot wind was more than I was willing to endure. But killing him right then and there would also have been impolite toward Olga. As I understood, she was the rightful owner of the premises, which meant she would have to deal with all the inevitable formalities — the police and the court. Besides, what if I killed him and she got upset, saying she didn't want him dead? Women are compassionate like that. They're often willing to give someone, even an asshole like Hugo, a second chance, in hopes that the situation would improve. I hoped she wasn't one of those. In any case, these issues are easy enough to resolve.

"Olga," I asked my descendant in a socialite's tone of voice, "do you know why the Velascos never get invited to houses of repute?"

"Why?" Olga asked, confused.

"Because they stink so much of manure, that they say the smell is passed down from one generation to the next," I explained calmly, not even looking at Hugo. "The founder of the Velasco clan worked for over two hundred years, tending horses for old man Armand Salazar. He was given his noble title as a reward for his service. But the stench has remained..."

Not everyone can accept the truth with dignity. Hugo could not. Hearing what I said, he turned crimson. "You!" He attempted to say something to me, but couldn't finish, so he turned to Olga. "What are you just standing there for, dummy?! Where did you find this clown?! Oh, it doesn't matter. I won't stand for this!" Then, once again interrupting his own fit, he turned back to me, and shot up his hands. Toxic-green sparks flew in all directions from the tips of his fingers, as he began to yell again, "No one insults the Velasco clan and gets away with it!"

I had immediately guessed the spell he had used against me. It was a light version of acid rain. I realized that even for a Velasco, he didn't have much by way of serious powers. But I could not allow him to ruin the atmosphere in my descendant's house, or worse, harm her.

Luckily, Olga immediately knew to hide behind the big armchair — she made it in the nick of time. With a revolting hiss, several drops of acid fell on the floor where she had just been standing, and burned a hole in the hardwood. I, too, had swerved away just in time. I was glad to discover my old battle instincts were still with me.

Just when Hugo was about to release a new acid attack, I lunged toward him, covering the distance in one bounding leap, and put my fingers to his neck. The abomination started to pump from his body into my energy channels.

The two cutthroats had not interfered in any of the proceedings until now, but at this point, they became alert. They exchanged glances and reached inside their lapels. 'Let's see what they've got in there,' I thought. I wasn't too worried about them, as the ungifted were not much of a threat to me, even if they were armed with a two-handed flamberge.

I grabbed Hugo harder, waiting for the energy to drain out of his body. The plan was to make him unable to resist anymore, and that's when we would have a real heart-to-heart. No yelling, no tantrums — because he would no longer have the energy for them. Then I would calmly question him about the lawfulness of his claim to my property. Or Olga's, which is the same thing — it was clan property, and I was the clan's chieftain.

At first, Velasco had resisted, but now, he went limp in my arms. I had to hold him up so he wouldn't fall on the floor. At the same time, I positioned myself in such a way that his ne'er-do-well bodyguards couldn't attack me without risking hurting their boss too. But when the last bits of abomination left Hugo's body, I suddenly realized something had gone wrong. As a necromancer, I knew it right away. Hugo died in my arms.

But why? All I had wanted to do was drain him of strength, I hadn't done anything more than what was necessary.

I would have to deal with this later. His entourage were being overly excitable, and I was concerned they may damage something valuable. By now, they had both produced some strange type of weapon that was completely unknown to me. It looked like a black boomerang, but much more complex, and apparently, metal. They lifted their arms and pointed one end of these weapons at me.

Just in case, I ducked. And I was right to do so: I heard two loud blasts, and something small, but very fast, whizzed by over my head. I couldn't wait to look into how these weapons worked when I got a chance.

I lunged toward one of them and packed the impact with some of my energy. That was enough to knock the ungifted guy backward two yards, and he would have kept flying if he hadn't been stopped by the wall he crashed into. One down.

But the second one...

Bam! Bam!!! Bam!!!!!!

The sound of the weapon was expressing the panic of the shooter. Why were these people all so loud and unreserved? What, they'd never seen a wraith before? I ordered Fred to attack the hoodlum.

And he, well... A level two wraith is not exactly the fastest and wiliest warrior out there, so I watched the surviving bodyguard launch several small projectiles into Fred from his 'boomerang.' He was extremely surprised when Fred had not the slightest reaction to this. I didn't even think of intervening — how often do you get the chance to see modern technology being used in conditions approaching battle?

Why only "approaching"? Because it's a battle when the opponent has at least the smallest chance of surviving; whereas this was decidedly just an exercise. While the slab of meat was trying to come to his senses, Fred took aim and launched a wrought iron skillet right at the poor guy's head. The next moment, the last of our enemies was dead.

I examined the scene of the battle. It wasn't exactly the outcome I had expected. Then again, you can never have too many servants. Olga got up from behind the armchair, and for some reason, whispered, "Are they alive?"

There was so much hope in her voice, that I

hated to disappoint her. "Alas," I shook my head. "But don't you worry about it, Fred will tidy up."

"You mean," Olga inquired, stupefied, "you want to get rid of the bodies?"

What a question! For the life of me, I couldn't get used to the fact that she hadn't studied necromancy.

"Who would I throw away valuable resources like that?" I said. "We'll simply put them in the cellar."

"The… cellar? There's no cellar here."

"So you don't even know about that? And you call yourself a homeowner? I guess we know who really owns this place."

Olga was in a huff, and momentarily even forgot about the three corpses lying there. "That's not proven yet. Show me first."

"Naturally," I smiled and walked toward what was now a veranda in the backyard of this stablehouse. Olga followed behind me, as did Fred, with Hugo's body slung over his shoulder.

When we got to the spot, I was sorry to say we would have to remove a few floorboards. Olga objected, "What if whatever was down there is long gone? I can't afford a renovation."

"Seems to me, that's the least of your worries right now," I noted, nodding toward the corpse. All further protest was nipped in the bud. She fetched a crowbar and some other tools from the closet. Then, Fred lay Hugo down to one side, and went to work on the floorboards.

I went back to the vestibule and shot an iota of my own energy into the other two corpses to stop them from decomposing. Also, I very much wanted to examine the weapons they had been firing from. I pried one from one of the cutthroats' dead fingers and studied it. From a distance, I hadn't seen how many small parts they had. Now that I held one in my hand, I was actually awed by the simplicity and elegance of the thing. It seemed the little lever on one of its parts launched a mechanism that shot a projectile from the long part. But what was it that created the pressure to push the projectile out with such force? It definitely wasn't magic.

Olga came into the room, and it was obvious she wasn't exactly comfortable in a room full of corpses, even if one of them was moving around and working.

"What is this?" I asked her about the weapon I was holding.

"Do you really not know? It's a handgun."

"How does it work?"

"You pull the trigger, and a bullet flies out," Olga answered, a little embarrassed.

This answer was not exactly comprehensive, I would have to study the subject in more detail later. Maybe seek out a specialist. The owners of the weapons were no longer in a position to explain them — after all, I'm a necromancer, not a medium.

"Let's go back," I said to her. "Fred must be done by now." She nodded and we went back to the veranda.

I kept going over the recent battle in my mind, and I was decidedly not happy about how it had gone down. I was horribly weak! I only had maybe one percent of my former power. That was enough to deal with these losers here, but, truth be told, I was currently at approximately the same level as pathetic old Hugo. I had slept too long, and the energy channels in my body could barely function — they were much worse at responding to the energy being transferred along them, and the volume of that energy was catastrophically low. I was used to operating with accumulations of magic energy that were orders of magnitude bigger, and now I felt like a parched traveler in the desert.

And, in this desert, there would be no oasis — more likely, a puddle of mercury.

As much as I hated to admit it, the only way I could restore my energy with relative haste right now was by taking in abomination. I couldn't lie in a coffin for another fifty years again, while the world hurled itself into the abyss. And, besides the world, there was...

I looked pensively at Olga. Was she really the very last Richter? How had my enemies been able to accomplish this? They had destroyed my descendants, and erased all memory of my clan, and of me, from history. Even my distant great-granddaughter — who knows how many generations away — had no idea of the rich heritage of her clan, and had never heard of Max Richter.

But I knew who she was! I knew who we were. And I was going to do everything in my power to make sure no one ever forgot it again. No one had the right to speak to members of my clan the way that puny bureaucrat had spoken to her. That was *his* last tantrum. But I still could not understand what had happened when I had taken all the abomination out of him. That shouldn't have killed him under any circumstances. If he was using abomination as magic power, which would have been an extremely rash and stupid thing for him to do, it should have made him weak, but no more than that. If only... Well, I would get to the bottom of this right now.

By now, Fred had removed all the necessary floorboards. When Olga saw the secret hatch under them, she gasped. Then, she looked at me admiringly. It appeared the last of her doubts had just been put to rest. I, in turn, was gratified to find that the magic lock spell I had left here a millennium ago had been preserved very well. This meant that no one had looted my cellar. Shame that there was nothing of value down there, but at least there was a small backup lab, which is where Fred was taking Hugo now.

I opened the lock, and jumped down the hatch first, raising clouds of dust. The cellar had kept much better than my crypt had. I was especially delighted to find that it was dry down here. Dust was OK — the wraith would have that cleaned up in no time.

I lit the torches by the entrance and waited as Olga and Fred descended.

The young lady gasped again. "There are several rooms down here?"

"As you see."

The first chamber of the cellar was a perfectly round room with three doors leading in different directions. The spiral staircase we had come down was right in the center. I walked over to one of the doors, and opened it, causing another upheaval of dust. There was so much of it here that it had made Olga cough — it was already causing more harm than Hugo ever did.

In the new room, there was a lot of magical lighting. These were not torches, but bright lamps. Actually, they needed to be charged a bit. I was loath to part with even the smallest amount of energy, but this was necessary.

There was also plumbing in the small laboratory, with water coming from a nearby stream. So, when Fred laid the dead viscount on the operating table, I gave him a new assignment: the wraith obediently headed upstairs to get rags and a bucket.

I walked around the room, examining the shelves. Almost everything that had been kept down here had rotted away. Gauze, instruments... even things that were kept in glass. Uncorking a few vials and sniffing the contents, I knew that none of the wealth of supplies down here was usable anymore. Which was a shame: the shelves contained many different ointments, potions, and elixirs. The poisons could still be usable, I supposed, but even those would probably no longer be as lethal after a thousand years.

Fred returned, and set about cleaning my work area. Despite the position I had found myself in, I had no desire to renounce my former habits. I like order and consistency, especially when it comes to a delicate matter like an autopsy. I'm not a butcher, I am accustomed to sterility and care.

When Fred finished cleaning, I began.

Olga hadn't said a word this entire time. She just watched me carefully and tried to process everything that had just happened. But now, when Fred removed Hugo's clothing and exposed his torso as I had ordered him to do, she couldn't contain herself anymore. "What are you going to do?" she asked.

"I'm going to take a look at what's inside him."

"I doubt his insides are different from anyone else's," Olga said, barely suppressing a nervous laugh.

"That's what we're going to find out."

Luckily, she didn't faint. Oh right, she's a healer, I remembered, or at least considers herself one.

I sent an energy stream to my hands, and created a simple little spell. A thin, non-material, but nevertheless visible, dark blade materialized at my fingertips. In a precise, measured motion, I drew it down Hugo's chest. Olga, who was watching intently, gasped again.

"That was so..." she didn't know what to say.

"...clean?" I offered.

"Yes, exactly. I've been present at many autopsies. I don't just have a diploma in magic medicine, but also in regular medicine," she explained. "But I've never seen someone perform it so ideally, without spilling even a drop of blood. And your spell — I've never seen something like that before, either."

"The spell is partly the reason it's so clean," I

explained to my granddaughter. "There's no physical tool that can compare in thinness to a shadow scalpel. Plus, it immediately seals the incised vessels and capillaries. This is one of the basic spells that every self-respecting necromancer must learn. All my experience helps, too, though."

"You mean," she pressed her fists to her chest in excitement, "I could do that, too?" Now she was beginning to see the light.

"Not only could, but will," I assured her. "If you want to, that is."

After our mini-lesson was over, I concentrated on my work, making small, careful incisions here and there, until I finally discovered what I had been looking for; what I had feared finding.

I turned my scalpel into tweezers, and carefully extracted a small, white, very hazy crystal, right from Hugo's chest. There could be no mistake: these were the very crystals I had mined from monster foci in the distant past. Could this mean the corpse before me was no longer human? A mutant like those whose lives run exclusively on abomination energy. That was why he had died as soon as I had sucked all the abomination out of him.

I made a few more careful incisions to make absolutely sure. Indeed, the body before me was not that of a man, but a monster in human form. Oh world, what had you turned into while I slept?!

Chapter 05

OLGA OBSERVED THE AUTOPSY intently, and what I had extracted from the dead viscount was not lost on her. Her reaction surprised me: "Holy crap, that's a grace stone!" she exclaimed. "Where did it come from?!"

"It formed from the abomination inside him," I explained. "That same energy you suck out of aristocrats. When it builds up, it concentrates into this gemstone. It's kind of like a magic source, only it's foreign and hostile to the normal human body. Why are you so surprised to see it?"

"That thing is worth a ton of money!" Olga reported.

"A whole ton?" I asked skeptically.

"About a month's wages for me," she

estimated. "That's on the black market, of course. If you go the legal route, it's like twenty percent of the price, which is still a lot of money."

I stared at Hugo pensively, and automatically calculated in my mind how much profit could be made from destroying the weak gifted. If each one of them is carrying around a crystal like this one inside them, then killing one a day would be more than enough, and then…"

I didn't have a chance to finish my thought, because my granddaughter had noticed something in my gaze that gave her a start and her face changed.

"Don't do it, uncle Max!" she pleaded.

"Don't do what?"

"Whatever you were just thinking of doing, don't do it."

Boy, these modern people were real shrinking violets! I wasn't about to stage an aristocrat genocide, I was just day-dreaming!

When I was young, I was acquainted with one Count Raskolnikov. He was a very daring and brave man. He hunted witches, armed only with an ax. Those were difficult times — poverty, drought… They only paid twenty silver pieces per old woman, so he would have to get a lot of them. "Five witches are worth a gold piece," he would mutter as he sharpened his ax. He always carried it with him just in case it came in handy. Anyway…

Finished with Hugo, I needed to see to something else. Luckily, there were several long tables in the lab, so I didn't have to jostle the corpses to and fro. I ordered Fred to take off his coat and lie down in the vacant spot.

"What's wrong with *him*?" inquired Olga. She really did have something of the healer in her — tons of curiosity, and no squeamishness at all. We necromancers did work with people, and made them feel better. For the first time, I thought maybe this new title of 'healer' suited us after all.

"Gotta take out the projectiles," I explained, carefully examining his torso.

The weapon he had been shot with had left very neat and precise little holes — not at all like the arrows and crossbow bolts I was used to. Those usually tore up the flesh so badly, a weak necromancer or healer would most likely not be able to patch up the victim without scarring.

"Bullets," Olga reminded me. "They're called bullets."

I grabbed one with my shadow tweezers and pulled it out. It was a small metal thingy, and it radiated abomination energy. I was getting used to that by now. I still couldn't understand how this tiny thing had such a charge in it. Fred was no longer living, so, as far as he was concerned, it was just a hunk of metal that had slightly damaged his already dead flesh. But, if a thing like this hit a living human being, survival would not be likely.

I pulled several more bullets out of his body, and cleaned the abomination out of the wounds. In my position, I could use any energy I could get.

"Max," Olga had chosen this moment for a pointed question, "who are you, really?"

"Founder and chief of our clan, naturally," I

answered without pause. "Haven't you figured it out yet?"

"I... Yes, but I don't understand. Where have you been all this time? What happened to our clan? Why..."

These were things that needed to be explained clearly and logically, and I didn't want to start answering a barrage of haphazard questions, so I gestured for her to stop. Besides, I would have a chance to tell her what I knew of the history of our clan later, along with all the other things about our gift and our capabilities that I needed to tell her. But first thing's first. I gave her a brief summary of the truth.

I told her that I had once defeated all the abomination in the world, after which I had to conduct a convalescence ritual that was supposed to last fifty years, but ended up lasting ten centuries. And, of course, I told her that on the day I descended into my magic slumber, we Richters were the most powerful clan in the world, and no one dared challenge us.

"So you see, Olga, I don't know everything," I concluded. "What has happened in the last thousand years is a mystery that I will now seek to solve."

As I spoke, my descendant's facial expression displayed a constantly shifting tableau of emotions. It seemed she was having a hard time believing a lot of what I was telling her. I wasn't surprised when she launched into asking whether I had really slept for a thousand years, and whether our clan had really been so powerful, and whether she would really be able to learn necromancy, and a lot of other things. She had thousands of questions, and I tried to patiently answer them all. Even the silly ones, like "Am I a vampire?" She had apparently read about these weird creatures in some book, where they were portrayed as immortal. Her world had literally turned upside down today, so I was tolerant of her probing. As I said, she was actually handling herself quite well. She was obviously my great-great-great-etcetera granddaughter.

"When are we going to start my lessons?" she asked after all the information she had just received had sunk in. I smiled. Olga's eyes were alight with impatience and passion. This girl was definitely going places. And how could it be any other way? She was a Richter.

But, before beginning her training, we had to settle a few pressing affairs. Plus, there was a lot for me to learn, as well.

I turned the abomination crystal around in my hand, and asked, "You called this a grace stone, right? Tell me, where are they mined right now?"

"Well, no one takes them out of dead aristocrats, if that's what you mean," she began, unsure.

"No, no," I shook my head, "tell me about the normal ways. Since these gemstones exist, are sold, and are considered valuable, that means they are procured from somewhere." I still felt I had to spell things out for her to allay her continuing suspicions that I may be a bloodthirsty maniac who wanted to serially kill aristocrats.

Book One

My taking things slowly with her worked. Olga relaxed, and began to explain enthusiastically: "Gemstones are usually mined by purifiers in special areas. Most of these areas belong to aristocrats, and they use their clan cleansers to purify them. However, there are some foci that are on state land, where independent professionals can get purification permits. Naturally, in those cases, the treasury buys up the harvest."

"Just the gemstones?"

"No, they buy up any useful or valuable trophies or ingredients."

"What about poachers? Who guards these areas from unlicensed cleansers? And who monitors the buyup of the harvest?

Olga seemed stumped. "I don't know the details of how they work, Max. It never even occurred to me to get involved with anything like that, so I never looked into the ins and outs. But I have a friend who's a cleanser. If you want, I can introduce you."

"I want," I nodded, "but not now."

Honestly, I had the urge to set out right there and then to hunt down the abomination monsters and harvest a lot of the trophies and energy I so badly needed from them. But the fact of the matter was that I barely had enough strength to purify even the smallest and weakest focus. I'd have to work a "healer" side-gig for the time being.

Normally, that thought would have thrown me into paroxysms of laughter. Max Richter, a healer! What could be funnier! Just the fact that I was now forced to be one meant something was terribly wrong with our world.

"So, what are you planning on doing now?" Olga's question made me stop and think. In my mind, I ran through all the permutations and levels on which the question could be answered, unsure which part to communicate to her. For example, existential issues would probably have to wait for now. Abomination was destroying the world, and had made a lot of headway in a thousand years' time. If it wasn't stopped, our civilization would inevitably perish.

And there was no way to tame it, or make it serve us. There was no reasoning with it. At one time, I, too, had thought about ways to use the abomination as an energy source, and considered leaving some of the foci undestroyed. I wanted to contain it. My comrades and I made thousands of calculations. But, no matter how many different ways we modeled the future, the conclusion was always the same: if the abomination was not destroyed completely, then it would slowly, but surely, take over the world.

Beating this nasty stuff was going to take some time. We needed a serious and complex approach. There was no point burdening my descendant with all this for now. Nor must I complain about my weakness. That was not to be displayed in front of anyone, under any circumstances. Recharging my energy was my first priority, and it had to be done as quickly as possible.

But there was something else, as well, that I expected to resonate with her with all the force of our blood.

Book One

"Olga Richter," I said her name with gravitas, "I have told you a lot about our people. But all that was in the past. Now, you and I are all we've got." She wanted to say something, but I motioned for her to be silent and let me continue. "What we have is a lot. You'll tell me everything you know about the modern world, you'll be my guide. I, in turn, will take your gift to a completely new level. You have powers you don't even suspect you have, but they are living inside you. They are in the Richter blood, waiting to be called forth. And together, Olga, you and I will punish all those who dared turn our clan into servants for other gifted. We will give it a new birth, resurrect it in all its glory."

Proud of my slightly puffed up, but, as I'd hoped, inspiring speech, I looked at Olga triumphantly. Strangely, she blushed. "New... birth?" she asked gingerly. "You and me?"

I nearly facepalmed. There was no way I could have ever perceived her as anything but my granddaughter, even if a distant one. When I was talking about giving new birth to the clan I didn't mean I wanted to turn Olga into an incubator for little Richters. It seemed that's what she had thought I meant. What a perv! I had meant new birth in a higher sense.

"Others must have survived," I answered calmly, with a paternal smile. "They may be distant relatives, but they'll have necromancer blood in them. We'll find them."

"Oh, yes, of course," Olga's mind was put to rest. Although, for a moment, a hint of disappointment did flash across her face.

the Dark healer

While we were talking, I had completely forgotten about Fred, who was still lying on the operating table in front of me. He needed to be stitched up. I figured I'd let him regenerate his own tissue. I redirected some of the now processed abomination energy I had gotten from Hugo into Fred — exactly the amount needed to take him to level three. Now, Fred was a stronger and more skillful wraith. He could now also remember more commands, and heal small wounds. By evening, there would be no trace left of his bullet wounds.

Once that was done, I ordered him to get up and get dressed. Actually, it wouldn't be a bad idea to get him something more suitable to wear than the rags he was wearing now. In fact, unfortunately, the same could be said for me, too. Thankfully, at least I didn't need to go to a barber — the spell that had protected my body also blocked hair and beard growth. If not for that, I would have woken up looking like an insane forest creature.

"Shall we go upstairs?" I said to Olga. "Meanwhile, Fred will bring the other bodies down here — our future servants. I want to take a look at this mortgage our late guest was bragging about," I indicated Hugo with a nod of my head.

"Sure!" My granddaughter hurried up the stairs. After our talk, she had clearly cheered up, and even displayed some enthusiasm. As I had hoped, my speech had had the desired effect. To be fair, she had also seen with her own eyes plenty of evidence to start trusting me and thinking of me as the senior family member.

Soon, we were standing in her studio, where

she worked. She began rummaging around in a small safe mounted on the wall, which was stuffed with papers. It didn't take her long to find what she was looking for. I noticed that despite the huge amount of papers, they were kept in perfect order, carefully organized in folders.

"Here," she extended one to me. "This is everything to do with the house."

While I studied the papers, she took some kind of rope from the shelf, and stuck one end of it into her... smartphone — wasn't that what she'd called it? Then, she stuck the other end of the rope into the wall. I couldn't resist asking what she was doing.

"I'm trying to charge my device," she said, furrowing her brow, "but it's not working. I think it's broken."

Indeed it was, and I even knew who had broken it. I had to come clean.

"Really?" Olga was surprised. "Okay... Good thing I copied everything valuable onto my laptop.

"Laptop?" I asked.

"Yes, this rectangular thing on my desk," my granddaughter pointed at the laptop. She gave me a quick rundown of how it worked. I realized I shouldn't touch it while I couldn't control the way I was draining things that ran on abomination. I did, however, stand behind Olga and quizzically watch her set up an appointment with a client for later that day, using text message.

I had also carefully studied the mortgage papers. According to them, my granddaughter owed a large sum of money to a noble clan called

Nilsson. I had never even heard that name before. They must have been entitled as nobles while I slept.

"All set," Olga announced, getting up from her desk. "Let me just grab my old phone and I'll call a cab."

When we came outside, I looked around again. On my way here, I could not have failed to notice how much everything had changed. The stable was the only building I recognized. In the past, all the land for miles in every direction had belonged to my clan. An enormous number of different buildings had once stood inside the castle walls: army barracks, craftsmen's shops, warehouses, archives, laboratories... And, of course, residential buildings — everything from my own palace wing with spectacular master bedrooms, to the humble servants' quarters. All of this was once an ecosystem that worked like a well-oiled machine. Even the placement of the buildings and rooms inside them had been designed for maximum efficiency. Along with my castle, a well-oiled production operation — practically a whole town, which provided the Richters with everything we needed — had also been ruefully lost.

I consider the castle the heart of the clan; a source of strength. As long as it's maintained in order, the family's affairs also move along swimmingly. And what did we have now? Olga's stable-house was on the same street as some sort of dirty shelter with seedy looking types hanging around outside it even during the day. There was a pub on the corner with even more dubious people inside.

Book One

The whole neighborhood was depressing. Something had to be done.

That is to say, I knew what had to be done: I unequivocally intended to reclaim all the Richter lands for myself.

The taxi drove up to the curb. I had noticed these new-fangled carriages, which ran without horses, the night before. Now, knowing what I knew about how things worked nowadays, and how a lot of stuff was fueled by abomination energy, it occurred to me that perhaps taxis did, too. But Olga casually opened the door, and dove into the scuffed up automobile (I now knew what they were called, too). So, I got in, too. Right away, I felt the abomination start to enter me. *Quel surprise!*

The driver, who looked similar to the hood-lummy types loitering in the street, produced a heartfelt profane exclamation when he realized his machine wasn't starting. Then, he assumed the mask of politeness again, apologized, and offered to call us another taxi. Olga agreed right away.

But, when we got out of the car, I proposed that we walk.

"Why?" she said. Then, she thought about it for a second. "I mean... we do have time. We could stop at the shopping center on the way, buy you something to wear. Sorry, uncle," she softly smiled, "but what you're wearing doesn't fit you anymore, and it's in tatters. You look like you took those clothes off a corpse."

Admirable powers of observation! She had said that last part on auto-pilot, and hadn't realized what she was saying, but when she did, she also realized I actually might have. I was about to tell her about the magical ways to sterilize cloth, when she sharply changed the subject: "I'll show you the clinic where I work as a volunteer, too. It's on our way."

"Do you have to rest after seeing ungifted clients too?" I asked.

She shook her head. "No. Even after a full day at the clinic, I feel only slightly tired. Nothing like what happens after I treat an aristocrat." Then, she suddenly said, "Actually, I believe I recharge faster than most healers. Now that I know you, I doubt that's a coincidence. I've always felt there was a special kind of atmosphere in my house..."

She was having a hard time finding the words, so I helped her out: "That's normal. You feel the energy streams intuitively, even if you don't realize it. Many power lines of energy criss-cross in this place, the magic practically oozes from the ground. That's why I chose this place for my castle."

She nodded gravely. "So I was right. But... here's the weird thing: this neighborhood is not popular. You can see for yourself how poor it is. Aristocrats definitely don't live here. Even regular people with a little bit of money don't set foot here, because they often get sick if they do. My friends kept trying to talk me into getting rid of the mortgage and moving somewhere else. But I have loved it here since the first moment I arrived."

I smiled. "You felt at home."

It was strange, though, that another magical clan had not claimed these lands for its own houses. Hadn't anyone except us sensed how unique this place was?

We walked a little more, and finally found ourselves before a large building that immediately stood out against the others, and not just because of its size. It was much newer than the rest, and screamed, "Look at me!"

"That's the shopping center, we can buy clothes here."

I nodded, and warned her just in case: "I'll have to pay you back after we get paid."

This did not surprise Olga. "Of course," she said. "Look around, choose some stuff. I make enough not to skimp on simple things, and you will also receive a tidy sum from our first session together."

Once we were inside the shiny building, she immediately flitted away, saying, "I'll go check out the electronics section real quick — I need a new smartphone." I nodded, and sent the lizard with her so we wouldn't get lost. The shadow scout jumped onto her backpack and blended in so well that she didn't even notice it.

I must admit, I was fascinated to look around and see what kinds of things were in demand in this new era. The shopping center as a thing in itself did not surprise me, it resembled a covered market or bazaar where a multitude of merchants offered all kinds of wares for sale. Some of the merchandise hadn't changed much since my time, and some I could guess what it was for. But there were also some things, I had never seen anything like them before. I would need Olga's help to get oriented.

A window display with watches caught my eye. I knew what they were right away, though they didn't make them yet in my day. All the ones I remembered were very large compared to these. These were affixed to the wrist with a little belt, like a bracelet. What an interesting and useful accessory! And, unlike many other modern inventions, I didn't feel any abomination coming from these watches, which gave them a big advantage in my book. I should probably acquire one of these elegant little trifles, I thought.

Having decided this, I was just about to seek out Olga, when the lizard sent me a thought-image. Olga was surrounded by three young guys somewhere in this shopping center. They looked like aristocrats. They were definitely gifted, but I couldn't determine how powerful they were from the image.

"Hey, honeycakes. What's the matter, don't you have anybody to buy you a smartphone?" a skinny ginger guy with messed up hair was harassing her. "You don't have a boyfriend?"

"Want three at once?" laughed his dark-skinned friend. "We won't hurt you. Come on, it'll be fun, and we'll make it worth your while."

"Don't insult the lady, she doesn't take money," the third one butted in. "She's down to party for free — isn't that right, pussycat?"

Olga was trying to ignore them while they buzzed around her like dung flies.

Their pickup lines were on the level of high schoolers, but what they lacked in maturity they made up for in brazenness.

The lizard showed me the shortest way to where Olga was, and that's where I headed, hastily.

Chapter 06

AS I TRAVERSED THE SHOPPING CENTER on my way to Olga, I kept receiving images from the lizard — fascinating scenes from 'civilized' modern life. The three aristocrats were all over her, it seemed like next they would start pulling on her braids like school kids. She had a well-practiced poker face on, and successfully ignored their dumb and utterly uninteresting come-ons, smoothly swerving away from their outstretched paws.

She was already making her way from the electronics department toward the exit, when a fourth guy blocked her way. He seemed to be a friend of the other three, though he was much larger and older than the rest. Or maybe it just seemed that way because he had a neatly trimmed goatee. A real fashionista.

"We've got to stop meeting like this!" he exclaimed, getting right in Olga's way.

"Sorry, I'm in a hurry," she said, and tried to squeeze past him. He grabbed her by the shoulders and shoved her toward the wall — not hard, but he *was* much bigger than her. This was getting serious, and I started walking faster. The other three punks were just going to get a talking to from me, or at most a spanking, but this asshole had already earned himself a permanent disability.

"Don't you recognize me, sweetheart?" he cooed, putting his face right in hers.

"How do you know her?" one of the other guys asked.

"She gave me a suck once," he laughed. "But she didn't finish. Ran off in the middle of the session."

"Well that's just asking for it!" the ginger one butted in gleefully.

"I guess so," the big one grinned, getting in Olga's face again. "So, what do you say? Want to finish the job? We can do it right here, in the fitting room."

Olga rolled her eyes. "I've treated a number of members of the Hoffman clan, but I have never had as disgusting an experience as I did with you. I will never provide my services to you again, and I demand that you immediately cease your vile innuendos," she said right to his face. She was calm, and not at all afraid or nervous with these horny animals. 'That's my girl,' I thought to myself.

I was surprised by the security and staff of

this shopping center, though. They were completely ignoring what was going on, pretending that several unhinged assholes hadn't just pressed a female customer, who was alone, into a corner. Were they so afraid of aristocrats? But Olga was no commoner either. It's just that she didn't have battle magic and a clan to rely on. Might makes right.

Beardo obviously considered himself the top of the local food chain, but, in addition to his lack of manners, I noticed another reason he was so unabashed. He was the type that was so overcharged with energy, you could see it with the naked eye. According to Olga, his aura had literally flashed orange, and he had barely been able to contain himself. I knew these symptoms well. He had overdone it on the abomination, but just a little. If he had really overdosed, he would feel very ill, or even fall into a coma from the excess of foreign energy. But this condition, when the organism had taken in too much, but had been able to digest it, was characterized by uncontrolled flashes of physical strength. It's like a kind of battle madness. And, if the energy isn't siphoned off right away, it will cause an explosion. The force of that explosion can vary by a lot, depending on the magician's own strength. And this guy was no weakling. He was a solid mid-level.

I wasn't the only one who noticed the state he was in. One of his buddies even told him, "Herman, be careful. Don't do magic here!" But this had the opposite of the intended effect. The hipster bully flashed again, this time with actual magic flame. Inadvertently, a ring of fire materialized right next to his hands, and disappeared again right away, but I noticed it. Fire was a good sign — as strange as it may sound, that's the element whose energy is easiest to take under control.

The bully exhaled loudly and closed his eyes. He might even have counted to ten in his head. That's a technique five-year-old magicians who have trouble maintaining focus practice, and this pituitary case hadn't outgrown them by much other than size.

Nevertheless, after a few seconds he got a little more grounded, and shot back at his friend, "I know, Charlie. It's under control. Besides, this sucker here is going to have to finish what she started whether she likes it or not. I really do need a session, and the sooner the better, so cut the crap," he grimaced. "I'll even pay you."

Olga burned a hole in him with her gaze, and answered, "You've been blacklisted from half the city. It's no wonder you're having energy fluctuations. I'm not interested in your money, and I have the right to refuse service without explanation."

"Oh no, you don't!" the goateed bully raged. "Look at you, acting like you're an aristocrat, when you're just a leech! You're coming with us right now."

I was just arriving, and heard the last part myself, without transmission from the shadow scout. I also saw the three ne'er-do-wells, and beardo's broad back. Olga and I even made eye contact, which gave her a start for some reason. I would have thought she would be happy to see me in a situation like this. The herd of lowlife aristocrats suddenly started laughing heartily. The ginger one said, "Now she's scared! Now you get what's up, honeybunch?"

For the first time in this whole episode, Olga showed an emotion: "Morons," she said, "I'm concerned for you, not for myself."

So that's how it was. I guess because of recent events, Olga was afraid there might be a few more corpses to deal with in a minute. She was wrong to feel that way. I wasn't an animal and I didn't kill without reason. And anyway, I had other methods, too.

"I heard someone was looking for a healer?" I snickered to the lowlife brigade who called themselves aristocrats.

"Who the hell are you?" the goateed giant spat out. "Get lost, no one invited you."

"Unfortunately," I continued to smile affably, "I can't just pass by and look the other way when I see people in dire need of help."

"Who are you?!" the ginger spoke up. "Have you looked in the mirror? Hobos hanging around a heating pipe dress better than you."

The outsized hipster started laughing like a horse. "That's for sure!" he said. "But even if he looked better, I prefer to get suck jobs from sweet young ladies like this shrewish little bitch here. The fuck am I gonna do with that freak?"

"Right on," the ginger brown-nosed.

Of course, I could have killed all four of them, and found a precious energy gemstone in each one. But if I did it here, in front of witnesses, we'd probably have to be detained and sign some sort of paperwork. It would ruin all our plans. I needed to knock him out somehow, in such a way that no one would realize what had happened.

"Well? What are you waiting for? Are you deaf or something? Go ahead on to wherever you were going," the outsized 'musketeer' took an intimidating step in my direction. Since magic was forbidden in the shopping center, he had decided to scare me off with his physical strength, the idiot. I was slightly taller, but much thinner than him. Like a fencer, as compared to a wrestler.

I took literally one step forward, and was right near him. "Sir," I exclaimed loudly, "you need urgent medical attention!"

The hulk grimaced and assumed a menacing stance. But I suspected he wouldn't let me get at him just like that, so I had already made sure that the shadow scout had gone up his pant leg.

"Aaaah" the bearded bully screamed, bending over and grabbing his privates. The other three just froze, exchanging glances and trying to figure out what kind of magic I had just used. They didn't have that kind.

Lizards have no teeth, but they bite pretty hard, and it's especially painful in the most sensitive parts of the body. My shadow scout squeezed his little jaws together like pincers on the bully's private parts.

"Oo-oo-oo-oo-oo!" the guy wailed.

I wasn't about to be too friendly with the dumbass, and causing him a little crotch injury was exactly what I needed to distract him and break his concentration. Now that he was wailing hysterically, I 'came to his aid' by placing the palm of my hand to his forehead. But not to suck the energy out of him. This prick wasn't getting off that easy.

On the contrary, I added some of my own energy to make him overflow and explode. The goat-faced fool's aura flashed so brightly that even the ungifted could see it. That's when I started absorbing the excess abomination as fast as I could.

A few seconds later, it was all over. Hoffman went limp in my arms, and I carefully laid him on the ground. He was alive — I had learned from my experience with Hugo to be careful and leave the ungifted some energy.

"Take him home," I said to the lackeys of the now comatose moron. "He's fine now, he just needs to restore his strength." I kept playing the doctor, and I even began to like it. The stunned expressions on my opponents' faces were a sight to see! Say whatever you want, but this "healer" thing was an excellent cover. You can wreak all kinds of havoc, and if you say you're a healer, people will believe and trust you!

After a lengthy silence, the ginger demanded, "What have you done, dickwad?! Do you know who you're dealing with?"

"That doesn't make any difference," I announced with gravity. "As a doctor, I don't have the right to walk past a person in need of help." Olga covered her mouth with her hand, trying to suppress laughter. But no one was paying her any attention at this point, they had all surrounded me instead. Which meant it was time to select the next victim. I was looking at their auras, trying to identify the strongest one. It was a real disappointment — none of them even remotely approached the big one's level. I could use all the energy I could get, so it would have been better if they'd had more of it to take.

Unfortunately, I didn't have a chance to take their energy, as a voice rang throughout the shopping center: "Disturbance in electronics. Stay where you are. Security is on its way. Any attempt to escape will be held against you in a court of law." I didn't feel any magic from the announcement, so it must have been another new-fangled invention.

No one had any intention of escaping. The hoodlums were disappointed not to have had a chance to hurt me. "You're lucky, dumbass!" the ginger spat out with hostility. "But only in that you're alive. You're in deep shit now, boy. You'll be sorry yet that we didn't just finish you off." I just shrugged my shoulders and waited patiently for security to arrive. All the better, I thought, to dispense with formalities sooner rather than later, and then resume our shopping. We had big plans, and the day only had so many hours in it.

There were only six security guards, and they weren't gifted, but they were armed, and had clan pins. The crest on these pins seemed vaguely familiar to me, but I couldn't remember right away who it belonged to. Even in my time, there was a multitude of small, little-known magical clans; I couldn't remember everybody.

Along with the security team, came a short

woman of about forty-five, with a displeased and furrowed facial expression. Unlike the others, she had a magic gift, but a very weak one — it was barely palpable. When she came closer, I read her name tag: Elsa Frank. Manager.

She bent over the goateed bully in the magical coma, concerned. "What's wrong with him? Is he dead?"

"He's alive," I reassured.

"Grace overdose," explained Olga.

"There was no overdose, they're full of it!" the ginger hooligan argued in outrage. The manager shook her head and looked around briefly. A crowd had formed around us, and the security detail had drawn even more rubberneckers.

"Follow me to the service wing," she ordered tersely, and we were led away from the shopping floor. Hoffman, too, was carried behind us, on a stretcher they had produced from somewhere. At some point, though, our paths diverged, as he was taken to the infirmary. Finally, it was just the five of us in the manager's office: me, Olga, and the three lackeys of the victim — the ginger, the curly one, and the dark-skinned one. The three of them were acting very sure of themselves, as though the situation had already been resolved in their favor.

As soon as the door closed behind us, the ginger again stepped to the fore and started peacocking in front of Elsa.

"Do you know who this cretin just harmed?" he asked, meaning me. "Herman Hoffman! Everyone in this neighborhood, and in this whole city, knows that name!"

"I understand your outrage, and, naturally, I know Mr. Hoffman. He is a VIP customer here," the woman began to placate. "But we need a little time to get to the bottom of this."

"What's there to get to the bottom of?!" the curly one butted in. "It's all clear as day!"

They sprawled on chairs, and leered at us with derision.

"Please introduce yourself," the woman said to me.

"My name is Max Richter," I answered curtly. Then, Olga introduced herself, and then, eagerly, the hoodlums. They had just been waiting to speak their names, which, along with the name Hoffman, I was hearing for the first time in my life. Too many bogus aristocrats had arisen in the last thousand years. Considering how weak these three were, I didn't even bother remembering their names — the nicknames I had given them would suffice.

Elsa the manager, however, was much more impressed with them than I was. Especially whenever the name Hoffman was mentioned, she would start smiling subserviently. So far, she had only heard their version of events.

"That Richter is a real psycho!" the curly one complained. "He attacked the three of us unprovoked, and almost killed Herman! You saw yourself what state he's in now."

"What will his father say!" the dark-skinned one proffered. This made Elsa go pale. I already knew she was not on our side.

"And in general, the Richters are nothing but leeches. They sure think highly of themselves though!" the ginger added, apparently in an attempt to maintain his status as chief lackey. "That Olga probably put her relative up to this to get back at Herman for not using her services anymore. He stopped calling her because of her unacceptable behavior."

Olga was angry, but she answered pretty calmly: "That is the exact opposite of the truth."

Elsa made a displeased grimace, but, so that everything was by the book, she said, "Alright, what do you have to say about the rest of it?"

Here, I decided to take the floor myself. "Are you gifted?" I asked the manager.

"Yes I am. How is that relevant?" she asked with resentment.

"Do you think you could have sent Herman Hoffman into a coma?" I asked.

She opened and closed her mouth several times, unable to understand what I was asking.

"Me? Hoffman?!"

"So why are you accusing me of doing that? I'm a healer, I'm not trained in battle spells. Herman Hoffman was on the verge of an energetic collapse. He was moments away from his power bursting out of him and damaging your shopping center's merchandise, or worse, hurting somebody."

"That's a crock," the ginger interrupted.

I just shook my head and added calmly: "Are you an expert? I am. It was extremely irresponsible of him to go to a public place in the state he was in."

The manager sighed heavily and rubbed her

temples. It was clear she didn't want to make any decisions in this case. When she did finally open her mouth to speak, she was only able to say half of the phrase, "Of course, we will take measures against Max Rich..." when the door opened, and a tall, upright dark-haired man in a business suit came in with a fast step. He didn't look any older than thirty, but the seriousness and concentration on his face belied a person accustomed to giving orders and solving problems. And he was a magician a level higher than even the poor Herman.

Seeing him, Elsa smiled broadly and her face betrayed blissful relief. She began to chatter: "Mr. Ali Demir, how good to see you! I called the main office about the incident right away, but I didn't think you'd come so soon. I've had a talk with the parties, and detained the culprit: Max Richter attacked these people."

The man named Ali froze in place, as though he had hit a wall. "Did you at least watch the security camera footage?" he asked, surprised.

"No, I didn't have a chance to," Elsa said, embarrassed, "but these respected people, regular customers of ours, unanimously attest..."

"These people here?" Ali Demir measured up the three little aristocrats.

"Yes, they're friends of Mr. Hoffman."

Ignoring her, the man turned to face me. "Mr. Richter, permit me to express the utmost gratitude to you on behalf of the Demir clan. You prevented a catastrophe just in the nick of time. We were fortunate that you happened to be nearby!"

"Not at all," I stated, "it's my duty as a healer."

"Uncle Max..." Olga rolled her eyes. It looked like I was the only healer who held such views. Ali Demir was surprised, too, but nevertheless rushed to shake my hand.

"Elsa," he commanded, "make sure our guests get a gift certificate on the house for the maximum possible amount. And see that they're happy with everything. You almost ended your career today, and its continuation depends on their satisfaction."

"How can you do this?" the ginger objected. "Mr. Hoffman suffered a serious injury from this leech."

Ali Demir didn't even look at him, but just said, "The Hoffmans will be fined for disturbing the peace on Demir property. No one has the right to come to another clan's turf in a state of near uncontrolled explosion."

"But..." Herman's buddies tried to keep arguing.

"Hoffman has already been handed off to his family, so there's no reason for you to hang around here, either. Pay your fine, and you're free to go."

"A fine?"

Demir didn't bother to answer, but turned to the manager and said, "Elsa, you can take over from here." Then, Ali exited the office as quickly as he had entered it.

Three pairs of enraged eyes were fixed on the manager. Luckily, I didn't have to listen to them yelling anymore. Elsa immediately handed Olga something — I guessed it was the gift certificate — and said she would be with us in a moment. Then, she politely saw us out of the office. She had obviously decided to take out the dressing down she had just received from her boss on the other three. I hoped they'd all have fun together!

* * *

Emre Demir, the leader of a big clan and owner of the chain of shopping centers, liked to keep tabs on all his businesses. He was an old-fashioned man, and he had worked hard to raise his clan to the level they were at now. He remembered the rise and fall of many a gifted person, and he knew that all could be lost in the blink of an eye, whereas to gain in life required talent, patience, willpower, and even luck. Emre considered himself a wise and resilient person, and he did not allow himself to relax even after many centuries of hard work. The only person he could really trust was himself.

Emre loved power and all its trappings. He loved his empire, the piles of money and the fabulous skyscraper he owned in the city center. He had an astounding view from his office window — the kind only a handful of people could afford. The decor inside the office was not too shabby, either. He had only custom-made designer furniture, and the paintings on the walls were as good as ones in museums. He was very proud of his private collection, but only displayed it to working class people as though it wasn't worth anything. He could afford to do that, and he saw it as part of his status. But, to enjoy all of this wealth, you have to work hard, and Emre did not shrink from hard work.

Every day, he was involved in every aspect of his business.

Today was no different. He opened the report on the day's incidents, lazily leafed through the part about how many shoplifters had been caught red-handed, and then he froze. The report on the incident with the shoppers had caught his eye.

It wasn't often that aristocrats would cause a scene on one of his properties, so he couldn't have missed this. And the name in the report made the color drain from his face, despite the fact that he was of dark complexion.

Max Richter...

Furrowing his brow, Emre studied the video from the security cameras, zooming in as much as possible on the healer who had shown himself so excellently. Finally, he shuddered, grabbed the phone, and dialed a number.

"Ali, I'm calling about today's incident. With the Hoffmans, yes. But that's not important. I want you to dig up everything you can on this Richter. Yes, you heard that right. I want you to find out everything there is to know about him. Report directly to me. Any time, day or night."

WE CAME OUT OF THE MANAGER'S OFFICE, gift certificate in hand. In my time, when someone apologized, they gifted something of consequence — horses, jewels, or villages. But the world had changed, so I had to take Olga's cue. It looked like a small blue energy sphere that floated through the air right behind her. She set about studying it right away. It was no bigger than a ping pong ball, but I could tell by the way my granddaughter's eyes lit up that they had not skimped.

"A hundred thousand coins!" she exclaimed. "That's way more than I expected!"

"Coins? So good old gold isn't current anymore?" I inquired.

"It is, but... it's complicated."

"Will you explain the situation to me?"

Money is important. If there's something complicated that needs to be understood, it's best to get to the bottom of it right away. Especially since the Richters were broke! I had already begun automatically thinking of Olga as a member of the clan, without even telling her.

She began to explain: "For the last couple hundred years, gold isn't in use anymore, and we use spheres instead. They're wallets, like this certificate, and they're different colors. Each sphere is magically tied to a single owner, which is very convenient. They're almost impossible to steal, and they take up no space. Everything you own is always with you. And you can convert gold into coins at any bank branch."

"So you've just been gifted coins?"

She shook her head. "No. Certificates are spheres with coins, but they're not tied to an owner like individual sphere wallets; instead, they are tied to a place where they have to be spent. This certificate can only be spent at Demir Group shopping centers."

"Will you show me your own sphere?" I asked.

"Sure." Olga held her hand out palm up, and another energy sphere kind of rose out of her skin. It was about the same size as the certificate, but green rather than blue.

Olga sighed, and said, "When I was little, my dream was to have a golden sphere, but I haven't earned one yet."

"What's the difference?" I couldn't resist asking.

"Only VIP clients of the bank can get a golden sphere. It comes with all kinds of bonuses, a personal assistant, and so on. But the main thing is, it opens a lot of doors..." She was suddenly embarrassed, but explained, "It's a status thing. A dream for a beautiful life type of thing."

As she spoke, I carefully studied her sphere. It was interesting magic, and I even thought I recognized the style. "Does the bank belong to the Schitzer clan?" I asked.

"Yes, how did you know?" Olga was surprised.

"I'd know their style anywhere," I guffawed. "Are you aware that this sphere is not tied only to you?"

"What do you mean?" my granddaughter asked, confused.

So the sly foxes didn't even tell people how these spheres worked! I wouldn't trust the Schitzers to shine my shoes. They'd steal them.

"Don't you know that some of the energy you're spending through your wallet is going to the Schitzers? They're the real leeches."

She became pensive. "So it's not just a rumor. I heard about something like that, but yeah, there's no official information about it. And the amount of energy they're siphoning off is too small for me to notice, I guess."

"Naturally," I confirmed. "The ungifted use these spheres, too, right? And even they have enough resources to skim from. A little bit from everyone adds up to a huge energy stream."

"But why hasn't anyone from the influential clans noticed this?" Olga asked as she tried to wrap her mind around this new information.

"Maybe because they have golden spheres," I supposed, "which work differently. The strong won't let themselves be robbed. Or maybe they have some other kind..."

"Platinum!" she made the connection. "The heads of all the strong clans have platinum ones, and their entourage does, too."

"There you go," I shook my head. "You see for yourself how simple it is."

For a while, Olga and I walked around the shopping center in silence. Then, she said, "Now I want to give up using spheres altogether. Too bad that's impossible."

I smiled. "Not necessarily. We'll talk about that later. For now, let's spend our gift."

"Let's start with clothes!" she said, her eyes lighting up. Then, she coyly asked, "Will you let me pick out a couple of looks for you?" Women can't get enough of dressing people up. I've heard it's a habit they learn as children. When their gift is in its seminal stages, they make dolls, dress them up, and put curses on them. Or whatever it is girls do with dolls — I've never actually looked into it.

I can't stand shopping for clothes. Like most upper-crust aristocrats, I have a disdain for the niceties. Once, one of the Villons — they were always a little wacky — forgot her purse as she left her house for the clans' spring ball, so instead she grabbed a woven basket on her way. And then? The whole capital started carrying baskets! All the tanners and leather workers went out of business and turned to piracy. The peasants had nothing to gather their peaches into, and the harvest rotted on the trees. All because of one idiot.

And then there was my granddad, founder of the Richter clan. He wore nothing but a burial shroud for the last three hundred years of his life. He even went to royal receptions like that, to see all twelve of the kings who ruled during that time. The last four didn't even believe in him, they considered him a ghost.

They were onto something, too. They couldn't lay Granddad to rest for another two hundred years after that.

These were the things I think about when I hear about trying on clothes. You can imagine how unpleasant I find it. I knew I had a chance to pawn off the shopping on Olga. The main thing was to supervise the situation, because women tend to get a little excitable when shopping.

"Looks?" I asked. In my day, you'd invite a tailor to your house and they would custom-fit everything to your liking. But now, it seemed you could choose from clothing that had already been made. I wondered how they did that, considering that everyone's body is different.

"Yeah," she said. She was no longer surprised by my questions, understanding that we were separated by many centuries. "That's what it's called when you're not just wearing regular clothes, but a coordinated image, put together according to the situation and the style of the wearer."

"Got it," I agreed, knowing this would save a ton of time and energy. "But I get to have the power of veto."

"Of course!" My granddaughter elatedly dragged me by the hand toward the clothing showrooms.

Two young women employees immediately jumped to help Olga, and they sized me up with their detail-oriented professional eye. Naturally, when both their gazes were drawn to the ring on my hand, their eyes widened a little. Then, they started running around the showroom, communicating in some language of their own.

"Raglan sleeve!"

"Polo neck!"

"Cardigan!"

"Hoodie!"

"I hope they don't accidentally invoke a demon," I was concerned.

They didn't. Olga commanded them confidently and decisively. She took the task seriously, and explained all her choices. After selecting a few suits for me to try on, she said, "You look young, uncle, but we should focus on the classic to emphasize your status and importance."

Status and importance didn't come from clothes, it came from the level to which your magic was developed, and how well your army could fight. But I wasn't about to rain on Olga's parade, she was trying so hard.

She chose a couple of suits for me — a dark gray one and a blue one, a pair of sturdy and comfortable shoes, and a wristwatch — the one I had liked. I would have chosen it myself, and was glad to see our tastes coincided. According to Olga, this was how well-appointed aristocrats dressed nowadays.

I chose another outfit myself. This included a pair of sturdy canvas pants, which were called jeans here, a thin "turtleneck" sweater, and a short black leather jacket. Until I created an army of undead servants, I'd have to do all my fighting myself. I was fine with that, but I wasn't going to do it wearing suits.

Olga approved of my selections, but said I looked like "a dangerous type." The saleswomen nodded, and their eyes became dreamy.

"You have such a great body," one sighed.

"It's such a pleasure dressing you," added the other.

Naturally, I wasn't going to put on my old rags anymore, so I left them right in the showroom. A pretty young saleswoman noticed, and chased us down at the department exit. "Wait! Mister! You forgot..." out of breath, she stretched out the bag to me.

"I don't need that anymore," I answered curtly and kept walking. But she caught up to me again, and, with a comically furrowed brow, asked, "What are we supposed to do with this?"

"Best to burn it," I advised, completely serious, and we walked on, leaving the confused young woman there.

"You're very... interesting, uncle," Olga commented, laughing. I just shrugged. It's better not to joke around with leftover magic.

I was happy with our purchases, and we had only spent barely half of the coins in the gift certificate. I let Olga keep the rest, let her buy a good smartphone — after all, I broke the old one. And she would need it for our business. She almost kissed me on the cheek, she was so happy, but then she thought better of it and ran off.

While she was discussing something with the salesman in the electronics department, I grabbed a whole pile of magazines with shiny covers off the shelf in the hall. They turned out to be free.

"Max, what are you going to do with all that trash?" Olga asked, widening her eyes in surprise.

"Study modern life," I answered honestly.

"But there's the internet!" my descendant exclaimed. "And TV."

I didn't say anything for now about the fact that her TV was now broken, and I was sure that her laptop would suffer the same fate if I touched it. "I'll do it the old-fashioned way," I said.

"Then we should find you a briefcase to put those in," Olga said. We found a durable and capacious one pretty fast. If I put a spell on it, I could even carry artifacts in it. I was happy with our shopping, but when we finally exited the shopping center, I was relieved. It was a necessary trip, but very fatiguing.

"Taxi?" Olga hopefully looked at me.

I shook my head. "I want to see the city," I said, not wanting to disclose just yet that until I acquired chimeras for us to ride on, we would always have to walk when we went out together.

"OK," she nodded, immediately changing the subject to the day's plans: "Our first client is Mrs. Agnessa Peddleton. She's a very lovely elderly lady. I've treated her before. You could say she's a regular of mine."

Again, the name didn't ring a bell, so I didn't expect to get much energy out of this session. But, I trusted Olga's judgment, and I was sure if she had had access to a bigger fish, she would have taken me to it.

We didn't have far to go, it was just a few blocks. But the environment changed very substantially. We were obviously now out of the blighted neighborhood, and in a pastoral landscape that could only be described as "heaven on earth" — a small corner of peaceful, rural life. Strange that two such different neighborhoods were right next to each other. This one was behind a high fence, and could only be entered with a pass.

All the plots here looked like pictures from lovely postcards: neat, doll-like houses with perfect little gardens in front. Some people cultivated flowers, others grew fruit trees, and the laziest ones had covered the space in front of their houses with a bright green lawn.

We stopped in front of a house whose owner perhaps loved plants the most out of anyone on her street. Ivy covered the walls of her house and its elegant wrought iron balconies. I counted no fewer than twelve flowerbeds with peonies, orchids, hortensias, and God knows what else, surrounding the path leading to the door of the house. Near a cozy gazebo, there were lilac bushes in bloom. I had never been a big lover of flowers, but I couldn't resist staring. As for Olga, she was devouring the garden with her eyes. And this wasn't even her first time here!

A prim butler in a coat with tails opened the door. He smiled pleasantly at Olga, and carefully examined me. Seeing nothing suspicious, he smiled at me, as well. 'Olga did a good job picking out my wardrobe,' I thought to myself. If it stood up to the scrutiny of a snob like this butler, then it was exactly what the doctor ordered.

Inside, the house looked no less lovely than outside. It was like a dollhouse, filled with paintings of blissful landscapes. Knitted decorative doilies covered the wooden surfaces, and the furniture looked so soft and comfortable that it was all I could do to keep from plopping down on it. Which is, actually, what the butler proposed that I do, and wait here while Mrs. Peddleton sees Olga. As soon as I landed on the fancy couch, an elegant porcelain cup of tea with a beautiful saucer, and a crystal vase full of candy appeared before me.

Not wanting to waste time, I started leafing through one of the magazines. I found out how to choose where to go on vacation, how to lose 20 pounds in two weeks while eating only cakes, and how to find a new husband without divorcing the previous one. I skimmed all of this, taking in the new names, traditions, and expressions. Finally, I found an article about automobiles, and it absorbed me totally.

"Can't get good help these days!" I heard near my ear. Looking up, I saw a snot-nosed brat dressed like a dandy. Old ladies always have all sorts of nephews and grandsons hovering around, and this was apparently one of those. Some things never change.

"I beg to differ," I said, slowly sipping my tea. "The help here is excellent. And the tea is good, too. Maybe you'll ask for some, and they'll bring it to you."

The brat froze in place, opening and closing his mouth silently like a fish. I could have challenged him to a duel for his first inane comment, but I felt like a bull in a china shop among the aristocrats of today, so I gave the moron a chance. Besides, the old lady wouldn't be too happy if I killed her grandson.

"I know!" the snot-nosed brat flew off the handle. "I live here! Who are you?"

"I'm a healer," I said, placing my tea and saucer on the table. "Are you feeling unwell? You seem high-strung — yelling, twitching. It's not good for your blood pressure, and raises your risk of hurting yourself."

I was beginning to enjoy this charade. You could explain away literally anything by saying you were a healer. Case in point, the neurotic little idiot in the monkey suit immediately changed his tune, and became a lot less aggressive. He was probably just nervous.

"But Grandma usually sees Olga Richter. Why does she need another healer?"

"Doctor-patient confidentiality," I continued to have fun at his expense.

"If that old hag is up to something..!" He formed his hands into fists and stormed out of the living room. That wasn't a very nice way to talk about the lady at whose expense the little insect existed. Then again, that was their problem. It was for her to teach her grandson manners, none of my business.

"Is this the uncle Max I've been hearing so much about?" I heard a pleasant female voice that sounded much younger than I'd expected.

"Yes, Mrs. Peddleton, he's the one I told you about!" Olga confirmed as she descended the stairs from the second floor. The lady of the house appeared as well. She was smiley, and wore an attractive silk house dress. She definitely didn't seem like an old lady. To look at her, I would give her maybe at most fifty. I saw, however, that in actual fact, she was around three hundred years old. She was gifted, and pretty strong. For her age, she actually looked strikingly bad. She wouldn't have been able to maintain her ideal youth for thousands of years like Katharine, for example, had done, but she did have at least another one or two hundred years before she was supposed to start truly wilting. Something was wrong here.

Olga caught my concerned look, but she decided not to say anything. The lady of the house started fussing around. She introduced herself floridly, then called the butler and asked him to top off my tea, and also bring the cakes, which had been baked under her strict supervision that morning. Agnessa was obviously very proud of her culinary and organizational talents, and adored entertaining guests.

Several times, I caught her looking at me with interest. "I didn't know Olga had such a charming uncle," she smiled.

"I didn't know myself," my granddaughter snickered. "Uncle Max's appearance was a complete surprise to me."

"A pleasant one, no doubt," Agnessa continued to shower me with compliments.

"How could it be any other way?" I held up my end.

"Mangia, mangia!" our hostess noticed how quickly I was devouring the cakes. "I love a man with a healthy appetite!"

It seemed like I could climb onto her coffee table and start screaming at the top of my lungs, and Mrs. Peddleton would praise my originality and musicality. The lady was clearly into younger men, and I looked at most 25.

That's why she was a grace addict, I realized — she was trying to use the foreign energy to look younger. Only, for some reason, it wasn't working. What was that reason? I continued to study Mrs. Peddleton carefully. In addition to the early aging, I noticed a few other strange signs: a reddish hue around the irises, and several unusual pigment spots on her hand.

"May I examine you?" I interrupted the small talk between Olga and our hostess.

"Examine?" Agnessa didn't quite understand. "But why? The treatment session went fine." She blushed. It seemed she had taken my words as a kind of flirtation.

"Oh, don't worry," my granddaughter quickly reassured her. "My uncle is an excellent specialist. If he is asking to examine you, then he has good reason."

"Of course I do," I confirmed. "I think you have some sort of energy problem."

"Do you think so?" the woman was concerned.

I bent down closer to her and took her hand. Olga had done a great job, I felt almost no abomination in Agnessa. Her own source was strong. She should look like an eighteen-year-old debutante right now! What was the problem?

Swiping with my fingers, I called the shadow scalpel, then immediately turned it into a needle, and lightly pierced her skin. Agnessa gasped and fixed her gaze on me, while I rubbed the drop of her blood between my fingertips. It was a wonder she was even alive! Mrs. Peddleton's organism was poisoned with numerous toxins of various types. The woman was being poisoned with variety and imagination. The only reason she was still alive was her own internal power source, which was strained to the max keeping her death at bay. Which is exactly what I told her.

"You must be joking," she said, stunned.

"Unfortunately, no," I shook my head. "Do you have any idea where and how poison is regularly entering your organism? I can clearly see that the toxins have been building up a long time. Maybe more than a year."

"I don't know, I have to think."

Agnessa spaced out, which was understandable. It's not every day you find out something like that about your own life. I didn't want to interfere with her collecting herself, so I focused on the cakes. They were very tasty. There were several kinds — apple spread, cherry preserves, and strawberry jam. It seemed like the filling had also been made in Mrs. Peddleton's kitchen. Maybe it was made from the harvest of her fruit trees.

I ate four whole cakes before our hostess spoke again: "Mr. Richter, if there's poison in a potion, would you be able to identify it?"

"I'm willing to try," I smiled.

Agnessa stood up decisively, and quickly walked out of the living room. She returned five minutes later, holding a small vial with medicine in it. At least, that's what it looked like. She handed it to me, saying, "I drink almost nothing except tea, and I don't eat anything that isn't made under my supervision. But this is a gift from my grandson." Her voice quivered. "He's been giving me this potion for over a year. He says it's a brand new innovative product of magical medicine. He's a structural magician, studying biochemistry."

I didn't know what a biochemist was yet, and I didn't ask. Instead, I focused on the "medicine." Its appearance and smell seemed fine. If this was poison, it was very well disguised. There was only one way to find out: I poured a drop of the liquid on my own finger, and licked it up. It was poison, no doubt about it. The taste had been masked using a lot of different ingredients, but I could still taste it.

"Killer stuff. You can use this to destroy all the pests in your garden," I said.

"Are you sure?" she asked, still struggling to believe it.

"Positive. Any alchemist will confirm it."

"Alchemist?" The woman was even more confused now.

Olga came to the rescue: "He means a lab. He's from far away, he doesn't know the language that well, and sometimes he uses the wrong word."

"So what do I do now?" Agnessa asked helplessly.

"If you mean the poisoning, that's no big deal," I reassured her. "Your organism is strong enough to clear out all the toxins in two weeks' time. The main thing is, don't drink all kinds of filth from others' hands."

"Oh, don't worry, I'm going to deal with that issue head on," Agnessa fumed, her eyes becoming bloodshot.

Chapter 08

SOMETIMES, THE PREY COMES to the hunter. No sooner had wc deduced the origin of Mrs. Peddleton's poisoning, than it appeared before us of its own accord. I doubted this was a coincidence. The grandson sensed his machinations were about to be discovered, and was hovering around to monitor the situation.

"Carl, sit down, sweetheart," Agnessa said in the sweetest of grandmotherly voices. I'm sure she wanted to smash something over his head, but she controlled herself. I wasn't surprised, either — you learn to maintain a grip on your emotions in three hundred years' time.

The grandson, however, was much younger, and did not see what was coming next. "I asked you not to call me that!" the 'sweetheart' barked, planting his behind in an armchair in a huff.

"Well, we should go," Olga tactfully began to make our excuses so we wouldn't be present for the family drama.

"I know you're in a hurry," I said, picking up another cake from the plate, "but please allow me to savor this. Mrs. Peddleton, your baking is simply exquisite. I haven't tasted anything so good in a thousand years."

The cakes really were good, but more importantly, there was a danger the grandson might finish her off right now, and then I would have wasted my time and energy on her for nothing. It was better to stick around and see what happened.

"I'm very glad," the hostess blushed with delight. "I hope you and Olga visit me whenever you want. No matter if we have an appointment or not. I would be delighted to have you anytime."

Hearing this, Carl the 'sweetheart' let out a snort, but didn't say anything. Just then, the doorbell rang. He jumped up, and ran to the door before the butler could get there. The living room in this house was in full view of the vestibule, so we could see everything that happened next. The courier Carl had been waiting for had arrived, and now the grandson was fussily signing some kind of paperwork. Then, when it was time to pay for the delivery, he activated his sphere — it was green, like Agnessa's. But something went wrong. The courier said the payment had not gone through. Carl tried again, and again the payment was declined.

He came back to the living room with a quick

step. "Gran, something's happened to my sphere," he said, furrowing his brow.

"Yes, it has," she confirmed gravely.

"Well, call the bank," the spoiled grandson demanded, "I need to pay for the package." I half expected him to actually stomp his foot.

"Sweetheart," Agnessa began with gravity.

"I asked you not to call me that!" he interrupted.

But Mrs. Peddleton continued, ignoring his outrage. "The time has come for you to make your own way," she said. "I have sponsored your entertainment, your education, and your whole life long enough. From now on, you'll have to support yourself, sweetheart."

"What?!" the dumbfounded grandson howled. "How can you do this, Gran? You promised..."

"Enough!" Agnessa barked, surprising even me. "You are not worthy of the Peddleton name! You should be glad I don't kill you right in front of the healers and your damned courier!"

Correctly assessing that the situation was about to rapidly escalate, the courier had begun slowly backing away, and Agnessa's last pronouncement caused him to sprint away altogether. The ungifted always try to stay away from magical conflicts.

"But why?" Carl asked, confused and irritated. You could see the gears grinding in his head, trying to figure out what the matter was, and it finally came to him. "You!" he pointed at us. "What have you been telling my granny?!" He strode up to me and got in my face.

"Just that your medicine is actually poison," I answered him calmly.

Carl the 'sweetheart' turned dark red. "How dare you! I'll have you jailed for libel! Gran, how can you believe these charlatans?!"

He was so good at playing the insulted innocent that Agnessa started to doubt whether he wasn't telling the truth. "Maybe it would be a good idea to call an independent expert," she muttered. But this frightened Carl even more. "You don't need an expert!" he panicked, "Don't you trust me?"

Agnessa shook her head, with an expression of profound disappointment. "That's enough. Get out of my house right now." The grandson swallowed hard and headed toward the stairs to the second floor. But the butler blocked his way, and Mrs. Peddleton added, "I said get out right now. With just what you've got on. Nothing in this house belongs to you, so there's nothing for you upstairs."

"You old bitch!" The grandson finally showed his true colors. "I hope you croak soon!" He turned his back and exited the house.

"Please forgive that disgusting scene," Agnessa said to us sadly. "And now, please excuse me, but I need to be alone. Don't forget, I'm expecting your visit anytime at all."

"Of course, Mrs. Peddleton," Olga smiled softly, and added sympathetically, "Please remember, all will be well. You'll recover quickly."

"Thank you, dear," Agnessa nodded.

With that, we finally left that peaceful abode.

That dollhouse had gone through a lot of changes today.

Before we walked too far, I called Olga to come over to me and touched her forehead to suck out the abomination. Just as I had thought, there wasn't much. Even less than Hoffman had had. But that was alright.

"That's an indescribable sensation," my granddaughter commented. "How do you do that? And doesn't it hurt at all?"

"All in due course, Olga, soon you'll be able to do it, too," I reassured her. "Don't worry about it for now. Where are we going next?"

"It's a slightly longer walk this time. Are you still against taking a cab?"

I nodded, and that same moment, I heard Carl the 'sweetheart's' outraged voice. "Did you really think I would let you just get away like that?!" The disowned grandson, left without his creature comforts, was making his way toward us menacingly.

I sighed. "Naturally, we didn't," I answered him. "I am of an exceedingly low opinion of your intelligence, kid, so the fact that you're here now doesn't surprise me in the least. However, it would be best for you to get out of our way before you lose something much more valuable than money."

He belly laughed. "Threats from some pathetic leech?!" He extended his hand forward and made a fist, around which flames immediately formed. Then, with a bounding leap, he lunged at me. But he wasn't fast enough, and he didn't have the technique. A typical hothouse flower.

The fire hands was one of the most common battle spells. It looked good, but was nowhere as dangerous as it seemed. I ducked, and punched him in the solar plexus. At the same time, I grabbed his elbow and twisted his arm behind his back. The 'sweetheart' groaned and bent into an unnatural pose, which made him even more vulnerable.

I was frustrated at having to waste my energy on this little fool. To twist him up the way I did, I had to use quite a bit of energy. Carl was no warrior, but he was pretty physically strong. His gift made him a magician of face-to-face combat, so he used energy to reinforce his body, too. Even though I was pumping energy out of him right now, its volume was insufficient to make up for what I was losing. My one comfort was that the added energy would stay with me for a whole twenty-four hours. Who knew what else would happen today? I might need it.

As though reading my mind, Olga pensively drew out, "I can't understand it — why do we attract so much trouble? Is that a trait of our clan, too?"

"It's a trait of any straightforward person who isn't afraid to defend their own interests, Olga."

I finished with Carl, and left him lying in the bushes near his grandmother's house. "What have you done to me?" he quietly whispered to us as we left, but no one gratified him with an answer.

Meanwhile, Olga continued thinking out loud: "It's interesting — I've done sessions with Agnessa many times, but I never felt anything out of the ordinary. I guess she'll need my help a lot less frequently now."

"Absolutely. Let me guess — did she use all kinds of dubious means to try to combat aging?"

"Uh-huh. Only..." she laughed, "If you keep treating people so effectively, I'll lose all my clients."

"If all goes according to plan, soon you won't have to do this business anymore, or treat anyone," I explained with the utmost seriousness. "Get used to the idea that you're a necromancer, not a healer." Olga furrowed her brow, but didn't argue.

Soon, we had left the dollhouse village and entered another new neighborhood. This one, too, was much more friendly than the one we lived in. We were on a neatly appointed street that clearly functioned as a commercial and entertainment strip. The buildings were tall, and the first floors of all of them were commercial spaces — stores, shops, and cafes. Consequently, there were a lot of people around.

Suddenly, I was enveloped in a very pleasant aroma. I inhaled it deeply, and asked, "What is that smell?"

"Coffee," Olga answered.

I looked at her, surprised. "What is that?"

"It's a beverage. It didn't exist in your time, either?"

"No, we mostly drank tea and wine."

"Coffee is kind of like tea. There's no alcohol. Some people add it, though. Do you want to try it?"

"You know I do," I answered. I love

discovering new things.

We went into one of the taverns. In fact, it was named after the beverage — it was called a coffeehouse. I figured this beverage must be popular.

A hostess took us to a table by the window. "This is a good place," Olga said, "I come here a lot. I recommend the cappuccino — it's really great here. But first, try an espresso — that's just pure coffee, with nothing else."

The coffeehouse was brightly lit and quite cozy. There were no noisy crowds or streetwalkers. The coffee drinking culture didn't favor them, I figured. The waitress brought Olga a huge mug with a heart drawn in the foam, and me — a tiny cup, about one tenth the size of Olga's. "Is it just me, or did I get ripped off?" I asked, jokingly.

I drank the dense, somewhat bitter and caustic beverage, and was amazed. The aroma was as good as gallic cognac, and the effect was astounding. My blood, thickened with the centuries, seemed to move through my body faster.

Before the waitress had a chance to walk away, I said, "Bring me another one, and one like she has, and what else have you got?"

"We have latte, we have thai coffee..."

"Bring them, too!"

"Max, you won't have a heart attack from the caffeine, will you?" Olga asked after I finished off the thai coffee — a thick, milky drink, and very sweet.

"You feel like that would be an inconvenience for me?" I answered. Seeing how her face changed after I said that, I added, "You're a healer, I'm sure you'll save me." Funny, she wasn't worried when I was trying the strongest of poisons. Still, it was nice that she cared.

Seeing that I was about to call the waitress again, Olga pleaded with me, "Max, let's go! I have a coffee machine at home. It may not be as good as here, but it's not bad."

On that positive note, we headed to the next client. It really was a long walk, and I had a chance to ask my granddaughter a few more questions. For example, why had that Hugo come to her place at all? As I understood it, he represented the city, and they dealt with affairs of the ungifted, whereas Olga was a magician and an aristocrat. The usual rules shouldn't apply to her. I had already figured out that the legal system hadn't changed much in a thousand years, and it contained a ton of privileges for the nobility. Even if a gifted kills a commoner, the most they would have to do is pay a fine. And maybe their reputation might suffer. Maybe they've decided to frighten the commoners and make themselves seem like monsters in their eyes for some reason. Not a far-sighted strategy, to be sure — the loyalty of the ungifted is a resource, too, which no one should squander.

And if a magician kills another aristocrat, then there's inter-clan conflict, with everything that goes with it, but still, the civic authorities don't go anywhere near it.

"Technically, that's true," Olga sadly agreed with me, "but I'm not part of any clan. There's no clan lawyers backing me, there's no one behind me. That's the destiny of loners — to be subject to all the regular rules, like everyone else."

"What if you officially create a clan?"

"That's possible," Olga affirmed, "but you have to submit an application, and that's expensive. Like, very expensive. I don't know exactly how much, I never looked into it, but it's a fortune — the kind of money I've never laid hands on."

"That can be remedied."

Olga nodded.

"Yeah, I think if we continue to see several patients a day, sooner or later I'll be able to save up the necessary amount. Only..." she was embarrassed.

"What's on your mind?" I asked.

"New clans don't have it that great, either. Usually, they join a larger clan and become part of their coalition. Basically, they become yesmen. But there's no other way," she threw up her hands. "I'm sure you know that any clan can declare war on another. And the weak ones that can't defend themselves yet risk losing not only all their property, but their life, too. Even if every last member is killed, no one will say a word. So there's no point creating a new clan until we can defend ourselves," she concluded.

"How can you be so sure?" I snickered.

Olga looked at me intently, and admitted, "I'm not sure of anything anymore."

Finally, we arrived at the next client's house. He lived in a tall apartment building and his family was obviously much poorer than Mrs. Peddleton's. Maybe they didn't even belong to a clan, same as Olga.

Book One

We were met by the parents of the guy who had ODed. The father was level-headed, but the mother was on the verge of hysterics. She began to explain: "I don't understand how this could have happened! Alec is such a smart boy. He gets straight As. He's always been so good at controlling his power..."

"What's there to understand," the father harumphed. "It's all because of your high expectations. You've convinced our son that if he doesn't get into the elite magic academy in Bridgeport, his life will be over. No wonder he overdosed on stimulants!"

"Well, am I wrong?!" she screamed. "Do you want him to spend his life working in a factory like you? Besides, I never said that to him directly."

"But you let him know it!"

"I didn't..."

It was one family drama after another today. This had nothing to do with the treatment we were there to offer, so I decided to intervene in the fighting. "Where's our patient?" I asked the couple, distracting them from their squabble.

"One second," the mother started fussing, "I'll take you there."

Finally, the woman took us to the kid, who was about sixteen. He was unresponsive. Evidently, the excess of abomination had put him in a coma. "May we be alone with him?" Olga asked the hostess, and she left us.

"Hard case," she said, touching the kid. "It's been a long time since I've absorbed so much grace."

"Please, call it abomination. It's much more fitting. And let me see him myself."

Olga willingly walked off a little bit, and I put my hand on the kid's forehead. It really was a significant overdose. So much so, that, had we arrived a couple hours later, he might have died.

"I'll take care of this one," I told Olga, and started to absorb the excess energy. My granddaughter did not object. Why should she? I had just saved her from pain. Even though I would have relieved her suffering very quickly afterward, she would still have had to endure many very unpleasant minutes, given the amount of work there was to be done here.

Finally, when we were done, we received a good amount of money from the parents of the unfortunate future student. "Is he definitely going to be alright?" his mother continued to worry.

"Absolutely," I assured her. "Just give him a chance to come back to himself. I don't recommend using stimulants for at least a week."

"I'll make sure, thank you, doctor!"

I nodded, and we left the apartment.

"Wow," Olga smiled, "we didn't even get in a fight with anyone!"

"You're right, that's strange," I agreed, laughing. "Where to now?"

"We just have one more call," she said. "It's not far from here, and they pay well." Olga opened a navigator program on her smartphone — a pretty interesting invention I had already had a chance to appreciate. The interactive map was very convenient, and I regretted not being able to use one myself yet.

Following the program's instructions, we dove into a mass of courtyards. The atmosphere around us began to get more overbearing, as if we were back in an underprivileged neighborhood. The block was not too friendly, and, judging by the navigator, our client lived in some sort of hole where we found nothing.

"Are you sure you have the right address?" I asked Olga as we approached some charred ruins.

"No, it can't be. The client must have sent me the wrong address. Let me write to him and double check." She furrowed her brow, and became absorbed in her smartphone. I, on the contrary, studied the surroundings. So, when we were surrounded by several dark figures, I wasn't the least bit surprised.

Chapter 09

THE WALL HAD CRUMBLED after the fire and its charred ruins now provided a convenient cover for two dark-skinned guys, aged twenty or twenty-five. The roof tile provided great visibility, a lot of space, and excellent shade to hide in, for those who were underneath it. If you didn't know it had been an accident, you might think it had been laid that way on purpose.

Naturally, as the gang leader, Kir took the best spot for himself. His second in command was his twin brother and right-hand man, Rik. It's true, their parents had a quirky sense of humor.

"I don't know, Kir, I don't think we should have agreed to do the gifted one." Rik was the voice of reason between them.

"Don't you ever stop whining? Chill!" Kir hissed. "You know how much we're getting for her." He hated his sibling's propensity for perpetual doubt. Rik had thought the gang was a stupid idea, but he'd put his foot in his mouth after they made easy money and didn't get caught, several times in a row. Kir was confident this time would be no different.

"What if she resists? Starts doing magic at us?" Rik continued to worry. "It's not too late to call it off."

"Don't be stupid, huh?" his brother attacked him. "She's just a leech — what magic is she gonna do to you?! They've never had any battle magic in them."

Rik got quiet. Kir was right, but still he had a bad feeling.

And that's when their victim appeared. Only she wasn't alone. Kir appealed to his twin again: "Look, she's got a guy with her."

"So what?" his brother dismissed him.

"What do you mean so what? Suppose he's gifted too?"

"Listen, Rik, remember when you fell down the stairs when you were twelve?"

"Yeah, what does that..."

"Sometimes I think you must have knocked all your brains out," interrupted Kir. "Just think — what magician in their right mind would get involved with a leech, and go to treatment sessions with her? I guarantee he's the same as her — a bottom feeder, or doesn't have any gift at all. We'll take him down, and grab the girl like we planned.

the Dark healer

They only paid us for one."

* * *

The dark figures did not encircle us all at once, but crawled, like spiders, out of every crevice in the charred ruins. "Olga, quick! Hide behind those!" I commanded, nodding at the upturned trash cans near the wall.

"What?" Olga looked up from her smartphone. Incredible carelessness! They don't train any battle qualities in the young people at all. Although, truth be told, there was nobody to raise Olga, so there was no one to blame for how she had turned out.

Eventually, she noticed the ambush and was now staring at the figures surrounding us, her eyes round from fear and surprise. "Maybe we should run?"

"No," I said unequivocally, and walked straight toward the gang of thugs. I didn't have time to explain why she shouldn't run away, and Olga respected me enough by now to listen. Anyway, it was simple — there were at least twenty cutthroats, and if she ran, some of them would run after her. Then, the fight would be more difficult for me, as I would have to chase after the ones who were chasing her. Imagining that circus-like battle scene, I immediately had that silly circus song playing in my head. Best to let them all concentrate on me.

I could feel a scowl involuntarily form on my face. Twenty bodies and not one gifted one — this was going to be a piece of cake. Thanks to that troglodyte Carl, I had pumped myself full of energy earlier in the day, and this had helped me identify the ambush faster than I otherwise could have. I wouldn't have been surprised if he had been the one who had sent these gentlemen here. I had left him almost unconscious, but he could have reached his cellphone. I already knew how those things worked.

I really had a taste for battle again. This skirmish could hardly be called a battle, but it would still be fun, and give my muscle memory a chance to recall some old moves. The fights I'd had until now had all been in tight quarters.

"Tough guy, eh?" I heard one of the gang members say. "Maybe he thinks we're playing hide and seek and wants to play, too." The others all laughed, even though the joke had not been funny. I guessed its author was a head honcho.

"Why not?" I snickered. "We could play hide and seek. Whoever doesn't hide, don't blame me for what happens next."

"You're a real maniac," the gang leader said again. I could see for sure now that that's what he was, because everyone was waiting for his signal to act. "But I don't have time for you. Get him, boys!"

"What about the girl?" one of them yelled out.

"She's not going anywhere."

I wondered who it was that was so interested in my granddaughter. We were going to have to find out. I went straight toward the leader. Not knowing whether he had some surprises up his sleeve, I moved slowly. I wanted to let the gang of losers show their colors. Why 'losers'? What else would you call those who would try to ambush me?

What was weird though, was that they weren't in a hurry to attack, either. Maybe they were so shocked by me walking toward them that they didn't know what to do. Finally, the leader overcame his stupor and grabbed his gun. He shot three times, slowly. Too slowly. Surging with energy for battle against the gifted, I easily calculated the bullets' trajectory, and just as easily got out of the way. But, at least five more of them got their guns out, too. In my time, too, the ungifted were big fans of the longbow, the crossbow, and anything else that would allow them to do battle at a distance. It was much less risky.

Right away, there were several times more bullets flying at me, and getting out of the way of all of them became a lot more tricky. They were mostly all aiming for the upper part of the body. So, I hunched down, and in one fast motion, was right in front of the nearest shooter. I gave him an uppercut so hard, the guy flew three feet up in the air, which is when I punched him again, in the stomach this time, sending him flying. But he was unconscious by then.

"What the fuck?" I heard several surprised voices exclaim. This was followed by a new avalanche of bullets. It seemed like maybe only seven or eight of the twenty attackers had guns, and the ones that didn't were staying out of the skirmish for now, afraid to get caught in the crossfire. But,

I saw each of them produce some weapon or other — knives, clubs, and other implements from the youth delinquent's arsenal. These were not serious gangsters.

The fight did become a little more entertaining, though, because of the multitude of bullets flying at me. I was enjoying studying this new weapon. Its speed and kill power were much higher than any longbow or crossbow. And it called for a somewhat different defense strategy.

I really didn't feel like ruining my new jacket, so I came up with a way to eliminate the shooters from the fight. It only took a few movements to get to the most aggressive one of them as he was reloading. In one instant move, I ducked away from the other shooters, and leapt over to him; the next instant, I cracked open his ribcage in such a way that the broken ribs went inward and instantaneously made a pulpy mess of his internal organs.

A sudden pain in my shoulder. One of the bastards got me after all. This wound was nothing to me — my body immediately blocked the nerve endings and blood vessels near the wound, pushed the bullet back out, and healed the wound.

Even though my jacket was now ruined anyway, I didn't feel like giving them the gratification of hitting me again, so I grabbed the guy as he fell and used him for a shield. Besides, for a necromancer, fighting with your own hands isn't really that normal — it's just that I personally didn't like to miss an opportunity to have some fun. But my experience was with hand-to-hand combat, backed by a chimera army of my own creation.

the Dark healer

These were creatures made from the dead flesh of my enemies. I didn't yet possess the requisite materials to create a whole army. However, I was about to demonstrate, with gusto, a lot of other surprises.

Using my shadow scalpel, I gave the head of the dead gangster two quick slices, and was now holding his ears in the palm of my hand. As always, thanks to the special qualities of the scalpels, there wasn't much blood — I didn't even get dirty. Pretty much any suitable pieces of flesh would have done for my purposes. I put a little power in the ears, and tossed them upward. The corpse flies was a basic little spell that beginner necromancers used — usually just for training, and sometimes for creating a diversion. Once upon a time, just for fun, I changed it a little: my flies were different — they wouldn't stop until they'd eaten my enemy whole.

Which is what they were now doing. Two cloud-like swarms of flies, one for each victim. At once, the flies covered their faces and necks. The other thugs were so shocked by what was happening that they forgot all about me, and ran to help their unfortunate brothers in arms. To no avail. Those two had already died a horrible death, and now the flies were attacking others, leaving the first two victims with nothing but bloody messes where their faces used to be.

"Holy shit!" the horrified screams started.

"Fuck this, I'm out of here!" one of the thugs exclaimed, but he did not have a chance to run.

One of them decided to give the rest a pep

talk: "Dumbasses! If we scatter now, he'll finish us off one by one!"

I guffawed, threw my earless victim to one side, and picked up the gun he had dropped. It was time to try shooting.

With several of their soldiers disabled, the rest decided it was a good opportunity to beat and stab me to death with knives and brass knuckles. They banded together and charged forward. "Get him! There's only one of him, and a lot of us!" they were yelling, trying to psych themselves up.

I aimed and took several shots at the crowd. It turned out to not be that difficult, and two of my enemies immediately fell to the ground like empty sacks. Unfortunately, after that the bullets were spent, and I hadn't yet learned how to reload this weapon. But I had another surprise for my attackers. As they ran at me, the flies had taken care of several of their shooters, which meant I could use them.

It's more efficient to resurrect through touch, but you can do it at a distance, too — you just spend more energy. So now, I just sat and waited for the trap to shut. There were only two shooters left, and they weren't about to keep fighting. Just the opposite, they wanted to split and abandon their gang. But they didn't have a chance. Their erstwhile friends, now zombies, rose up, and quickly dropped them on the ground, breaking their necks. People who say zombies are clumsy just don't know how to make zombies properly. It's true that they're not very good at balancing on two legs, but when they run on all fours, they more than make up for it.

A swarm of six zombies was now approaching their buddies with great speed. The others had surrounded me, but were not attacking. Maybe they were confused by the fact that I didn't try to resist their attack at all, but instead just sat there, smiling at them.

"He's a nutcase," one of them muttered, voicing all of their fears. "He's rabid."

"That's alright, we can take him together. What are we waiting for? Let's get him!"

The bravest of them lunged at me, but at precisely that moment a zombie jumped on his back and knocked him off his feet. The same happened to several others, and all that could be heard was screaming and swearing.

I felt great amidst this chaos. All I had to do now was finish off the ones the zombies had not gotten to. I even had time to calculate all the most effective blows to lay the lowlifes flat in one move, while doing minimal harm to my future servants' flesh. It was all over quickly. Or maybe not...

There were two aristocrats headed straight for us, as I found out from my shadow scout in the middle of the fight. They had decided to intervene, but I was not sure of their intentions. They might have just been observers. Maybe they had just happened by, but then started placing bets on the skirmish.

But now, I understood everything about them, including the level of power they wielded. They were both at least magister level — much higher than the fool Hoffman, and especially Carl, or Hugo had been.

"So much for your idea of using gangs made up only of the ungifted," sighed one of them to the other. "It's the same thing every time."

The other shrugged indifferently and tore away, moving toward me. His body began to develop steel armor, and his hands turned into blades, which he extended in front of him. He was from one of the metal clans. Those guys were good at close combat — they're like a weapon themselves, plus they're almost impossible to kill, even if you shoot them out of a catapult. I didn't think bullets from the ungifted thugs' guns would even scratch the armor on this guy, and he knew it. He was going whole-hog. I only had a fraction of a second to do something before he ran me through with his two swords. So, I just allowed him to. The jacket was already ruined anyway, and a few seconds of pain were worth it to catch him in my trap.

The son of a bitch was too fast, I saw that right away. I wasn't physically strong enough yet to fight him hand-to-hand on equal terms. Nor did I have the weapons — the gangsters' wooden clubs were no match for steel blades. So, I decided to let him wound me. Now, he was in my hands, staring at me, confused. He couldn't understand why I wasn't dying, or at least doubling over in pain.

I smiled, put my palm on his forehead, and drank up all his energy to the last drop. I took away all his energy and absorbed it myself. After all, his armor was just modified flesh, and didn't protect him from physical contact. The metallic armor peeled off of his skin, his hands became regular hands again, and he fell to the ground life-less.

"What have you done to him?" another one screamed.

"Try to guess," I answered, as I started moving toward him. But, when I saw the thin ice needles form between his fingers, I realized this one wasn't a fan of hand-to-hand combat. A second later, they were flying at me, followed by a barrage of more and more of them. That kind of environmental magic is quite unpleasant even for me, so I had to prevent myself from being struck, but in such a way that he wouldn't lose sight of me visually. At one point, he made a deadly downpour right above me, and almost got me — I got out from under the steady wall of falling knives just in time. He also kept trying to freeze me, and was constantly surprised that it wasn't working. To prevent that from working, and from turning into a shameful snowman when there was an enemy to fight, I had to push my blood through my circulatory system by force. In general, he made me constantly move. I was purposely getting closer to him, then getting farther away, so he wouldn't take his eyes off me. Meanwhile, one of the zombies made its way toward him from behind. Of course, you can't pull the same trick on a gifted that you can on a regular thug, so no one was about to jump on his back and try to bring him to the ground. I had more interesting spells up my sleeve.

Bam! As soon as the zombie was within punching distance of the magician, its body quickly inflated, then exploded. The sharp shards of bone pierced the enemy's body, while the torn pieces of flesh had turned into corpse flies, rats, bats, leeches, and even spiders. That whole mass of flesh started moving toward my opponent. He tried to fight it off, managing to freeze a few of the creatures. But, each one of the necro-creatures, as well as each bone knife, carried poison in it, which made the magician weaker with each new wound he sustained. This was one of my favorite spells, though it didn't come in handy too often. It was too destructive — a body like that takes a lot of energy to create, and once it's exploded, it can't be used again.

I wasn't going to let my creatures finish off the magician by themselves. I got in close, scattered them, and took what remained of his energy.

And that was it. I looked around the battlefield, and called to Olga, "It's over, you can come out."

She emerged frightened, but in one piece. I think I had shocked her again. To me, the corpses scattered before us were a source of revenue that I now coldly calculated in my mind; but she was not used to this kind of thing yet.

Olga swallowed hard, then asked, "What happened? Who are these people?"

I shrugged. "That's what we're going to ask."

"Ask who?" the young lady started looking around, frightened. "Is one of them alive?"

"Yeah, that guy over there, sitting under the collapsed balcony. He had the presence of mind not to get involved in the scuffle, but not enough to run away in time. Maybe he thought if he didn't move I wouldn't see him."

"I can't see him," Olga whined, disappointed.

"It's dark over there. I wouldn't have seen him either if I hadn't augmented my reflexes with magic."

"You can do that, too?"

"Naturally," I answered. Then, I yelled to the survivor: "Come on out. Or do you want my servants to drag you out?"

His silhouette jumped — it was the first movement he had made the entire time. To be fair, he had just witnessed such a clusterfuck of destruction that I don't even know how he had been able to stay still like that the whole time.

But I had noticed him right away — his loss, my gain. The fact that he was there had freed me up during the fighting, as it meant I didn't have to bother leaving one of the combatants alive to interrogate.

Chapter 10

"LET'S SEE WHAT YOU'VE got!" I egged on the thug. He kept milling from one foot to the other, frightened by the zombie.

"We're not gonna kill you," Olga called out. Then, she looked at me. "We're not, right?" What a kind soul. It made me want to give her a noogie, and I did, which embarrassed her for some reason.

"Of course we're going to kill him, no two ways about it. The fact that he's a coward and stayed out of the fighting doesn't mean he would have spared you if the shoe was on the other foot," I explained. "Still, I'll give him a choice: he can earn a quick and easy death if he tells us everything right now. Otherwise, he'll die slowly and painfully." I purposely spoke loud enough for the prick to hear us. Then, I looked back at him, and was clearly addressing him when I said, "I can see you're looking for an escape route. Look at those eyes darting around. But if you do that, then you'll have no options that don't involve getting intimate with all your former comrades here. Believe me, you won't like it when they start eating you and your brains alive."

The thug started trembling, but continued approaching, slowly. I guessed my arguments had resonated with him. "I…I barely know anything," he stuttered. "I'm n-not one of th-these… I just happened to be walking by."

"Right, and the gun in your coat also just happens to be there," I said, just as my lizard dislodged his gun from its holster and it fell to the ground with a dull metallic clunk.

"That doesn't prove anything!" he suddenly yelled, temporarily no longer stuttering.

"I'm not interested in proving anything," I cut him off. "What I've seen is proof enough. So, what's it going to be? Are you going to talk, or should we go straight to dinner?" I ordered a few zombies to get closer and surround the bandit like a pack of hungry dogs. It wasn't a sight for the faint-hearted. I could tell it even made Olga a bit queasy, even though she was not in any danger. I had to hand it to her, though: she was acclimating fast.

Unsurprisingly under the circumstances, our new friend started talking real fast. "O-OK! J-just g-get them away from me!" he recoiled in horror from his former comrades. I shrugged my shoulders and ordered the zombies to back off a little bit.

"We didn't really do anything," he began. "Just small-time kidnappings. We'd find someone rich — a lawyer, an architect, I don't know, even a who... we did a model once. She was a beginner, but not bad."

"You call that not doing anything?" Olga asked, horrified.

"See?" I answered her, "And you wanted to spare him."

Hearing that, he shivered again. "How about letting me go, huh? I'll tell you everything. And anyway, I was always against all this. My brother made me participate!"

"How old are you?" I asked him.

"Twenty-six."

"Does your mom still dress you, too?"

He swallowed hard. "But I... I really..."

"Keep talking," I interrupted him. Say what you want, but I never felt any pity or sympathy for his type. Even if he was telling the truth, he was no less guilty than the rest. Just a stooge who went with the flow and did horrible things, rationalizing it to himself by claiming he was forced to do it. Besides, I was sure he was lying. Maybe it was true that he wasn't that into the kind of stuff their gang got up to, but certainly no one forced him to get involved, that was for sure. I always see right through his type.

"Once, we managed to kidnap a magician." Then, leering at Olga, he added, "She was a leech, too."

Something dangerous flared up in her eyes.

"A leech! You're ungifted altogether," she snorted.

"Sorry, that's what everyone says," the thug started to apologize.

"Don't get distracted," I ordered him. "Who are you working for?"

"Y-yes, of c-course. I don't actually know exactly who. They worked with m-my brother, and didn't say anything about themselves. And he didn't ask, either! W-we just needed the money."

"It is in your best interests to remember every single thing you ever saw or knew," I warned him, calling a couple of the zombies to come closer again.

"They had requirements. The subjects had to be delivered in ideal condition, with no signs of mistreatment, health fully intact."

"Subjects," Olga snorted again, her pity for this specimen waning.

"S-sorry, v-victims," the thug started stuttering again.

"Is that all you remember?" I asked him.

"Y-yes."

Olga said, "Maybe they're organ traders. Otherwise, why would they have to deliver their victims in ideal health? There have been rumors about that in healer circles. There are rich commoners who extend their lives by getting organ transplants. It's hard to find the right donor through the official channels, and you have to wait a really long time. But this way..."

"Exactly!" the gangster exclaimed. "I remember seeing some kind of medical equipment when we were delivering the last victim."

Book One

Olga nodded gravely. "Yes, that's it. And I know why they came after me specifically. First of all, unlike many other gifted, healers can't really resist," she explained. "Second, our bodies are in ideal condition and we are immune to practically everything. I've never been sick even once in my whole life." Hearing herself say all that out loud really gave her pause. "My God, I could have been a victim!" she said.

I gave her another noogie. "But you weren't," I said. "As long as you're with me, you're in no danger." Then, I turned back to the thug to ask him a few more questions. But, unfortunately, I couldn't get much more out of him. He had no idea who the gifted who had attacked us were. He just delivered victims to them, and that's it. Even when one of my zombies lightly tugged on his pant leg and gave him a careful bite, he screamed, but didn't come up with any new information. I was going to have to conduct my own investigation. After all, an attempt had been made on my life, and on that of a member of my clan, and letting that go unpunished was out of the question. Furthermore, all the other healers, or 'leeches' as they were called, were untrained necromancers like Olga. They were my potential students and allies. I wasn't about to let them get butchered.

"So, are you going to let me go? I told you everything I know," the thug said hopefully.

"No. But, as I promised, your death will be quick and painless."

The cutthroat stared at me in horror. In one lightning fast motion, I was near him. I put my hand on his head, and the life force immediately left his body.

"I think I'm starting to get used to all the killing," Olga said, "This creep really had it coming. What kind of lowlife do you have to be to kidnap and deliver people to have their organs harvested!"

I nodded, and went over to the gifted ones to see if there were crystals inside them like Hugo had.

"Uncle Max," Olga called out to me again, "do zombies really eat brains?"

I laughed. "Only when ordered to. They don't need to, they feed off the energy of the necromancer who raised them. But it sounds nice and scary, doesn't it?"

* * *

Phil was smiling so wide you could see all twenty-four of his teeth. He wasn't too lucky in street brawls, but what was that now, when everything was going good? A great day had turned into a great evening. He and his 'bro' had just returned to the city from a fishing trip on which he hadn't caught a single fish. But he had caught a beauty named Kitty on his hook, and she was now in his bed. That catch was worth all the fish in the world!

The best thing of all was that the buddies had no plans to curtail their activities. On the contrary, right now they both had a pretty good buzz on, and were about to go bar-hopping and picking up girls. Nature and Kitty were great and everything, but these two were freedom-loving guys — real nightcrawlers. Swaying slightly and belly-laughing, the two of them walked the late night city streets where everyone knew them, looking for someone to... basically, they were making sure they hadn't been forgotten in the neighborhood in the few days they'd been out of town.

"Phil, look," Hans poked him in the side, "ahead there, looks like a tourist."

"Yeah, and stoned, too."

The figure that was slowly progressing up the street really was swaying back and forth quite a lot. It looked like a sailor who had just come on land, or someone really drunk.

"Let's find out what the deal is. Maybe take his dope."

"Yeah," Phil snickered, "collect a toll, so to speak."

Hans laughed like a horse, even though the two of them were the only ones who thought what Phil said was funny. Drunk friends think anything is funny.

They sped up, and soon Phil put his hand on the junkie's shoulder and said, "Hey scumbag, where you from?"

The junkie had no intention of stopping, he just kept stubbornly walking forward, oblivious.

"Hey, I'm talking to you," Phil yelled. Then, he caught up with him, and went white as a sheet. The face of the man he was harassing was disfigured by a huge bloody gash. The blood no longer flowed, but he saw literally a torn piece of meat where skin should have been, and could even see bones through it here and there.

"What the fuck is that, Hans?!" Phil even rubbed his eyes, thinking he was hallucinating. "I'm not losing it, right? You see that too, don't you?"

"What the..." his friend caught up to the junkie too, and stared at his face. "Well, I'll be dipped in shit! What the fuck is that?! How is he even alive?!"

Meanwhile, the 'junkie' paid absolutely no attention to them, and continued walking forward unperturbed.

"What's wrong with you, dude?" Phil was literally running after him. "Are you alive?" He had forgotten all about his plans of shaking the guy down for dope or money. Truth be told, he didn't know what the hell he was doing.

"Can you speak at least?" Hans pursued.

Zero response.

Finally, they left him alone and went their way, a lot slower now. "That's one unlucky guy," Phil said pensively. "I'd rather die than walk around like that. No wonder he's on drugs."

"Yeah," Hans agreed. Then, he suddenly exclaimed, "Look! Here come two more!"

Phil turned and saw them. Their walk was very similar to that of the fucked up junkie. The faces on these seemed to be intact, however. He and Hans stopped and waited for the other two to approach. When they did, the two friends got a fright once again. There was something weird about these people. Their movements, the indifference on their faces, and their unnatural pallor.

"They look like zombies in movies," Phil made

an effort to say.

"Oh, come on," Hans displayed his bravado. "We'll take care of them in two seconds." He purposely pushed one of them with his shoulder, but they just continued walking forward, undaunted. Then, he grabbed one of them by the hand, but very quickly jerked his hand away again.

"Fuck! Phil, he's ice cold! He's a corpse!"

"I told you! Let's get out of here!"

The two friends hurried to the other side of the street, farther away from these weird pedestrians, but only ended up running into a whole procession of similar uglies. There were about fifteen of them. Some of them also had gorey messes instead of faces, while others had visible fresh bullet holes in their bodies. And then, there were those that had no extremities. Their comrades helped them to move.

"Holy shit! Holy shit!" the two degenerates repeated over and over as the crowd of zombies walked toward them.

"Fuck them! Let's get out of here!" Phil said.

Hans nodded, and they ducked into the nearest entryway. The creatures — they weren't people anymore — didn't display any aggression, but then again, the friends didn't want to risk it. Once they were at a safe distance, Hans asked, "Did you take a photo?"

"No."

"Me neither. Shit. No one will believe us!"

"Let's go back?"

"Let's. We'll at least get a snapshot from a distance."

The two buddies hurried back, but they were only brave enough to take a photo of the undead crowd from the back, and from far away. The photo didn't really come out. It was dusk, and they had a cheap phone with a crappy camera. So much for capturing definitive proof of what they had seen.

"Hey Phil," Hans started up the conversation again, "maybe we should call the cops? Let them sort it out."

Phil agreed. They called the police, but the only response they got was that there's no such thing as zombies, and that if they prank call the police again, they'll have the drug squad come out and search them.

"Jackasses!" Phil seethed. "There might be a zombie apocalypse happening, and they don't even give a shit."

"It's our civic duty to warn the people!" Hans stated with pomp. "If the cops don't get it, then let's go to the papers!"

All the press offices were closed, but that did not deter the errant friends. They spent all night drinking at bars and telling everyone who would listen about the zombie invasion. Then, in the morning, they went to the newspapers, where no one believed them and their photo was laughed at. Only one reporter from a tabloid rag was interested, but they could tell by his utterly tedious face that he didn't believe their story either. Despite which, after questioning them, he promised to print it.

Book One

*   *   *

After the interrogation, we didn't delay in leaving the battleground. As I had expected, I had extracted a grace gemstone from the chests of both gifted. Then, I had used a decay spell to clean up the blood and other evidence of the skirmish. It's very convenient, it decomposes absolutely anything organic into untraceable dust. As for the inorganic stuff, like the guns and ammo, and the knives, these were gathered up by one of my new servants. Something might have gotten stuck in the walls, but I doubted anyone was going to dig for it. The street looked just as we had found it — dirty, abandoned, disgusting. Once I had raised all the corpses, I sent them all directly to my stable. Luckily, it was already dark out, so I knew they wouldn't be seen by many. Besides, Olga had shown me a route through the bad neighborhoods, where not too many people walked late at night. Frankly, I couldn't understand what was so difficult about lighting the street lights and putting guards there to keep things safe. The descendants had certainly let the city go, it was embarrassing.

We didn't go home right away, but decided to stay in the city for a while. Olga proposed that we walk to her favorite pub. "I need a drink," she said earnestly, "and my cleanser friend hangs out there a lot — the one I promised I'd introduce you to."

Seeing no reason to refuse, I nodded acquiescence. I had found the cuisine of this time pretty good, and was curious to see what the alcohol was like. Like any poison, I can digest and neutralize alcohol instantly. But I don't always use that ability.

Soon, we entered a pretty cozy establishment. Despite being for commoners, it was very clean inside, and smelled pleasantly of fresh beer and fried sausages. A buxom blonde waitress dressed as a valkyrie showed us to a table in the dining room, and we ordered right away. The smells were just too tempting, and I could barely contain myself. I ordered sausages, and another fried meat, and also something called a burger to try. That dish did not exist in my time.

"Uncle," Olga said when the waitress left, "won't you pop? I wouldn't have figured you for an overeater."

"A necromancer's figure doesn't depend on the amount of food they consume," I raised my index finger in a gesture of importance. "I can control my own metabolism and keep myself at my most comfortable weight."

"Oooh" my granddaughter said. She was definitely interested in learning necromancy now.

"I want to check the news," Olga said, "see if there's anything about kidnappings."

I nodded, and she became absorbed in her phone. It was dark in the pub, so no one noticed my not quite intact jacket. Or maybe that was customary? I had seen jeans on one young lady that were so torn, you could see not only the color, but the style of her underwear. Noticing my interest, she had smiled broadly, but seeing Olga, she tightened her lips and looked away, disappointed. I guessed she had taken me for someone from something like a lovers of torn clothing guild. Commoners always have silly stuff like that on their minds. Olga didn't notice anything, as she had been staring at the screen of her phone the whole time.

"Aha! I got it. Two healers have gone missing. Oh no, I remember that girl! We went on a difficult call together once. I thought she was very nice, and behaved very humbly and politely. Man! Do you think she's been killed already?!" she said the last part in a whisper.

"Do you know where she lived?"

"No, but I know who knows, I can ask."

"Ask," I said supportingly. "We'll go there tomorrow, maybe we'll find out something."

Olga started typing. Just then, the waitress brought a tray of food and beer, making eyes at me all the while. As soon as she walked away from our table, a tall, broad-shouldered man appeared next to our table, wearing a brown leather jacket with studs and a shepherd's hat — the kind they liked to wear in the New World, with the bent brim. I guessed no one had taught him to remove his hat indoors.

"Olga, so good to see you!" He smiled broadly at my granddaughter, and shot me a side glance.

Olga looked up and was also glad. "Prokhor, hi!" She smiled. "How lucky to run into you here. I wanted to introduce you to someone."

"Prokhor," the man leaned heavily over the table, extending his meaty hand to me. You can tell a lot about someone by their hands. A pianist's or a surgeon's hand is as different from that of a construction worker or a ditch digger, as wings are from hooves. Prokhor had the hands of a warrior.

"Maximillian Richter," I nodded and shook his hand. Prokhor naturally tried to play 'squash the hand', but was unable to, which left him very surprised.

Tired of flexing his muscles and disheartened by the failed handsquashing, he moved a chair over to our table, saying, "I won't be in your way here, will I? Maybe this is a romantic outing?" I almost laughed. Given the way he melted when he looked at Olga, and how unhappy he had been to see me with her, his question was not the least bit surprising. He wanted to know whether I was competition.

Olga skillfully evaded the question: "You won't be in our way at all! On the contrary, Max has something he needs to speak to you about."

"What's that?" Prokhor squinted.

"This," I said, producing one of the gemstones from my pocket, then tossing and catching it in my hand. "I want to sell a couple of these."

Prokhor examined me again with doubt and hostility in his eyes. Still, he answered civilly: "We can't do this here. Come to my base tomorrow." We agreed on a time and he soon left, saying his friends were here and he had to go meet them. I wasn't too upset, because they had brought the sausages, and I wasn't interested in sharing. As I remembered, this guy didn't order anything, so let him go hungry.

$\mathcal{B}$ook $\mathcal{O}$ne

* * *

Before leaving the bar, Olga went to the bathroom, where Prokhor intercepted her by the door. "Are you aware your friend has bullet holes in his jacket?" he asked, bending over Olga. "I don't like that guy. He looks like a poacher. Otherwise, where would he have gotten the gemstones?"

Olga smiled and shook her head. "Come on! That's my uncle."

"Uncle? Aren't you an orphan?" Prokhor said, surprised.

"Yes, but that doesn't mean I don't have any family at all," Olga said.

"Alright, I understand," the cleanser reluctantly agreed. "See you tomorrow then."

Olga went into the bathroom, and then she and her 'uncle' left. Prokhor was sitting in his car, and he saw them exiting the bar, chatting happily. They weren't even holding hands. But his distrust and animosity toward the other man continued to grow. He and Olga were just friends, but he had to watch over her and protect her from trouble. Which included sketchy types with aristocratic airs. This wasn't because he was jealous. No, of course not!

* * *

Back at home, we were greeted by an imperturbable crowd of my new servants. Olga recoiled from them at first, but got a grip pretty quickly. Seeing her reaction, I promised, "Don't worry, I'll move them to the cellar. Fred is enough help here in this little stable. We'll fetch the others when we need them."

She nodded agreement, and said with readiness, "Do as you will. I... you saved my life today!"

"A mere trifle," I smiled.

"No, it's not a trifle! And I realized that I very much want to learn from you!" she persisted. "I want to know how to protect myself! Please, let's start as soon as possible!"

Her enthusiasm was admirable, but today I had other plans.

"Aren't you tired?" I asked.

"Not at all! On the contrary, I feel more alert than ever! So many things happened today... how could I rest when... things like that... like THAT... are happening!" Olga looked agitated. All day, she had contained herself and been very reasonable and well-behaved. Now, she opened the valve and released the emotions that had built up inside her. Her voice was quivering, she had fire in her eyes, and her movements were spasmodic and impatient. She was rearing for battle.

"Alright," I smiled. "Let's start simple. Any self-respecting necromancer must first and foremost control their own body, manage all its systems. Every muscle, every cell." Olga listened carefully, and soon I suggested we move from theory to practice.

Relaxation. An absolutely basic spell that allows you to gain strength and cleanse your organism, as well as process abomination faster. Even my slumber had been a sophisticated version of precisely this magic. That fact won Olga over, and she started trying to replicate it.

She was able to almost immediately. Her eyes began to close, and in a moment, she was out. All I could do was catch her as she fell, and carefully hand her off to Fred. Let him carry her to bed. As for me, I hurried to the cellar. I still had a lot of stuff — and a lot of stiffs — to deal with.

Chapter 11

BY THIS TIME, FRED HAD FINISHED cleaning all the rooms in my cellar. There definitely wasn't enough room down there to store all of the day's undead catch. Besides, I needed the lab to work with the bodies.

Flesh is a universal element. A necromancer can create practically anything from it, given the requisite magical mastery, sufficient energy, and suitable equipment. With enough skill, it can be done without equipment, too. My skills enabled me to do almost everything from scratch, but I still preferred to work in well-equipped spaces. It was a shame all the laboratories I had assembled so painstakingly had disappeared while I slept. The stable cellar was only one of the precautions I had taken. I hate it when things don't go according to plan, so, whenever possible, I always provide for plans B, C, and D.

There was no need to do everything at the cutting edge of technology. I had only the most basic implements at my disposal now, but I couldn't complain. When Frank Stein, the most famous necromancer of antiquity, created his first chimera, he had even less to work with. He was armed only with the dream of breathing his life force into not just a zombie or wraith, but a man-made creature the like of which the world had never known. Our gift is akin to that of the painter or sculptor, and the old man knew this better than anybody. It was even a little sad that after his death, which happened before I was born, the Stein clan fell into decline and, like all the other clans with similar talents, fell under the expansion of the Richters. It was a shame, because I often missed having worthy competition. I'm of the conviction that competing with a worthy opponent is a great way to accomplish a lot, simply out of a desire for progress.

When the zombies had reached the house, I had blocked their access to my energy and they turned into regular corpses again, except they wouldn't rot. Fred was now transporting them to the cellar.

I gave him some of the energy I had amassed that day, bringing him to the next level. I would need a good assistant now. With his new abilities, the wraith would be able to conduct subtle operations that required sophisticated micro-motor control. I could do what needed to be done without the extra hands, but it would be a lot quicker and easier with them.

Before getting down to business, I checked all the equipment again: the saw stations, sewing machines, needles, crafting tables, and even the mechanical press. Everything worked well, which meant I wouldn't need to spend as much energy doing everything with magic. I wasn't afraid of simple solutions or physical labor. Besides, I was still applying my necromancer skills, or else I wouldn't have been able to keep the space clean and tidy. And I can't stand a mess. Blood and other bodily fluids were an inevitable nuisance in my business. Blood can be useful in some spells, but definitely not for creating chimeras.

Finally, Fred carried the last body into the cellar and I went to work. I was used to being in the company of a multitude of students and assistants when I was creating, so I had a habit of commenting out loud as I worked. I hate silence, so if I was working alone and there was no one there to learn and assist, I would invite the bravest bards alive then to play as I worked.

Now, there would be no students, musicians, or assistants. All I had now was Fred. He was an ideal conversationalist, by the way: he listened very intently, and never interrupted, or offered his 'valuable' opinion.

"It's ironic, isn't it, Fred? If necromancers don't exist anymore, then neither do chimeras. At the same time, magicians of all specializations have dreamt of creating them for many years. Granted, their attempts to cross-breed living creatures to create man-made monsters like griffins and manticores didn't lead to anything," I told my imperturbable helper as I selected the material I would be working with. "Except the poor creatures' deaths, of course. Living bodies resist that kind of treatment, but dead ones are like marble under the sculptor's chisel. A strong necromancer can attain amazing results and achieve astonishing forms."

Just then, I finished skinning one of the gangsters and looked at Fred. He was doing a great job sawing the bones into pieces.

"No offense, Fred," I continued, "chimeras also have their faults. They're a... specialized instrument. Not one of them is capable of the kind of complex work you're doing right now. That's because of their damaged nervous system. A creature assembled from two or more separate organisms cannot maintain the mobility of its extremities on the level required for performing complex tasks. They can't do anything that involves accuracy or precision, like making jewelry, for example. A chimera would never be able to assist during surgery, or play the lute. For brute force, though, they are unmatched."

So that my sudden lecture didn't go to waste, I also raised the level of my shadow scout. My lizard could now not only broadcast thought-images to me in real time, but record some of them. Olga would need this information later, and I don't like to repeat myself.

"The strength of the chimera also depends on the talent of its maker, however. The more perfect the creature, the less energy it spends," I continued. "The art of necromancy is unforgiving of shoddy work — a magician can easily lose all their energy in no time flat. The chimera will look dangerous and imposing, but if you distribute the energy channels carelessly, a fiasco is inevitable. A monster created by a loser like that will collapse before it can perform its duties, and its master will soon follow."

Fred had finished the prep work, and was awaiting my verdict. I once again took a walk around all the bodies I had to work with. There were already more than twenty of them, but their quality left a lot to be desired. Even the dead magicians weren't too impressive.

"You need the right raw materials to create chimeras with," I continued the lesson. "The best are magical monsters, but for now, all we have is people, so I'm going to create a very simple guardian chimera — a bone-handed reaper. All you need to create that kind of chimera is one body. It's pretty durable and strong, and requires very little energy to control and maintain in battleworthy condition. It can also store energy and act autonomously."

I walked past the rows of bodies again, dropping professional comments about the advantages and disadvantages of each one. "Most of them are only good enough to be zombies," I concluded. "A beginner necromancer would most likely commit this common mistake: they would use one of the magicians, presuming their bodies to be stronger. But they aren't. Magic provides no advantages after death. Only the size and athleticism of the body makes any difference — the state of its muscles, bones, and tendons at the time of death."

I stopped near the magician who had fought me hand-to-hand. "This one's not too bad. But, like most gifted, he was accustomed to relying on his magic too much, so his reflexes and strength are more the result of strength spells than of physical training."

Finally, I selected one of the cutthroats who had accompanied Hugo. "This one never had magic, so his body is in much better condition. Plus, he's taller and more massive than any of the available former magicians. He's the best candidate to be the reaper."

After that, I got so involved in the process that I almost forgot to keep commenting as I worked, and the lizard stopped recording. Its memory capacity was pretty limited for now.

It didn't take long to create a first reaper to guard my stable. The most time-consuming part had been sharpening the bone blades. It was important that their sharpness and strength were no less than those of steel. Naturally, to fortify them to such a degree requires magic. As for the rest, all I had to do was program him with the right behavior pattern.

As I've said, chimeras — especially really simple ones — aren't capable of truly complex actions. They only memorize a sequence of moves. But I was able to mitigate this fault somewhat. The spectrum of chimera tasks can be pictured as a chain of simple repeating actions. Most necromancers simply increased the number of possible patterns as long as the chimera could remember all of them. I modified this approach by making the chain unlinked so that any action could connect to any other, which made my chimeras truly unpredictable and dangerous.

Now that I was finished with the reaper, there was another, much more complex, and therefore more interesting piece of business to attend to. I went upstairs and picked up one of the magazines I had acquired that day. About an hour later, I knew exactly what to do. The main thing was to finish by morning.

*   *   *

When she woke up, Olga found me in the kitchen, reading a magazine and sipping aromatic coffee. Happily, her coffee machine was fully mechanical, so I could use it without immediately breaking it. Fred was able to use it, on my orders, over and over. I must have drunk at least twenty cups overnight, confirming once again for myself that it was not only a very tasty beverage, but possessed a tonic effect that was very handy at a time like this. Not that the sleepless night had affected my body. I only needed sleep to absorb large amounts of energy. Still, the coffee had a nice rousing effect.

After finishing in the cellar, I had decided not to waste time, but to devote the rest of the night to learning more about this new era I was in. I had drunk cup after cup of coffee all night, leafing through magazines.

Book One

Fred was already making breakfast. This time, I had entrusted him with eggs benedict — a more difficult dish than pancakes, requiring concentration and grace from the cook. Just yesterday, my assistant wouldn't have been able to even mix the sauce correctly; now, the whole process of meal preparation was a simple matter for him. Even the presentation was superb. The golden brown muffins looked delectable. The bacon laid on top smelled so appetizing that I salivated involuntarily. And the ideally prepared eggs were a clear testament to the improved skill of the chef.

"It smells so good!" Olga recognized the growing skill of the wraith as she planted herself at the table. When Fred put the plate in front of her, she smiled at him so brightly that any suitor of hers would have been jealous of the undead servant. I guessed the way to her heart was through her stomach. She inhaled the breakfast, and praised it again: "Very tasty."

I ate with similar vigor. I already knew that she and I could both really eat, so Fred was finishing up making our seconds.

"Why didn't I have my own cook before?" Olga said when we finished our breakfast and came out of the house.

"Because you can't even bring a dead mouse back to life yet?" I offered.

Olga snickered. Then, her attention was immediately caught by something and she opened her eyes wide. She had finally seen the main surprise. "What is that?!"

"Our new automobile," I said calmly. "A

chimeramobile."

"Wow!" Olga circled the car, unable to come to her senses. "It looks just... incredible."

I smiled proudly. I had not expected any other reaction. It was a totally new construction, one of a kind. At the same time, it looked exactly like a regular automobile. Or maybe not totally regular, judging by Olga's reaction. I had carefully studied several car magazines, and then Fred and I had spent several hours bringing my plan to life, so that now I was the proud owner of a respectable-looking ivory-colored car whose shape was reminiscent of the latest model of Lamba.

I gallantly opened the door, which opened upward like a beetle's wing, and Olga got inside.

"But... how?" she still couldn't believe her eyes. "A chimeromobile... so it's..."

"Yes," I nodded, getting in the driver's seat.

My granddaughter carefully studied the interior and ran her hands along the upholstery. "Ooh, leather seats," she began, and then realized: "Oh wait, is this... what I think it is?"

"Naturally. The very well disinfected and tanned skin of a human organs dealer. Ironic, no?"

"Are you joking?"

Catching her eye, I realized she wasn't ready for the full truth yet. "Of course I am," I smiled slyly. "You think just one gangster is enough for a whole car interior?"

"Right," she relaxed a little. "After yesterday, I guess there's a lot of... material. But they all have different colored skin," she continued to self-soothe. I just nodded. She didn't need to know yet that there had been two twins in the gang.

Driving the chimeramobile was very easy. Basically, you just had to imagine where you wanted to go and at what speed, and it would do your will. It was the same as any transport chimera, except this one didn't have legs; instead, its fortified muscles and tendons acted as wheels. Nor was I worried about it being stolen. There were no other necromancers in the world now who could drive a chimera. I explained all of this to my granddaughter. The city had changed a lot, so she had to navigate as I drove. The address Prokhor had given yesterday meant nothing to me.

"Oh! You were supposed to stop at that traffic light!" Olga suddenly exclaimed.

"Traffic light?" I raised my eyebrow in surprise. There had been nothing about this in the magazines.

"Yeah, it's a thing that turns on different colors to regulate traffic. You can only go through the intersection when it's green. Ah!" she exclaimed again. "You can't turn that way! There's a sign right there!" I had to stop the chimeramobile. Not that I was too concerned with traffic rules, but we were going to attract too much attention this way. I didn't need that, I had too many plans today. So, I proposed that Olga drive.

"Wow, it really listens, all you have to do is send a little bit of energy. You don't even have to steer!" She kept commenting as we drove. For a while, she kept intently watching the road and holding on to the steering wheel, but soon her hand reached for her smartphone, then her purse, and then she started digging around in there. She learned very quickly the wonders of a self-driving chimeramobile. When we finally reached our destination, she almost didn't want to get out, saying "It's a dream car!"

I studied the small building near which we had stopped. It wasn't exactly elegant. A regular one-storey box, but with a pretentious sign that read "Purgatory" and featured a skull with burning red eyes that reminded me a lot of something.

Inside, everything went smoothly. A completely normal interior, boring even. A pretty girl in a strict business suit quickly showed us to Prokhor's office. He was dressed much more strictly and practically than the day before — no hats, or any of that nonsense. He wore a quasi-military uniform with a great deal of pockets and decals, which included the same skull again, as well as his blood group for some reason. What was this guy, preparing for a meetup with vampires?

How did I know it was a uniform? In all ages, military clothing is created based on one principle: thick fabric, simplicity, and the ability to carry as much useful stuff on your person as possible.

Behind Prokhor's back, several screens were affixed to the wall. I saw my 'Lamba' on one of them. "Not a bad car," said Prokhor, indicating it with his head, "and an unusual license plate number." I shrugged. That had been one of the unexpected tasks I had encountered when creating the chimeramobile. I had no idea how these numbers were generated, so I just wrote "Richter" and drew a scythe symbol at the end.

But I wasn't interested in discussing this with Prokhor, so I cut right to the chase: "Here are the gemstones," I said, producing all three of them out of my pocket and laying them on my open palm.

"Can I take a look?" Prokhor asked, furrowing his brow.

"Of course," I said, extending the rocks to him. The potential buyer examined them very closely, even producing a magnifying glass and looking at every facet. I could see that he hoped the whole thing was a prank and there was no way I could be in possession of goods like that.

When he was convinced that the stones were real, he immediately deflated. "I can buy them for a hundred and fifty thousand coins each," he said, frowning.

"That's a shame," I shrugged. "I had hoped Olga's friend would quote us a fair price, but since that's not the case, we'll have to take our business to another cleansing company."

I had no idea what gemstones were worth, but I knew what people were like. Assuming the stones had come into my possession by illegal means, Prokhor was inevitably lowballing me. It's a kind of test: if I agreed, then he would consider his assumption correct, and take that as a sign to lowball me even more.

I took a step toward the door, but Prokhor stopped me just as I had expected. "That is a fair price," he said, "but it's on the low end. You didn't hear me out."

I stopped walking and waited to see how he would backpedal. Clearly, the last thing he wanted was to be diminished in Olga's eyes, and now that I had caught on to that fact, he was going to have to find a fast justification for himself.

"I said that's how much I can pay right now. I'll have the rest in about a week. How about two hundred and thirty thousand?"

"Make it two hundred fifty and we have a deal," I decided to shake him down for more as punishment for his attempt to rip us off. Prokhor got even more downtrodden, but threw a glance at Olga and didn't argue.

So I had interpreted all his weirdness yesterday correctly. People are so predictable!

"It's a deal." He turned his palm upward and called forth his sphere, which was a regular one, not a golden one. I guessed Purgatory wasn't doing too well.

Prokhor was looking at me expectantly. "I don't have a sphere, I use gold," I said, shrugging my shoulders.

"That's... unusual," he got tense again. "Then I'll have it delivered to you by the end of the day. I have to withdraw it first. Where should I have it taken to?"

"You know my address," Olga spoke up. "Have it taken there."

Prokhor wasn't very good at concealing his emotions, and I could clearly see him struggling to remove the suspicion and hostility from his face. Happily, I couldn't care less how he felt about me. Olga was an unwitting lever of influence for me over her friend, which was fine with me.

"Furthermore, I wanted to discuss one more

thing," I threw in.

"What's that?"

"I want to inspect an abomination focus." It turned out this term was still in use, but it had been transformed for their convenience. Abomination monsters were considered evil, but the gemstones gathered from them were 'grace'. Fucking hypocrites.

"You want to hire me and my team?" Prokhor asked. Right now, he had a handle over himself and was behaving professionally, which automatically elevated him in my eyes.

"No, I want to go myself."

"What do you mean? With a different team?"

I sighed, astounded at how dumb he was. "Alone."

"What do you mean alone?" Prokhor was bemused. "Cleansers always go to foci in teams of at least ten. Even full magicians with battle gifts don't go alone."

I noted his use of the word "full." Prokhor obviously didn't consider himself a 'full' magician, even though he had a gift, however humble. In fact, his power was related to ours — he also had a natural resistance to abomination. But, I guessed, he didn't want to be a healer, and didn't know how else to develop it, so he chose the path of the cleanser.

"How is my problem," I said. "All I need from Purgatory is permission."

Prokhor drummed on the desk with his fingers. "I can't allow that. I have two teams of professional cleansers," he offered. "Take either one of them. I'll even give you a discount because you're a friend of Olga's. But going alone? That's suicide."

"I am not here to negotiate," I answered. "I have experience in this, and I'll either make a deal with Purgatory, or with someone else who isn't so concerned for my safety."

Prokhor visibly hunched over, which is exactly what I had counted on. Only a blind person could fail to see how much he disliked me. Finally, he dropped the noble act. "Fine, have it your way," he said. "But don't say I didn't warn you. Let's just work out the conditions. Everything you find, you sell through us, or we'll both have problems. Plus, twenty percent of the find goes to us as well. Those are standard freelance vendor contract terms. You can't gain access to a focus without a license, and that's what we charge for."

"Deal."

We discussed a few more details and shook hands. That's when he noticed my ring. "What is that?" he asked, a little clumsily. "It's a pretty rare design."

"It's my clan crest," I explained.

"There's no such clan," he argued. "Purgatory has owned the rights to that image for several centuries now, and it's an inherited business." I just shrugged in response. It was not time for the truth yet.

Having failed to get any explanation from me, Prokhor told me where to go tomorrow and what time to be there to enter the abomination focus. Olga listened actively, memorizing the directions.

Finally, we exited Purgatory much richer, and

with a solid lead for future doings. When we were back in the chimeramobile, Olga said pensively, "Just think — only three gemstones, and they're worth seven hundred thousand. That's almost one eighth of my mortgage."

"Wait till tomorrow, there's much more to come," I smiled.

Olga nodded acknowledgement. Then, she said, "Now, should we go see the parents of my friend who disappeared?"

"Yes, only let's stop for coffee," I said. The day was going beautifully; why not make it even better?

* * *

Jorge Velasco was really pissed off. Not only had he been paired with the useless Mario again, but also saddled with a totally useless assignment.

A member of the youngest branch of the Velasco clan had disappeared, and the clan's security service had appointed Jorge to get to the bottom of it. The most annoying thing was that most of the time, when one of these dingbats went missing, he was usually just passed out in a bar or a whorehouse somewhere. Jorge was certain that what had befallen Hugo was no more serious than that.

However, after driving over to most of Hugo's friends' and acquaintances' places, he began to doubt this. It turned out Hugo had gone missing in the line of duty. Could someone have whacked him for the bad news he had brought? That job of his was really something. Now, everyone he was supposed to visit yesterday had to be checked out.

So, Jorge and Mario, the youngest combatant investigators of the Velasco clan, found themselves standing in front of the Richter stable-house.

As suspected, Hugo's car was parked there. Mario poked him in the side, letting out a dumb laugh, and pointing at the sign advertising Olga's services. "Maybe he got sucked in?" he said.

Jorge sighed. Mario was not only young and inexperienced, but also a goddamn moron. What made him maddest of all, was that Mario's magical potential was higher than his, which meant that most likely, in a few years, he would have to take orders from the imbecile!

"Let's go find out," he answered simply and walked toward the door.

"You're no fun," Mario snorted, but followed.

The door was locked, but this did not deter the investigators. Ignoring legalities and private property, they broke in and entered.

"Hey! Anyone home?" Jorge called out from the foyer.

"What if we find you?" Mario belly-laughed.

At that moment, the bone-handed reaper — the chimera created for the sole purpose of killing, which was peacefully sleeping in the cellar, opened its eyes.

Chapter 12

"DOESN'T LOOK LIKE THERE'S anyone home," Mario said, drumming his fingers on the dresser by the front door.

"You're always in a hurry," Jorge scowled. "We need to check out the whole place."

"I wouldn't be surprised if he shacked up somewhere with that girl."

"Yeah, or else he's high and passed out in her bed here."

At least Jorge and Mario agreed on something. Both couldn't stand these disappearance cases. Ninety-nine percent of the time, they went missing for the stupidest of reasons, and by their own fault. And they didn't contribute anything to the clan, either, goddamnit!

the Dark healer

They heard a noise from somewhere inside the house. "I guess Hugo's here after all," Jorge guffawed. "Let's take a look, shall we?"

But they only made it as far as the living room. There, they froze next to a big, long table, because they saw an enormous man standing in the doorway on the other side. He looked really weird. If Jorge had been called upon to describe what was weird about him, he wouldn't even have been able to. It was an array of details assembled into an absolutely brain-breaking image.

Firstly, the man was bald and undressed to the waist. Granted, this alone wouldn't have been that strange, given that they had come upon him at home, unannounced, and he might have been on drugs. However, his skin was gray and sickly, and he stood in an unnatural pose, as though he was crouching from acute pain, or preparing to jump. He held his hands in front of his chest like a mantis, and, instead of fingers, he had weird blades, like scythes.

"What the fuck?" Jorge exclaimed, "That's not Hugo! Hey guy, who are you?!"

"Hold on, I know him," Mario said. "That's Brad, the clan's mercenary, I've seen him a few times. But he's ungifted. How did he..."

He didn't have a chance to finish his question, as the monster lunged. Disregarding all obstacles it bounded toward them with giant leaps, six feet each. Its bone blade instantly split in two the table that was in its way.

The freaked out 'guests' barely had time to jump out of its way.

$\mathcal{B}$ o o k $\mathcal{O}$ n e

"Brad, what are you doing?!" Mario screamed.

"Open your eyes! That's not Brad, it's probably not even human," Jorge said, assuming battle form.

The Velasco clan specialized in poisons and everything that produces them. The drops of acid Hugo had been throwing around only represented the lowest rung on the ladder of their capabilities. Their patriarchs could turn into actual poisonous wyverns, and the others could become small basilisk lizards, or some sort of acid spitting monitor lizard on hind legs. Jorge was of the latter category.

In a situation like this, it was unrealistic to expect to have time to turn all the way. He transformed only partially. His skin became hard and scaly, his tongue got bigger and split into two, and claws grew from his fingers. And, of course, he could now produce venom.

Bam! A basketball sized ball of poison flew straight at the reaper. The reaper jumped out of the way, toward Mario. The projectile missed as Mario finally began to appreciate the seriousness of the situation. He ducked out of the reaper's way and called his magic weapon — the studded whip.

Unlike Jorge, Mario was a support warrior. However, his abilities were prized very highly by their clan. He could call especially poisonous plants with very strong vines that could be extremely unpleasant for the enemy.

Mario snapped his whip in the reaper's direction, and its tendrils extended outward rapidly, trying to bind the monster and restrain him. Jorge, meanwhile, started actively helping by drawing the monster's attention to himself. Mario called another whip, and was now working simultaneously with two. He was trying to bind the enemy's legs with one, and wrap the other around his shoulders.

"Something's wrong," Jorge roared. "My poison isn't working on him." He had already hit the reaper with two balls of venom, but this had had no effect. This was unprecedented — even very powerful magicians had always been at least injured by Velasco venom if they hadn't procured an antidote in advance.

"Tear him to pieces with your claws! Don't just stand there! Can't you see we're fucked?!" Mario screamed hysterically. His whips secreted somnambulant sap, which he had noticed also didn't have any effect on the enemy. Normally, that sap would slow down a gifted, and altogether knock out a regular person. And this Brad was definitely not gifted. He was now a monster, and that monster seemed to move faster and faster with every passing minute. He had seemed clumsy at first, but now his blows were each more dangerous than the last. It was as if he was learning as he went. It was all Mario could do to get out of the way of the steel blades. As for catching him with a whip, that was clearly not even an option. So, he very much hoped Jorge would come up with something.

It was now or never, and Jorge realized this, too, so he found an opportunity to jump on the monster's back, and even toppled it to the ground.

Then, he started tearing its flesh with his huge claws.

"Kill the bastard!" Mario egged him on, and was finally able to tie the monster up. He had called a third whip, and the monster was now on the floor, wrapped in a sort of cocoon. "Phew, I thought that was the end," Mario admitted, wiping the sweat from his forehead.

"I'll finish him off," roared Jorge, who was still lying astride the monster, and reached for the monster's neck with his clawed hands.

Just then, he felt the monster flex its whole body. The next instant, torn green bits of what had been the whips flew every which way. The monster was free.

"Shit!" Mario exclaimed. "The blades!"

But Jorge could no longer answer. Somehow, the reaper had bent in some strange way and instantly pinned him down. Then, two steel-hard bone blades pierced his scales like cardboard, ending the life of the Velasco clan fixer.

"You motherfucker!" Mario screamed at the top of his lungs as he fled. However, the creature had blocked the path to the exit, so he ran for the stairs to the second floor, scattering poisonous bombs and traps on the steps as he went. He already knew the poison in them wouldn't work, but they were also sticky, so they could buy him a little time. His plan was simply to jump out of the window and escape by car as fast as he possibly could.

But, as he reached the top of the stairs, he felt the ground falling out from under him. With a huge racket, the massive wood staircase buckled and came crashing down.

At the bottom, awaited the reaper: a merciless machine of death and destruction.

* * *

"Maybe we shouldn't have turned down Prokhor's help?" Olga said, taking a sip of coffee from a mug. "I noticed the two of you weren't big fans of each other, but first impressions can be deceiving. He's not a bad guy. I hope you hit your stride."

We were sitting in a cozy coffee shop — a different one, where they had types of coffee I hadn't tried yet. Say what you want, but I was absolutely besotted with this beverage. Nothing that had appeared since I'd been away had made me as happy as coffee.

I also ordered a couple of salmon sandwiches and scarfed them down. My body needed a lot of food, so it was a good thing you could now buy it on every corner.

"I'm sure," I said. "I know you wouldn't have introduced me to just anyone. But why do I need to hire him?"

Olga was embarrassed. "What do you mean? Didn't you hear him say that usually they go abomination hunting in large groups? A little backup wouldn't hurt."

I smiled. "Olga, are you underestimating me again?"

"No!" she hotly protested. "I'm just worried. To be honest..." she got so embarrassed, that she even blushed a little, "I haven't had a family in a long time. And…"

"I will be fine," I reached across the table and gave her a paternal pat on the head. We were both becoming more accustomed to that father-daughter dynamic, and it was becoming more and more natural. I really liked Olga a lot. At moments like these, she was as cute as a kitten.

Once we finished dinner, as we walked to the address we had, Olga told me a little bit of what she knew. The girl who had disappeared was called Alina Aster. She was twenty-two, very young. An only child, living with her parents, who were both in their late forties. The mother's name was Linda, the father was Ignatius.

Alina had a very insular lifestyle and couldn't stand parties. However, she wanted to contribute to society, so, like Olga, she volunteered, albeit at a different clinic. An all-around positive type of young woman. My granddaughter didn't have one dubious word to say about her. The chances that she had met a tall dark stranger and ridden off into the sunset were null.

When we arrived in the neighborhood where our destination was, even though this street looked way nicer than the one where my stable stood, I immediately knew the young woman's family lived humbly. They had a small private house with a neat little yard.

We jumped out of the chimeramobile and Olga rang the doorbell. A minute later, a dark-haired, painfully pale woman with bags under her eyes from crying, opened the door.

"Are you friends of Alina's?" she asked in a

weak voice.

"Yes. I wrote to you just a little while ago," Olga started. "We're very concerned and would like to know where you saw her last. Maybe we can do something to help."

"Come in," the woman said.

Soon, we were in the living room, being offered tea and meeting Ignatius. He was a stocky man who had gone grey early. His mood was as dark as a stormcloud. I could tell right away he was gifted, though not very powerful.

"Does Alina get her gift from you?" I asked him right away.

"Yes," he nodded, "there were no magicians at all in Linda's family. I have some on my father's side."

"Are you a healer like your daughter?"

"Garbage man," he answered curtly.

Olga had already told me that garbage men were people who processed and cleared objects contaminated with abomination. It was a thankless job. Like healers, they were people with a gift similar to ours, but who didn't really know how that gift worked, and they usually ended up burning out very quickly. The immunity that facilitates necromancy preserves a magician from mutations, but not from pain. You would need to master the appropriate practices for that, but all information about those practices had been lost or purposely destroyed.

I looked at Olga, and immediately knew something was wrong with the woman. She wasn't just devastated because of her daughter; I was now certain she had abomination poisoning. Which wasn't surprising, considering the whole family constantly worked with that gross stuff. And, like father, like daughter: despite being a healer, Alina had not been able to see that and help her mother.

"What do you do?" I asked Linda.

"I'm a housewife," she said, feeling a little invaded. "I used to be a lawyer, but..."

"Linda has been very sick," Ignatius added, his voice quivering a little. "Treatment is very expensive. If I could make enough to pay for it myself, then Alina wouldn't have to take so many calls. That night, she took an emergency call and left in a hurry."

Linda softly put her hand on his. "Don't say that," she said. "It isn't anybody's fault."

"What about the police?" I asked.

Ignatius slammed his fist down on the table and exclaimed, "They're useless! They say Alina is an adult and could have just gone somewhere and not told us. But we know she wouldn't do that!"

"Did you see exactly where she was going before she disappeared?"

The mother shook her head. "No," she said, "the only thing she said was that it was a new client, and he had promised to pay double for the emergency call."

Olga nudged me with her elbow barely perceptibly, and from her face I understood that that was the exact same scheme they had tried to use to set her up.

"Well," I said, "we're not the police, but we'll see what we can do."

"What do you mean? Aren't you just friends of hers?" Linda asked, surprised.

"Not quite," Olga said, saving the situation, "we're also representatives… of the Healers Union. If you find out anything else, please call me right away."

"A union?" Ignatius asked, lifting his eyebrow. "Never heard of it."

"I'm not surprised. It was just created recently," my granddaughter continued to lie. This was much simpler than convincing someone that we were acting on our own.

"To be honest," Ignatius shook his head, "I don't care if you're from the union, or from the moon, or if you're the devil himself. If you can save my daughter, I… I would do anything for you. I would be your servant for eternity."

Linda squeezed his hand again, and I could see she felt exactly the same way. These were simple, honest people, and I appreciated that they really meant it.

I nodded, and said gravely, "Your oath has been accepted."

Olga looked at me in surprise, but didn't say anything. Alina's parents also didn't know what to say in response to that, so I helped them out: "Linda, I'm a high-ranking healer, and I can give you some relief. Will you let me?"

"I…" she hesitated, "I'm afraid we don't have the money to pay for your services right now."

"Don't worry about that. I'm a volunteer like your daughter, I don't only treat people for money."

She was still unsure, but Ignatius said,

"Linda is a very humble person, and she doesn't like to ask for anything. It can be hard for her to accept help. But any relief would be a blessing for her."

I nodded and spoke to our hostess: "Linda, please lie down. After the treatment session, you'll probably lose consciousness for a little while, and then you'll sleep for a long time. But when you awake, you'll feel a lot better."

She did what I said, but first I proposed that Olga give treating her a try. Clearing abomination out of the ungifted was much harder than out of magicians, and I wanted to see how well she could do it. You have to be a lot more careful because regular people's organisms are much weaker.

Everything went more smoothly than I had expected. Olga was able to help the woman a little. But this was only the first step. After Olga was done, I took over.

It didn't take long — after a few minutes, we were saying goodbye to Ignatius and returning to our chimeramobile. "You're kinder to strangers than I thought," Olga said, getting into the now familiar passenger seat.

I smiled slyly. "You don't think I got nothing out of that, do you?"

"What do you mean?"

I remembered that I hadn't really explained to her why I was pretending to be a healer that was working with her. She was probably still thinking I had agreed to do it for the commission. Now, it was time to reveal the truth to her.

"Necromancers can process abomination into

regular magic energy. Now, Linda is sick with poisoning. But while the gifted can use even such a dirty power source for their spells, all a regular person can do is accumulate the poison inside them until it destroys them."

"And you could really treat her? Because of the difference in energy systems, healers can usually only relieve the symptoms of the ungifted. In magicians, surplus grace... I mean abomination, flows along energetic channels that healers can tune to easily, but regular people don't have anything like that."

I nodded. "Exactly. They don't have their own power that could counteract abomination even a little bit, or stave off it penetrating the tissues and organs of the body. But energy is energy, and one day you'll learn to feel it regardless of what form it's stored in."

Olga was listening attentively, and had stopped watching the road altogether, now accustomed to the chimeramobile driving itself. So, when it swerved suddenly, she yelped in surprise.

"What the hell was that?" She looked at the road. "Oh, a dog. That was close!"

The chimeramobile had been able to brake and swerve away from the rust-colored mongrel that had decided for some reason to cross the road right in front of us. Olga swallowed hard, and said, "I should pay more attention."

"That's a strange conclusion to come to," I replied. "Don't you realize the chimeramobile isn't a regular car? It can make decisions by itself. Like it did just now. So don't worry."

Olga nodded affirmatively, but for a while she looked at the road more frequently. Soon, however, she got sucked into her smartphone again. One always gets used to good things fast.

She didn't look up until we pulled up to the stable-house. "I think we have visitors," my granddaughter furrowed her brow, looking at the unknown car parked in front.

"I take it, you weren't expecting anyone?" I said.

"Of course not. Shit!" she exclaimed, "That's the Velasco crest on their car. Of course they're looking for him! Especially since his car is parked literally eight feet from my house!" She nervously clasped her hands. "What do we say to them?"

While she had been looking at their car, I had been looking at the broken down door. "I doubt there'll be anything to say at this point. Let's go."

"What? What do you mean?" Olga didn't understand what I was saying, but hurried inside after me. A couple seconds later, she saw the completely trashed dining room and lost it. "What the hell happened here?! Did the Velascos do this to intimidate me?! What did my kitchen table do to them?!"

I went further inside, into the living room, and was now witnessing a truly idyllic scene: my reaper was proudly standing over two corpses, which it had laid in a neat row, exactly like a cat showing off the mice he'd caught to his owner.

The pile of wood rubble that had until recently been the staircase lay a little further on. And the icing on the cake was Fred, who was calmly cleaning blood from the wall.

"I can't believe my own eyes," Olga muttered in shock when she walked into the living room. "Max, what does this mean?" She almost squealed the last part from genuine outrage and overwhelm.

"I told you we wouldn't need to explain anything to anyone," I concluded.

"Umm... What about me?! Even looking the other way on the destroyed table, I don't have a staircase anymore! But I do have two more Velasco corpses." Olga covered her face with her hands and breathed heavily, as though trying to ward off an oncoming panic attack. Considering how much had happened in the short time since we'd met, I was surprised she'd lasted this long.

"Don't worry about the staircase," I cheered her up. "Two corpses means two gemstones — that's enough for a renovation and then some." Olga exhaled loudly, and got ahold of herself.

"I don't know what amazes me more — this trashing of my place, or your way of thinking. Are you planning on killing off the entire Velasco clan this way?"

I shrugged. "Whose fault is it if they keep coming themselves?"

Having said that, I created a decomposition spell, and all the bloody stains disappeared from the house. Fred froze in place with his rag, then, just as neutrally, walked with it deeper into the house.

"You don't have some magic that'll put the staircase back together, do you?" Olga asked as she watched what I was doing.

"I'm a necromancer, not a carpenter. But you can always raise some workers that'll fix everything by hand. For example, Fred will now repair the door."

Indeed, Fred had armed himself with tools, and was now measuring the doorway for new door hinges. It turned out Olga was a very industrious young lady, and had a lot of different stuff in her closet.

"We don't even need a door," she said, nodding at the reaper. "With that as a bodyguard, it's the people outside who should be scared. What do I do about my bedroom on the second floor? Will Fred fix the staircase?"

I nodded. "Just order the materials," I said. "The gold from Prokhor should be delivered soon."

"Then I'll start on that right away. It needs to be completed by nighttime." Olga became enveloped in her smartphone again.

This small object had become a whole universe for modern man. It was the way people communicated, ordered goods and services, used their money, and who knows what else. The only drawback was, it ran on abomination. I'd have to think about how to recreate the technology, but without using abomination. But that was not a priority right now. Today, we had to prepare for the next day. And, yeah, OK, fix the stairs.

Olga worked fast. An hour and a half later, all the materials were delivered. I temporarily raised another wraith to help Fred. I needed them to get this over with quickly, as I would need his help in the cellar later.

the Dark healer

As the construction was underway, I read magazines again, while Olga watched the staircase repair with great curiosity.

"Wow," she said when the work was nearly done, "Fred did a great job. You didn't even have to watch him or help him out. Or... order him? However it is that you communicate with him."

"The higher level the wraith, the more complex tasks it can perform."

"When will I learn to raise and control them?" she asked, looking at me hopefully.

"Soon. First, you have to learn to polish basic spells like the one you learned yesterday."

She furrowed her brow. "OK, but I didn't quite get what was so useful about it. I mean, I got a good night's sleep, but is that it?"

"Did you notice anything today when you were treating Linda?"

"Hmm... yeah, you're right!" Olga said, astounded. "I felt almost no pain. There's always less with the ungifted than when treating magicians, but today I only felt the slightest prick."

I nodded. "Now you get it? Relaxation is, among other things, a way to make your energy system stronger. With it, you can learn how to cleanse your organism and process abomination."

"Just like you?"

"In time."

"Ah! The staircase is finished. I'll go practice in the bedroom."

I think my answer had really inspired her. Olga ran upstairs, while Fred and I descended to the cellar. I had another all-nighter ahead of me.

ℬook One

* * *

"I won't be surprised if he doesn't show up at all," said Prokhor's closest comrade Alan, putting out his cigarette on an already charred tree stump. "Maybe he's just a psycho, or a fucking showoff? Scaredy cat hiding in the bushes."

Prokhor and his detachment stopped their jeep about three hundred yards from the focus, but you could see its edge clearly from there. Instead of the usual green forest, everything had been seized by rotten crags, predator plants masked as harmless flowers, yellow grass, and unnaturally blackened soil. Even the sky above the focus was different somehow — darker and bleeker.

"Maybe he just doesn't appreciate the danger," Prokhor shrugged. "Oh well, let him go find out for himself. The local monsters will talk some sense into him in no time."

"Are you sure? They'll kill him."

"What are we, priests, to bless him on his final journey?"

"I'd definitely make a shitty priest," Alan laughed.

"It wasn't for nothing I ordered you guys to bring equipment," Prokhor explained. "We're going to have to get that idiot out of there. But let him get a good dose first."

"I'm all in favor of that," said Alan. "I can't stand dandies. Hey look, here he comes!"

Indeed, a car that looked more like it was

meant for going to upscale nightclubs than driving around the forest, was barreling toward them from an opening in the woods. A closed trailer was attached to the back of the car.

The automobile stopped in front of them, but Max only got out to say hello and leave Olga with them. Try as they might, Prokhor and his team could not discover even a hint of doubt in the arrogant stranger. He got back in the car and directed it into the nearest bushes, barreling right into the thick of the ailing forest.

By the cleansers' calculations, Max should start screaming loudly and calling out for his mommy in just a couple of minutes.

Chapter 13

I HAD NOT EXPECTED TO EVER have to visit an abomination focus again, especially such a weak version of one. These small problems — alpha-class foci — used to be taken care of by junior members of the Richter clan for practice. But now, the only clan member available to me was Olga, who was not even weak, she was untrained. And anyway, why should I send someone else in there instead of going myself? No, I was just disappointed that this focus wouldn't bring much harvest — either in terms of energy, or ingredients. Prokhor had probably chosen a simple one on purpose. I could see that he thought I couldn't even handle this much. Whereas I was sure that if I was careful, I could easily clear beta- and even gamma-class foci right now. They would take a bit longer though. Oh well, that would have to be next time.

I wanted to get as deep as possible into the poisoned forest, so as not to tempt the Purgatory team to surveil me. My reapers were likely the only ones in the world right now, and I didn't want to advertise them, or stir excitement among the cleansers.

My chimeramobile was rolling forward with gusto. It didn't need a road, it feared no scratches, and it simply chopped down small trees in its path with its sharpened bumper. Interestingly, the focus monsters hadn't noticed me yet. That explained a lot — I had noticed even before my thousand-year slumber that they were extremely sluggish in reacting to chimeras, or any other undead creature. And back then, I used to ride chimeras bareback, whereas now, I was sitting inside of one, so I must have been completely invisible to the local mutant life.

As soon as I got out of the car, however, every small beast within a certain radius gravitated toward me. Before the focus appeared, they had probably been rabbits, foxes, and other small forest creatures. Now, it was practically impossible to guess what they had looked like originally. Their fur was now a dirty burgundy color, and their eyes were red and poison-green. Their teeth and claws had become murderous weapons. I saw many corpses of fools who had gotten lost in the woods, only to have their bones picked clean in no time, as if by piranhas. All that was left were scattered bones.

A dozen of these things were speeding toward me, wanting to tear me to pieces. But I was ready, having charged up my body with energy in advance. With a single kick, I sent the first two monsters flying like furry soccer balls. Unlike soccer balls, however, when the monsters hit trees as they flew, they would literally pop in an explosion of blood, flesh, and bone. That was another feature of these little guys.

But their most insidious talent was that they could jump six or even nine feet in the air. I had to sweat to avoid the eight that remained. Three of them jumped, their maws already gaping open. If they caught me, they'd be on me like bulldogs and I'd have to tear them away — skin, meat, and all. Naturally, this option did not suit me, so I ducked and stepped to the side, while calling a slightly improved version of the shadow scalpel — a kind of two-sided shadow hatchet, about a foot long. Unfortunately, I didn't have enough energy to call a morc powerful weapon, so this would have to do.

I was in it to win it. As I ducked the beasts, I sliced a few of them with the shadow blade, then took a couple more steps to the side to avoid having them explode all over me. Their comrades were less fortunate. Two of them were within the forcefield of the explosions, and it set off a chain reaction. In the end, only one out of the original ten was still alive.

The remaining one charged me, as stubborn as a lemming. I made short work of him the same way as I had the first two, sending him flying with a kick.

the Dark healer

Now, I had one to five minutes before the next party of mutants arrived. Or maybe more than one party. They usually ran in armies of ten or twenty groups, about a hundred yards apart. The one nearest to me was probably already aware of my presence. Not wishing to waste time, I took the tent down from the trailer, and charged three reapers that I had made the night before, especially for this hunt, with energy. I could have ordered them to come out during the skirmish, but then they would have inevitably damaged the tent, and it would have cost more energy. It's always more draining to raise servants at a distance. Besides, the jumpers were basically harmless if you knew how to deal with them.

I was interested neither in wasting time combatting endless waves of them, however, nor in gathering up the gemstones that fell out of each of them myself. I had more interesting stuff to do. I was after the grand prize.

Every focus gets its energy from a crystal at its center. It's just like the gemstones inside the mutants, but much, much bigger. The longer a focus exists, the stronger it becomes, desiccating the surrounding lands and turning all living things into their servants and bodyguards. The thing the mutants fear most is a living person getting to the crystal and ruining it. They're ready to literally scatter their own bones on the battlefield to prevent that from happening. There was a time when I seriously investigated the possibility that these crystals were sentient, but I never found any real proof.

I needed the reapers to help me get to the center of the focus faster. While two of them fought off the jumpers, the third one chopped my way through the thickets of predator plants. Naturally, it wasn't just the animals that had mutated. The abomination left nothing unchanged. Those who underestimated the power of the living poison ivy, or of the giant brown flowers that looked like flytraps, regularly perished in their embrace. To an unprepared magician — never mind a regular person! — the mutant plants were even more dangerous than the mutant animals. The latter were more predictable. The local flora was full of surprises: thorn traps that jumped out from underground, poisonous spores just waiting to be inhaled, pincer-ended vines that normal steel couldn't chop through, and a whole host of other things.

The reward for fighting these things was gemstones. To get them, you had to not only chop up the mutant plants, but dig up their roots — that's where the poison crystal was, where the bulb should be. After the reaper finished with one of the predator plants in my path, I ordered him to dig up the bonus, but I quickly realized that was a bad idea. I had forgotten how deep down these crystals were kept. It would take longer than a day to clear all the trees here and dig up the stones. I didn't have that kind of time, so I would have to content myself with the stones I got from the jumpers.

The reapers were dicing them up quickly and with relish. I even had a chance to get bored because none of them were getting through to me so that I would have to fight them myself. When another mutant appeared, I decided to take it on.

I hadn't counted on seeing anything bigger than jumpers here, but now it looked like this focus might actually be beta-class. The closer I got to the crystal at the center, the more advanced monsters began to show up. Fatties, as they were usually called, had also once been animals, but I didn't know whether they had been larger animals, like bears, for example, or whether they had been assembled from several smaller ones like my chimera. It could be either one. The stronger the crystal, the bigger transformation all living things inside the focus underwent.

Looking at these things, it was anybody's guess how they had come to be. One thing was for sure: fatties' fur didn't look homogenous. Their bodies could be covered in some sort of scabies in one place, thorns and needles in another, and scales in a third. Jumpers were all made in the same image, and in high-level foci they were all indistinguishable from one another; fatties, on the other hand, were each unique in some way.

The first one we encountered looked like a beaver with a pituitary disorder, about the size of a bear. It had huge front teeth and tiny eyes, and it moved like a typical rodent. This thing was not to be underestimated. Those teeth could easily puncture not only flesh and trees, but even bone blades protected by a magic spell. I knew that from previous experience. That's part of the reason I decided not to let the reapers near them. I didn't have enough material yet to risk losing servants. So, I decisively headed for the fatty myself.

They weren't as fast as jumpers, so I wasn't afraid of it getting the better of me through sudden movements, considering the reflexes I had. Their endurance, however, was unmatched. I knew the fight would last a while, especially since the best weapon I had was the shadow hatchet. That meant I would have to hit the monster many times before it fell. To speed up that process a little bit, I made the hatchet blade serrated. Now, it not only cut, but tore the flesh, and every chop would lead to the fatty losing more blood.

But, even with ten or more torn wounds bleeding from its skin, it didn't look even a little bit tired. I had to attack it over and over again. And I had to be careful. It was no great task to avoid the monster's powerful jaws and claws, but the fatty had other surprises in store. One time, it almost got me. I had not noticed right away that it had two niches under its long fur, which it was using to shoot long thin venomous needles. These flew at speeds even the fastest jumpers couldn't match.

Finally, he croaked. Right before he breathed his last, he rasped something like, "Bearvr bitch, I fartred." Who the hell knows what that was supposed to mean.

The reapers and I kept working our way deeper into the infected forest, making for the heart of the abomination focus.

the Dark healer

* * *

"OK, this is weird." Prokhor was getting visibly nervous when ten minutes had passed and no screams of horror had been heard. By the Purgatory boss's estimation, the arrogant Richter should have encountered at least one herd of jumpers, probably two, by now, and should be running for dear life out of the focus. That is, if he didn't get caught in one of the poisonous predator tree traps, or worse.

What confused him even more was the imperturbable expression on Olga's face. Didn't she understand that her relative, or whoever he was, was facing certain death?

"What's weird?" she asked innocently.

"That we're not hearing any sounds of battle. Maybe they ate him already?" he added tensely. He didn't like Max, but for Olga's 'uncle' to die here in such a stupid way would be unacceptable. Especially in front of her. The last thing Prokhor wanted was for her to be upset. If this Max character died, he'd feel guilty for letting him go on this suicidal mission.

But Olga only waved it away nonchalantly. "Don't worry," she said, "you don't know my uncle. He can take care of himself."

Her careless attitude pissed Prokhor off. Was this a family trait of theirs or something? He answered in an unexpectedly snarky tone: "You don't realize how dangerous mutants in foci are! Even the grass in there is dangerous!" He was so agitated, he started pacing back and forth. "A herd of monsters the size of cats can chew up practically anyone, even a battle magician below magister level. And those aren't even the most dangerous creatures in there!"

Concern flashed momentarily across Olga's face, but it was soon replaced with certainty. "I'm willing to bet he's alright," she smiled.

How could she be so sure? Prokhor could not understand this at all. Why did she trust Max more than his own professional opinion? It drove him crazy.

Oh well, it didn't matter. He would be proven right imminently. Besides, there was no more time to wait — it might be too late already.

He made a gesture to his team of four warriors, and said, "Boys, we're rolling out. We have to see what's in there."

Then, he turned to Olga and ordered curtly, "You stay here. Don't move a step closer to the focus." He tossed her the keys to the jeep, and added, "In fact, best to just get in the car, and at the first sign of trouble, get out of here."

Olga shrugged. She was still sure Prokhor was wasting his time, but she didn't want to argue with him anymore. These men — once they got an idea in their heads, it was impossible to change their minds. So, without a care, she quietly got inside the car and started watching the latest episode of her favorite series on her phone.

the Dark healer

* * *

As we made our way toward the center of the focus, two more fatties sprang up in front of us. These looked like a giant wild boar, and a raccoon. They attacked simultaneously, and were also joined at the same time by two whole herds of jumpers. Which was to be expected. The mutant animals were trying to keep me from reaching the nucleus.

I ordered the reapers again to fight only the jumpers and aggressive plants that were grabbing at our feet, and took on the fatties myself. The one that looked like a boar came up with an interesting surprise. He was almost as fast as the little jumpers, and he was especially fast at attacking with his fanged maw and sharp horns. He made sharp movements the naked human eye wouldn't even be able to discern. I had to duck away from the raging animal, feeling like a bullfighter or a lion tamer.

And then there was the other one. Luckily, the raccoon, or it was probably actually a skunk, didn't have any serious surprises for me — it just kept releasing clouds of poison in between attempts to chew my leg off. For a necromancer, poison is nothing. You could say we have an innate resistance to most of them. Especially after training. So, I didn't even bother ducking away from it, concentrating instead on the boar.

I was already expecting to spend twice as much time on these two as I had on the beaver, but I guess the perverted nature in this place tended toward restoring some sort of balance, so the boar turned out a lot less resilient than its comrades in tooth and claw. I only had to hit it twelve times to kill it.

The raccoon took more hits, but turned out to be so un-agile that I could literally stab it over and over again, and it wouldn't get out of the way.

But this was not all the focus had in store for me. In the clearing where the crystal was supposed to be, there were at least six herds of jumpers waiting. They all moved toward us as one enormous mass. I had to get all my reapers in a group so we could hold a four-sided defense, back to back.

All it took was killing about ten of them for a chain reaction of jumper explosions to begin again. This time, because of how many of them there were, this was dangerous even to me, but especially to my reapers. I had to strain my energy reserves and cover us with a shadow dome as the monsters' bodies popped all around us like popcorn. I had had to use all my energy reserves for that spell, and I was now literally running on fumes. But what was the energy for, if not cleansing foci?

When the jumpers had all exploded, I sent the reapers to patrol the clearing to make sure there were no more surprises. I walked to the crystal. Now, I could see everything clearly. It wasn't the biggest, but it was the size of a good fist. It was a murky white, just like the gemstones I had seen so far. Oh well, what else could be expected from an alpha forest?

Without wasting time, I picked up the stone from the ground. The battle was over and it was time to collect our spoils. I planned to take everything I could find from this focus. I could dig around in the earth some more, or send the reapers to get the gemstones from the monsters we had killed.

But, I didn't have a chance to decide where to start, as I received a signal from two of the reapers. Not only are chimeras able to take my commands, but they can also send me information, as long as it's very simple. It was nothing like what my shadow scout could do, but nevertheless.

Could it be that we had missed one of the monsters? That was strange, they never did ambushes. They would always try to get themselves killed when I was clearing.

Furrowing my brow, I walked toward the chimeras. To my surprise, I saw not more monsters, but Prokhor and his helpers. It was a good thing I hadn't ordered the chimeras to destroy everything living in sight, and they had therefore not killed the humans.

Instead, they now held their blade hands to the men's necks, making it clear that it was best for them not to make any sudden moves.

Chapter 14

I COULD HAVE USED A LITTLE MORE time to gather all the trophies before Prokhor and his guys showed up. Then again, their appearance sooner rather than later was to be expected. Firstly, he didn't believe for a second I could clear the focus by myself, but at the same time my confidence that I could gave him pause, so he was curious to see for himself how I could be so sure of myself. His second reason was potentially more devious. He maybe wanted to either save me to seem like a hero in front of Olga, or maybe what he intended was to aid in my demise and make it look like a hunting accident, pocketing anything useful I had managed to find out here. I chose to give him the benefit of the doubt because he was Olga's friend, but I kept my eyes open to the possibility that he had ulterior motives. He obviously didn't believe the "uncle" story, so I was a thorn in his side.

I slowly approached my unwitting hostages, and asked, "Is this enough people to clear a focus? Didn't you say you needed at least fifteen?"

"There are two more, and they have you in their crosshairs right now," Prokhor answered challengingly. That was the truth: two of his guys were sitting in the bushes nearby, aiming some sort of metal things at me that were bigger and more hefty looking than the pistols had been.

"I know," I said. "And you should know that's not a problem for me. Whereas, these guys over here," I nodded toward the reapers, "will tear your and your helpers' heads off in a fraction of a second."

"Who the hell are they? And, more importantly, who the hell are you?" Prokhor asked. I was beginning to like the guy. He was handling himself quite bravely and remaining even-keeled given the situation he was in. Many in his place would be panicking right now and would either become aggressive, or freak out.

In fact, one of his helpers — the one I thought Prokhor called Alan — was doing just that. All his hair stood on end, and his eyes were full of fear and a desire to do something rash. Alan was one of those people who don't run away and hide when they're frightened, but instead double down and act big and tough. It was all he could do to keep from saying something dumb.

I wasn't going to conceal my identity

anymore, and this was a good time to clear the air. I turned back to Prokhor and said, "I am Prince Richter. Head of the Clan of Necromancers. I was away for a while, but now I'm back."

Alan could no longer contain himself. "Bullshit! Who's gonna believe that?"

Prokhor threw him a warning glance, and said, "That's hard to believe. But what I'm seeing right now with my own eyes is even harder to believe. The shredded remains of thousands of monsters are lying all around us, and you don't have a scratch on you." He was silent for a few moments, then looked over at the reapers. "So they're not people?"

"They *were* people," I explained. "But they're not magicians or mutants, if that's what you mean. I created these servants from my dead enemies." This made Alan shiver so hard that his movement almost provoked one of the reapers. Prokhor was doing a much better job outwardly controlling himself than his friend was, but his eyes gave him away. He was scared. Perfect opportunity to screw with them a little more. "Now that you know so much," I said, "I have no choice but to 'lose' you here."

"What?!" Alan exclaimed.

I ignored him and continued, "Don't worry, I'll tell everyone you died like heroes, bravely fighting monsters. I'll even donate some of my harvest to your families."

Now, they were worried. Alan reached for his weapon, apparently wanting to commit suicide by attacking me. I wasn't interested in killing him, so

I telepathically ordered the reaper to take it easy on him if he started to make waves. What I was most interested in right now was Prokhor's response: I was waiting to see whether I was right about him.

"Alan, calm down," he barked. Then, to me, he said, "How about other options? You could have killed us at any moment, but haven't yet. That means we can negotiate."

I nodded in satisfaction. "You're right. We do have one other option. I'll let you live if you pledge allegiance to my clan right here and now, and become clan servants."

Let me clarify that there was nothing insulting in my proposal. Ungifted, which these two were, and even magicians who weren't related to us by blood, could enter the clan only as servants. The offer was an honor I was bestowing upon the two men.

Prokhor started considering, but Alan guffawed histrionically. "There's no such thing as a Richter clan! What are you talking about?"

"Alan!" Prokhor barked at him again.

Prokhor was facing a difficult decision, and needed help making it. I lifted my hand and held it up with my palm facing outward. I saw a flash of recognition in Prokhor's eyes when he saw my ring. "You think this is a coincidence?" I asked him.

"I don't understand," he insisted.

"Yes you do. That's the symbol of your organization, Purgatory."

"I still don't understand why you're wearing

that," he persisted.

"Because it's the symbol of my clan. The Richter Clan. And you, Prokhor Kalinin, are a distant descendant of my assistant Simon Kalinin, head of the clan's guard. And a pretty powerful executor level magician."

"What do you mean?" Prokhor perked up. "I'm an aristocrat? I didn't know I had any magicians in my family."

"You're a magician yourself. As is Alan, and the other two in the bushes. You all have a gift, but it is undeveloped. That's what allows you to clear foci and handle the abomination exposure."

"Oh yeah? I'm going to have to chew on that for a while."

I signaled the reapers to put their blades away. There was no point threatening them anymore — if something went wrong, like Alan decided to have another tantrum, it wouldn't be hard to handle these four.

"Thanks," Prokhor turned his head from side to side. "My neck was sore already."

"This doesn't mean you don't have to decide right now," I reminded him of my ultimatum.

"Of course," he acknowledged cooperatively. "May I ask a couple more questions?"

"You may," I agreed graciously.

"This Simon — when did he live?"

"A thousand years ago."

"Is that how long you've been away?" Prokhor's exclamation betrayed his surprise.

Alan's eye twitched.

"Approximately," I answered elusively.

"And you'll help us develop our gift?"

I smiled. That was a good question. Practical. I liked this approach. "Naturally," I answered. "I don't need any weaklings around."

Prokhor's ire was piqued momentarily. He didn't like the jab about the weaklings. He didn't think of himself as a weakling, but it would have been absurd to argue the abyss between our powers and capabilities did not exist. So, he swallowed his pride. "I'm ready to serve you," he said.

"Wise decision. I didn't really feel like killing you. But remember: you and your subordinates," I motioned in the direction of the armed ones, "are entering into a magical contract with me. You will swear an oath that can never be broken."

Prokhor was ready, but the others leered at me in surprise, fear, and confusion. I added, "Naturally, I'm prepared to extend the choice to the rest of you. If one of you prefers death to service, I have nothing against it."

While the others thought, Prokhor said, "These guys here are my closest comrades. What about my other soldiers? Will they have to swear allegiance to you, too?"

"No. The others didn't see anything they shouldn't have. It's enough that they work for you."

"I don't suppose we have a choice," concluded one of the two whose names I didn't know yet. "I'll do it," he added.

The other one nodded. "Me too."

Only Alan remained undecided. After a little while, he gave a dismissive wave of the hand. "To hell with it. I'll do it, too. Where do I sign in blood?" he snorted, trying to conceal his anxiety behind bravado.

"It's simple," I answered. "I'll place a magical seal on each of you. It's complex mental magic, practiced by generations of Richters. That way, I'll be certain you cannot harm me or my clan."

"I've never heard of other great princes using anything like that," Alan grumbled.

I gave a snort, amused by his naivety. "You think they'd make a public show of this?" I said. That shut him up.

Prokhor asked with a serious tone, "Is there anything else we should know about this seal?"

"A couple of small things. For example, it will be visible on your body, like a tattoo."

"Can we choose where?" one of the others — it was about time I learned their names — asked, sounding concerned.

"Yes," I said. The guy looked relieved.

Alan sneered and said, "Then I want mine on my ass."

"As you wish," I shrugged. "But are you sure you'll be prepared to show it to the guards every time you want to enter clan property?" His friends all laughed out loud, even Prokhor couldn't help himself.

"I was joking, jeez," Alan backpedaled.

"Well," I concluded, "if there are no more questions, then let's proceed."

I directed my ring, which contained the spell, at each of them. The ritual went off without a hitch. My new servants especially relaxed when they realized that their new tattoo was simply their already familiar Purgatory logo.

And I finally learned the names of the other two — Constantine and Brandon.

After it was all over, Prokhor said, "I don't get it — is it just me, or is the seal actually making me feel different?"

"Better?" I smiled slyly.

"That's what's weird about it — yes."

"That's a little surprise for you," I answered. "Consider it an onboarding bonus. The Richter clan seal is a very complex structure that has many functions. It embeds itself in the carrier's organism and optimizes many biological processes. You will now get less tired and recover faster from any exertions — both mental, and physical."

"I guess we've made the right choice," Brandon whistled and said.

I had decided not to reveal the second surprise yet. The seal was also a conductor of energy between me and my servants. I could pump them full of energy if I needed to, and likewise drain it from them easily. I didn't even have to be near them to do it. Luckily for them, I only drained my servants extremely rarely, almost never. But the ability to do that guaranteed me their loyalty.

"Well," I announced, "now that we're done with the formalities, let's get back to gathering our trophies. Since you're here, and now working for me, we can stay a bit longer than I had planned to take everything out of this focus that it has to offer."

"I still can't believe you cleared it by yourself,"

Book One

Prokhor shook his head. "I have to admit, Purgatory would have needed a whole battalion, or even two, to do it, and it would have taken several days. And we would have inevitably sustained injuries. Not lethal ones," he hurried to clarify, "but we get wounded almost every time we go in."

I shrugged, and responded to part of his tirade: "I barely touched the plants, so your team still has work to do."

"If I get some Purgatory guys down here, the cleanup will go a lot faster," he proffered. "Same arrangement — 80 percent to you, twenty to us, so you don't lose anything, but you save time. It comes with the package, I just..."

"You just didn't think it would come to that," I finished his sentence. I was curious to see how a cleared focus cleanup was done in this day and age, so I decided to hang out longer than I had planned. Besides, the whole endeavor had just turned much more lucrative. "Great," I said, "go ahead."

About an hour later, a few more cars drove up and a lot of activity ensued. By that point, we had finished clearing the monsters and only the predator plants remained. The garbage men who had come could now get to work without fear of being attacked by remnants of the focus.

I studied the equipment they had brought with them. I was especially interested in the machine for cleaning air. In my time, we just took all the crystals out of the focus, especially the central crystal, and the abomination would dissipate by itself. Now, they had a whole technology for sucking the maximum 'grace' out of the infected earth. They used everything at their command, including what were, from my perspective, weird machines. They not only dug up the gemstones under the mutant plants, but also gathered the plants themselves for reprocessing. The ground was so tilled over after they were finished that you could plant potatoes in it.

You don't even want to know about the mangled monster corpses. The exploded bodies of the jumpers had to be literally scraped off of all the surfaces that had been around them when they blew up. The puddles of blood under them, too. It was all useful.

The garbage men gathered the gemstones, to which I did not object. Prokhor wouldn't be able to pull the wool over my eyes now because of the seal, so I knew I would get my full cut, and I wouldn't have to dig in the dirt for it, either. I was winning on all fronts.

Nor had I forgotten to calculate the approximate profits in advance. Unfortunately, not counting the main one, there were only four relatively large gemstones, and those were only the size of a pea. The jumpers contained only really tiny ones, like little diamonds. But there were so many of them, plus the trophies from the trees and other ingredients, that I expected to get at least five million coins.

As I watched them work, Prokhor came up to me again. I could see in his eyes that he wanted to ask me something, but was having trouble getting up the courage. I guessed that after everything that had happened, he didn't quite know how to act with me yet. Which was natural — only an hour ago, he had been on his own, the only leader of his own business. Now, he was in a completely new and unaccustomed situation, where he was going to have to learn to be subordinate.

I could see that Prokhor was a reasonable man, but also ambitious. I didn't want him to worry too much about this or think of his role as some strictly etiquette-regulated dance on egg-shells. Besides, I preferred to resolve things as soon as they came up. That's why I always taught my servants, if they had something to say, to say it right away, without beating around the bush or thinking too much about how to present it. And that's what I told him.

Then, Prokhor finally relaxed and asked, "How often could you clear foci like this one?"

I could see what he was getting at. I almost laughed, but answered seriously: "Every day if you want."

You could practically hear the gears working in his head as he calculated how much money he could make. "That's..."

"Yes, that's correct. Start looking for the next focus."

"I've got a couple lined up."

"Great. I have a question for you, too, though. How soon will I receive my cut?"

He furrowed his brow and said, "Probably within the week. I can't say for sure. Maybe tomorrow, maybe in a few days. We can only sell to the clan's buyers. Once we've gathered everything here, the ball's in their court."

"I see," I said. "What about registering a clan? How is that done?" Olga had unfortunately been unable to tell me the details of this, so maybe Prokhor knew. But his first response was the same as my granddaughter's had been.

"Are you serious? There's only two of you. Or is there something I don't know?"

"Just us two," I answered unfazed, "but technically, Purgatory are also my people now. And anyway, it's not a question of how many. Or does the law forbid creating clans with fewer than a certain number of members?"

"I don't think so. It's just unusual, that's all." He thought for a second, then suddenly something dawned on him, and he asked, "How long ago did you wake up?"

"A couple of days ago," I answered honestly, trying to guess why he was asking.

"Then... what about your papers? Have you gotten them?"

I raised my eyebrow questioningly.

"I see," he said. "The first thing you need to do is get your papers, then pass a test for a magic license. Then, you can apply to register your clan.

"Then let's go?" I immediately proposed. "Or do they need you here?"

Prokhor looked over at all the workers around us. "No, the guys can handle this on their own. But are you sure you want to go right now? You don't need to rest?" he asked skeptically. He must have still been under a strong impression from how quickly I had dispatched all the local monsters.

"Man, all you descendants are so lazy," I gave an exaggerated sigh. Prokhor didn't take the bait.

Very soon, we were in my chimeramobile. I had hidden the reapers back in the trunk before the garbage men had shown up, so now all we had to do was pick up Olga, who was still waiting for us in Prokhor's car near the entrance to the focus. I hoped she hadn't died of boredom.

It turned out she was doing great. With these smartphones, people never had to be bored anymore, even when they were alone. She smiled and got into the car with us. I let her have the driver's seat, as always. I would need to learn the rules of the road so I could drive, but that wasn't a priority for now.

"I told you there was no need to worry about Max so much," Olga said to Prokhor in a celebratory voice. Then, she asked, "Where are we going?"

A shadow crossed Prokhor's face. It hadn't occurred to him until now that he would have to admit to her that he was now working for me. I decided to graciously tell Olga the whole story, in a light that was maximally flattering to Prokhor. By the end of my narrative, he looked at me in gratitude. He might have thought I was going to try to make him look pathetic to my granddaughter.

Once we were on the highway, he relaxed, and started studying the car's interior. He noticed Olga not looking at the road at all, and asked about it. She looked at me, not knowing what to say to him, so I answered for her: "I created this car with my magic," I said. It was an honest answer, but without too many details.

"You can do that?" Prokhor was gaining more respect for me all the time. "Wait, what about all the meters on the dashboard? Is it just me, or are they just jumping around randomly?"

Hmm... I guessed I was going to have to learn more about this mode of transport so I could perfect the chimeramobile and give it more credibility.

* * *

"What a stupid day," thought Dave Fast of the Road Patrol Service. Not only had he fought with his wife, but now he'd been posted in a real shithole area on the outskirts of town. He wanted to take his mind off things by focusing on work, but there was so little traffic out here that that was impossible. But neither could he abandon his post watching the road, as there was a camera right over where he was, and his superiors wouldn't be happy with him if he slacked off. All he could do was stare blankly at the highway, hating the world.

Wow, what a car! You don't see one of those very often. Dave stared at the attractive ivory Lamba, then noticed the driver. The young woman was not only not watching the road, she wasn't even holding the steering wheel, instead completely consumed by her smartphone. Weirdly, the car was driving straight and not even wavering.

She obviously thinks she's above the law. Well, she's got another thing coming!

 Chapter 15

PROKHOR WAS THE FIRST TO NOTICE the police officer. "Olga," he called out from the back seat, "there's a cop there." She gave a start, looked up from her smartphone, and put her hands on the wheel, but it was too late. The traffic cop was already pulling her over. My granddaughter was nervous, but when the cop came over to the stopped car, she smiled very broadly.

"Did I do something wrong?" she innocently batted her eyes. But by the stern expression on the policeman's face, you could tell right away that he wouldn't be so easily manipulated.

"Officer Dave Fast," he introduced himself. "Driver's license."

"Yes, of course," Olga opened her purse

cooperatively, produced her papers, and gave them to the officer, who started carefully studying every letter on them. This made Olga nervous again.

Max, on the contrary, looked very relaxed. "What does this guard want from you?" he asked lazily. "Just give him some money. They always want money."

Though Dave had apparently not heard him, Olga became very tense, and poked Max in the side with her elbow, with a look on her face that said "please don't!"

Prokhor was busily scheming in his head how to get her off the hook if Officer Dave asked for the car registration. As far as he understood, Max had not bought this Lamba, but made it himself.

"Registration," said Officer Fast.

Olga reached for her purse again, then pretended to be embarrassed: "Uh oh, I think I left it at home."

"In that case..." Dave Fast started in a celebratory voice.

But he he was interrupted by Max sighing heavily. "We don't have time for this," he said. "I told you, just give him some money." With that, he got out of the car, and started walking right toward the cop.

"Uncle!" Olga called out pleadingly, apparently frightened of something. But nothing terrible happened. Max took a bag out from inside his shirt, and dumped a handful of gold nuggets out onto the hood of the police car. Prokhor actually saw the cop's eyes widen and his jaw drop further down with each clink the metal made as it fell out of the bag.

Once this procedure was over, Max calmly got back in the car, and said to Olga, "Let's go." She was in shock, but didn't argue. The Richter Lamba rapidly distanced itself from the still dumbfounded highway cop.

Rumor has it, he's still standing there with his eyes and mouth wide open to this day.

* * *

After our brief encounter with law enforcement, Olga and Prokhor were both staring at me like they'd seen a ghost. Or like they'd never bribed a cop before. Strange people. It's bad tone to scare or kill a keeper of the public order. How else are they supposed to perform their duties?

For a while, it was silent in the chimeramobile. Then, my granddaughter said, "I hope he doesn't chase after us. Plus, he saw my papers."

"You think I didn't give him enough?" I asked. "Modern price points still confuse me a little."

"No," she shook her head, "it was more than enough. It's just that bribes are, um... illegal."

I shrugged my shoulders. For better or worse, when has the law ever stopped anyone from doing anything? It's just a given: money always opens doors, saves time, and provides opportunities. And the more of it there is, the faster it does those things.

"By the way," Prokhor spoke up, "why don't you use a sphere? No one keeps a lot of gold on them now. It's way more convenient..." he stopped mid-sentence, remembering, "oh, right — you have no papers."

"You don't *have* to have a sphere," Olga huffed. I snickered. Since I had told Olga about the Schitzer scam, where they were skimming money off of every user of the financial system, she had re-evaluated her opinion of how important those things were. "I was thinking about closing mine, too," she added.

I smiled and messed up her hair with my hand. "Don't be silly, it really is a convenient thing to have. And as for that other thing, we'll see to that in due time. So, yes, Prokhor, when I get papers, I'll get a sphere. I'm fascinated to learn all about that magic."

"That other thing?" my new comrade asked. "What's that?"

Olga looked at me questioningly, and seeing that I didn't object, explained: "The Schitzers don't just take a commission in coins for us using the sphere; they also take energy. That's what."

Prokhor was unimpressed. "So? It's still convenient. They probably take just a little bit, since no one notices." But, seeing that Olga was unhappy with this turn of the conversation, he changed the subject.

This was a culture clash between a commoner and a gifted. We value energy above all else because that's what makes up our power. But it meant nothing to Prokhor, who didn't know how to use his gift.

"So, where are we going?" Olga asked.

Prokhor looked at his watch. "It's too late to go to the office, and there's no point pushing it directly." He guffawed, and continued, "You're right, Max, about time and money. I know a woman who can save us the former in exchange for the latter."

"Who's this woman?" Olga's eyes flashed.

"She works at the agency," Prokhor explained. "Sometimes, she helps me get lucrative orders in exchange for additional compensation. We can set up a meeting with her at a nightclub, explain our problem, I'm sure she can help. And we can celebrate clearing the focus!"

I could see that Prokhor was excited by this idea. He had lost his independence to some degree, but he was a reasonable man, and accustomed to the clan system, so he saw more advantages to this than disadvantages. He had made a good amount of money in one fell swoop, and secured a future of clearing foci on a regular basis. Besides, he now had occasion to see Olga more often, which obviously made him happy. So, most likely, he just decided not to worry. I approved of that decision. A good servant shouldn't fill his head with unnecessary doubts.

"Let's meet her," I agreed. I had nothing against it. Even in my time, the best deals were always made over a feast and libations.

Olga, however, wasn't so sure. "Then we'll need to get ready. Buy you a jacket, for example. The other one is ruined, remember?"

I laughed. "Olga, don't turn into my mom, it doesn't suit you."

My mother also had a habit she could not

overcome of micromanaging what all her children wore, and panicking if one of us didn't dress according to the latest fashion. I would quickly change the subject with her.

Olga was taken aback. I added, "We don't seem to be having any money problems, so don't worry. We'll buy everything we need." Then, I asked Prokhor to tell us about the woman we were going to see.

"She's just a regular girl," he answered readily. "A little older than Olga. Likes to party, so she'll go to a nightclub anytime. Especially if we hint that it's our treat."

"Is she gifted?" I asked.

"Yes, but she's only an adept, and that's her ceiling. The clan was disappointed in her, so she's an aristocrat in name only. That's why she works at the agency. They don't hire ungifted, even though the work isn't exactly prestigious. She always complains that her salary isn't enough, so it shouldn't be too hard to make an arrangement with her. Especially if you use the same trick you did with that police officer!" he laughed.

"Police officer?"

"The keeper of the peace who stopped us on the road," Prokhor said.

With that, we arranged a time and place to meet the next day, and dropped him off at home.

* * *

I didn't really understand what a bar was until we got there. It was basically a big, loud tavern with a few modern amendments. The owners were extremely greedy and brazen, skimping on dancers by making the patrons dance themselves.

I liked the music right away, it was upbeat and rhythmic and reminded me of the war songs of northern tribes. I also realized why Olga had been so concerned about my clothing, and not only mine. When we had stopped at the shopping center, she ran around all the clothing departments for at least an hour, probably trying on everything they had that was her size. I didn't object, as this gave me an opportunity to explore other wares. I was especially interested in books and magazines. I selected them more carefully this time, as I now understood what knowledge about the modern world I still lacked.

The time she had spent at the store had not been enough for my granddaughter. When we got home, she spent another hour trying things on in front of the mirror, trying to get the most out of her wardrobe and accessories. Finally, she decided on some short black shorts, an attractive white top, and a black blazer.

Olga glowed as we walked toward the club, and she would catch the interested gazes of the people standing in the long line to get in.

Aristocrats have privileges. They let us in through a side door. Inside, my four new servants already awaited us. They had occupied a great little table with a soft half-circle couch and an ideal view of the dancing girls. I discovered this last advantage as I sat down. What they lacked in dancing skill, they made up for in enthusiasm. And some of their outfits were such that the odalisks from the harems of the rulers of the Levant would have blushed in shame.

"Beer?" Prokhor asked. "Or something stronger?" Each of them already had a big mug and a small plate with appetizers in front of them.

"I want a cocktail," Olga said. "Want to try one, too, uncle?" She knew I was curious to learn anything new.

They brought us two garish glasses — she had a bright green one, and mine contained something strange and striped. I found the beverage itself disappointing. The alcohol in it was of very low quality, which they had tried to mask with other additives. So, I switched to single malt whisky — a drink that time has been unable to ruin.

Soon after that, Prokhor briefly excused himself, and returned with his acquaintance. Her name was Lara Allen, a curly-haired, light-hearted looking blonde wearing a red dress that fit too tightly and a lot of large jewelry. It was easy to see why this free spirit had not been granted an official position.

Seeing me, she flirtatiously extended her hand for a kiss. I was pleasantly surprised by this, as it was the first time I had seen any evidence that the traditions of my time had survived. Olga, on the contrary, immediately became tense, and was now staring at Lara like she was an enemy of the people.

Lara was loud, laughed a lot, and liked attention. She sat between Prokhor and me, ordered a cocktail, and fit right in to our party.

Book One

The Purgatory guys were as happy as little kids about today's harvest. From this, I deduced that clearing a whole focus was not an everyday thing for them.

Prokhor could not take his eyes off Olga, which made her tense.

Lara had apparently considered my kissing her hand enough of a preamble to assume attack position. "So you're the tall, dark stranger with the documentation problems?" She asked, bending over me.

"I don't have any problems," I asked, "because I don't have any documents."

"How did that happen?" she asked.

"You won't tell anybody?" I asked, squinting in a mock sly way.

"No waaaaaay," she said, "my lips are sealed." She made a very serious face, and made a 'zipped up lips' gesture with her hand, while also licking her lips seductively. It was so contrived that I almost laughed out loud. I had met every type of temptress in my time, so Lara's attempts to seduce me were just risible. Like any attractive young woman, she was still very lovely and attractive, but I didn't like to mix business with pleasure. I was supposed to have a business relationship with Lara, and there was no reason to ruin that.

I came up with the most normal excuse I could: "I'm from far away, and went through a difficult path to get here. My papers disappeared along the way. Now, it's easier to get new ones than restore the old ones."

"Uh huh. Are you definitely related?" Lara

was staring at Olga.

"He's my uncle," Olga answered, resentful of Lara's implication.

"Is that what they're calling it these days?" the blonde giggled. "It's none of my business. But I do have to warn you that I can't make papers for any level higher than adept. Because for higher levels, you have to pass exams, defend a dissertation... it's a whole thing. I wouldn't recommend it," she concluded seriously.

"That's no problem," I answered her. "It's not hard to dumb down our powers. Let's do it."

"Hmm..." she said, drawing her finger down the length of my shoulder. "What's your actual level?"

"Unclassified," I told the truth.

"Then you have to show me a few spells," the blonde said, for some reason taking my words as a flirtation. I heard Olga groan quietly. I don't think she was jealous, I think she was bothered by how forward Lara was being. Olga felt her uncle deserved better.

"So how are you going to do this?" I changed the subject. "Are the papers going to be falsified?"

"It's all completely legal!" Lara stated proudly. "First, we submit your statement that you lost your ID, and send an inquiry about whether there's a record of you in our archives."

"There isn't," I said.

"Right," Lara continued," but my friend, who works there — you don't need to know his name — sends a reply that there is. Then, I grant you a passport, and send him a report that a new document has been issued, and he enters your name in the archive, backdated. And voilá!

I was once again impressed by the wiliness and greed of government officials. No matter how airtight a system you have, they will find every loophole and use it.

"Great, let's do it."

"It's going to cost two hundred thousand coins," Lara said. "Don't be surprised it's so expensive, I don't keep all the money myself. Can you afford that?" she asked, looking at Prokhor — after all, he had recommended me.

"Yeah," Prokhor laughed, "Max is literally littering gold everywhere he goes."

"Legal gold, I hope?" the young woman asked. I'm sure her services had been solicited by all sorts of people.

"Absolutely," Prokhor confirmed. "Did I tell you we're celebrating clearing a focus? Max was the one who did most of the work. We basically just stood there and watched."

It seemed like she had been waiting for this moment. "Ooooh, congratulations!" Lara lunged at me with a hug, and I had to tear her away like predator ivy.

"Let's dance!" Olga said, grabbing Lara by the hand and dragging her out from behind the table. "Come on, give me some support, girlfriend!"

Lara was mad at first, but then she decided that dancing was a good way to show off her body, so the two young women headed for the dance floor.

the Dark healer

* * *

Herman Hoffman had finally gotten back on his feet after the unfortunate incident in the shopping center, and was now chilling out in a nightclub with his pals. That dickhead with the Richter bitch kept not leaving his mind. In fact, they were the topic of tonight's hot debate over strong drinks.

"Those leeches are all wrong!" the ginger yelled.

"Exactly," Herman agreed, "some pathetic servant is going to choose who she works for? No one turns up their nose at a Hoffman!" He slammed his beer mug down on the table, splashing the beer everywhere, and almost shattering the mug.

"She's a nobody!" his minions nodded along.

"They should be punished. Let's find them and..." the ginger drew his index finger across his throat.

"And take turns with the girl!"

"Yeah!"

"Speak of the devil, there she is!" said the curly one, who had been silent until now. They all turned at once to look in the direction he had pointed in. Indeed, it was Olga Richter in the flesh, dancing her ass off with some fancy bitch.

"Maybe the other one is here too?" the dark-skinned one said.

"Let's find out," said Hoffman. "Let's watch them and see where they go."

A little while later, the young ladies returned

to the table, where indeed the thugs saw Max Richter himself, along with some ungifted people. "It's now or never!" yelled the ginger. "Let's…"

He didn't have a chance to finish, as Herman Hoffman interrupted him. He still remembered the talking to he had received from the clan elders, and he wasn't about to go to loggerheads. He didn't need another scandal. "Let's not hurry," he said. "We won't be able to get our proper revenge with all these witnesses around. Let's ambush him somewhere more private."

"That's right!" the ginger said. "Let's finish him in a public bathroom somewhere!"

Chapter 16

A PUBLIC BATHROOM WAS the perfect place to calm these fucktards down.

I wouldn't be true to myself if I had missed the opportunity to explore the club through the eyes of my shadow scout. As a result, I was aware of the potential problem Hoffman and his gang of shitheads represented. I didn't really feel like wasting time on them, but since a peaceful parting didn't seem likely, I was going to have to take precautions to make sure they didn't scare Lara off. I didn't need her getting cold feet and refusing to help with the papers.

And in general, I didn't believe in second chances. If they didn't understand or couldn't appreciate their luck, they had only themselves to blame. I wasn't about to give these dickheads even a hypothetical opportunity to harass my granddaughter again.

She returned from the dance floor, looking quite disturbed. She must have noticed them, too. Sitting down next to me, she whispered in my ear, "Hoffman is over there."

This made Lara flare up in jealousy, and she moved even closer to me.

Prokhor also became interested in what we were talking about, and before even knowing what it was, he instinctively became tense and alert. But he didn't say anything out loud, which earned him another point in my book. Instead, he leaned over to Alan and whispered something to him. A few minutes later, Alan invited Lara to dance.

The blonde threw me a challenging glance and departed with Alan for the dance floor, seductively swinging her rear end. I guess she was trying to cither make me jealous, or demonstrate how flexible her body was. The usual flirty girl behavior, in other words.

As soon as we were alone at the table, Prokhor immediately cut to the chase. "Is something wrong?" he asked.

"Herman Hoffman is here," Olga explained. "The fuckface who's been harassing me for a long time. Max really made him eat it recently, so he'll probably be looking for trouble."

"I've heard of him," Prokhor shook his head in disapproval. "I know he's fucked in the head. Maybe we should wrap it up here quickly, or go to another bar." Olga nodded passionately in support of his proposal.

"Why not just kill him?" I asked, surprised. "Since he's asking for it so insistently."

Prokhor and his pals laughed, apparently thinking I was kidding. But then, Prokhor spoke up. "It would be great to be able to solve our problems so simply," he said, "but even if we get in a scuffle with them right now, later the Hoffman clan will seek retribution. No clan would let a thing like that rest without seeking revenge. Especially if the perpetrators were ungifted, or healers."

Olga nodded in agreement again, and added quietly, so the others wouldn't hear, "We already have problems with the Velascos as it is."

Scoffing, I answered Prokhor, "That's if anyone finds out. All we have to do is not leave any witnesses."

Prokhor smiled again, still thinking I was voicing hypotheticals. "I wasn't sure before, but now I see that you really were asleep for a thousand years. There are security cameras everywhere now," he said, "and everyone has a smartphone. If there's a scuffle, we will immediately be recorded on at least ten devices, and a few minutes later the whole world will know what happened."

"Hmm... that's not good," I said. I remembered that the dark-skinned guy at the shopping center had also said something about security cameras and watching the footage from them. Demir... Demir... There was something vaguely connected to that clan spinning around in my head, but I couldn't quite remember what. It must not have been that important.

"Olga," I asked, "do the cameras also run on abomination, the same as smartphones?"

"Yeah," she answered instantly. Then, clarity slowly came to her face. "Don't tell me you're thinking what I think you're thinking."

"Of course not!" I said, playing innocent. "Me?! Never! I just suddenly need to go to the bathroom."

Olga's eyes met my gaze, and she realized there was no point arguing, so she stepped down.

Prokhor giggled lightheartedly again. He obviously didn't know me very well yet.

I got up and made for the bathroom, making sure to pass by Hoffman's table and demonstratively ignore him and his crew. I had sent my shadow scout to the bathroom ahead of me, so I could catch a moment when the bathroom was empty. As soon as the door closed behind me, I immediately found all the cameras and broke them with one touch. They had tried to make them hidden, but they were radiating so much abomination that I had no trouble finding them.

Once that was done, I looked around more attentively. I didn't find anything unusual, it was just a regular bathroom. There were a few stalls and a mirror over the sinks. It wasn't too clean, but that was normal for places like this. It might be an upscale nightclub, but there's always a drunk who'll piss past the toilet. So, it didn't smell too good, either. But I was willing to tolerate that for a couple of minutes. Hoffman would not be able to withstand the temptation of following me in here. I don't know why, but lowlifes love to resolve their issues in bathrooms.

I had a flashback to magic school, where I had been sent when I was twelve, promoted straight to senior. The rules were such that otherwise I wouldn't have been able to take the magister exam. My idiot eighteen-year-old classmates at the time had decided that I was being cocky, so they organized an ambush in the bathroom to "put me in my place."

Four clans lost their heirs that day, and eight more had to undergo lengthy treatment and rehabilitation. The bathroom had to be rebuilt, on the losers' dime.

The lovely elderly headmaster feared I would lay waste to something else if they didn't pass me, so the school considered the bathroom incident equivalent to my exam, passed me, and sent me home.

Hoffman didn't make me wait long. Within thirty seconds, their whole crew piled into the bathroom, all grinning.

"Did you think we were finished with you, douchebag?" the goateed Herman got in my face.

"We would have found you no matter where you hid," the ginger gloated.

The other two positioned themselves so that I wouldn't be able to get past them and exit the bathroom. But they should have been the ones to worry about fleeing.

"Whatsammater? Pissed your pants from fear?" Hoffman proffered again. "If you beg for forgiveness on your knees, I'll consider not ripping your nuts off. Well? What are you waiting for?" With those words, he turned the palm of his hand upward and started creating a ball of fire over it. This was not surprising, I had realized back in the shopping center that his element was fire. As for the rest, all his attempts to provoke me were so childish, it was as if I was back at magic school.

Be that as it may, the dumbass now deserved execution. Even though I had spent most of my energy clearing the focus, this did not slow me down one bit. The energy boost I had used before was to remain active for twenty-four hours, and it still coursed through me. Plus, now I had new energy donors practically jumping right into my lap. It would have been stupid to turn them down. The main thing was not to let the bearded fool spend too much energy before I took the rest away from him.

I waited until he threw his fireball. Then, without giving him a chance to make a new one, I ducked out of the way, and his spell flew right past me, shattering against the wet tile with a loud hiss. Hoffman's already intellectually underdeveloped face took on an even more idiotic expression. He had obviously not expected a regular healer to have chops like mine.

Now, he was about to be surprised again. My shadow grew, turning into clawed hands, and tore into the galoot's legs, jerking him toward me hard. Hoffman collapsed to the floor, without even trying to remain upright. Then, my shadow dragged him closer to me like he was nothing but a crumpled rag.

I didn't use that trick too often. A normal magician would never let an enemy's shadow get to him so easily. But with these imitators, and in a confined space, it worked perfectly.

"What the hell!" he and his crew exclaimed. They hadn't yet realized what was in store for them next, or else they would have grabbed ankle and split from the bathroom as fast as physically possible.

I put my foot on Hoffman's head and started sucking out his life force. It was easier through the hand, but a trained necromancer can do it either way without too much difficulty. A few moments later, Herman Hoffman was finished.

I looked up at the others. Their eyes were round with fear. They finally realized it was time to get out of there, but my shadow had already blocked their way to the exit. Again — had they been real magicians, this would have deterred them for no more than a second. Then again, I wouldn't have been surprised if shadow magic had been forgotten in this new time, too, along with necromancy itself. After all, only necromancers knew how to use that magic.

"Don't fall for it, boys!" the ginger yelled, trying to encourage the others. "Herman is alive! I'm sure of it!" If not for the loud music, the whole bar would have been able to hear him. As it was, he did not attract any witnesses. "The three of us can take him!" he continued to yell. But no one was in a hurry to second his enthusiasm. Instead, they were swearing loudly and trying to figure out how to move the shadow away from the door, because it was getting in their way of feeling around for the handle.

The ginger put his hand in front of him and sent a stream of air at me, making it into a mini-twister the size of a soccer ball. It was so cute, it almost made me cry. Even Hoffman's little fireball was a nuclear bomb by comparison. I didn't even bother to dodge it, I just took one step toward him and drained his feeble little source with my touch.

Alas, his two friends didn't have much to offer me, either. In fact, they were even weaker. Hoffman had clearly been using them for entirely ego-driven purposes.

It was time to wrap it up in here before someone else tried to enter the bathroom.

It was time for phase two of my plan.

* * *

"Good thing we quit drinking, Hans!" Phil said happily to his friend.

"That's for sure. My brain has never been so clear."

The pair were sitting on the pier, their legs dangling, eating ice cream. It was a warm and starry night. They had just finished their chin-ups in a nearby courtyard.

Ever since they had realized that a zombie apocalypse could start any minute, and no one was about to do anything about it, they had decided to take matters into their own hands. Even if they couldn't stop the inevitable, they could at least be ready for it, they figured. For that same reason, they had started saving money for a garage with a cellar, where they were going to build a bunker for themselves and stock it with canned food and water. They were going to approach this whole problem seriously.

Suddenly, they heard heavy footsteps behind them. Who could it be at this late hour? It would have been better for them if they hadn't turned to look. The scene they saw, already familiar to them, made Hans shudder, and an unpleasant chill ran up Phil's spine. There were four figures moving toward them along the pier. To all outward appearances, they were just drunk. But Hans and Phil knew better. They definitely had the walk of zombies. Exactly the same as the ones on that other, memorable night. They wouldn't have mistaken it for anything else, and this time they were totally sober.

While Phil seriously considered jumping into the sea to get away from the trouble, the zombies walked right past them, exactly like last time, paying them absolutely no attention. But then, something even weirder happened. They approached the end of the pier, and… plop! One by one, they jumped into the water, each raising a big splash.

After being quiet for a minute, Hans said, "Are they planning on attacking the city after rising from the depths like an army of the drowned?" From the shock of what he was seeing, he had even started talking differently, in a kind of contrived literary style.

"Obviously," Phil said. "Otherwise, why would they be jumping in there? They probably have their headquarters down there, or whatever zombies have."

"Maybe next we'll see ghost ships."

"We're in deep shit," Phil concluded. Then he palmed himself on the forehead. "Did you get a video? Or at least a photo?"

"Damnit! Foiled again! No one will believe us!"

"Nah, bro, ours is the way of the survivor."

* * *

I came back to the table with a blissful smile on my face, which fooled everyone except Olga. She firmly grabbed my arm and quietly asked what I had done. It didn't seem like she wanted to let go until I told her. Lara and Alan had already returned from the dance floor, and the blonde was staring daggers at my granddaughter again.

"Everything is fine, Olga," I told her. "Hoffman won't bother us again."

A shadow passed across her face, but she didn't ask for details in front of the others.

Prokhor had heard what I had said, too, but only lifted his eyebrow in surprise, without saying anything else.

I got back to my whisky and relaxing. My people and I had nothing to worry about, I had taken care of everything. Since no one believed in zombies in this era, no investigation would come up with anything. Especially since the Hoffman clan had appeared during my millennial slumber, so I doubted they knew anything about the Richters. It had been a productive day and a pleasant evening.

I wasn't about to disrupt it because of some stupid nonsense.

When I was plotting how to get rid of Hoffman without anyone noticing, I had remembered an amusing story about my old acquaintance, Viscount Christie. He slept around a lot, and always needed to prove to his wife that he hadn't cheated on her. Every time I saw him, he was always concerned with having an alibi. But, unluckily for him, his wife Agatha was no fool. She was always catching him red-handed. Plus her gift was far superior to Christie's, so he was regularly in the dog house. But he never let up — he was both brave, and stupid.

I told Olga that story, and I think she understood why I kept repeating the word "alibi." After that, she calmed down and relaxed again.

However, it was Lara who had been made most happy by the story. She liked to laugh a lot. I could have just held up my index finger, and she would have started laughing her heart out.

Prokhor spent all evening trying hard to get me drunk. He kept pouring me more whisky, and I kept saying let's have another one. Whereas I easily controlled the level of alcohol in my blood, and remained at a point of being pleasantly buzzed and fun, Prokhor kept getting more and more shitfaced with every shot. Finally, he fell asleep with his head on his folded hands. His Purgatory employees took him with them, and literally loaded him into the car. They even apologized to Olga and me, saying they had never seen Prokhor so drunk before. In fact, until that night, they had been certain no one could get him drunk.

I could easily have relieved him of the murderous hangover he would experience the next morning, but I purposely refrained from doing so. I figured it was a good lesson for him: if you're no match for your opponent, know when to stop.

Lara, too, had become an accidental victim of Prokhor's alcohol marathon. The young woman turned out to be even stronger than Purgatory's owner — she was still trying to stand and talk. She even wanted to keep "chilling." Olga and I had to drive her home and unload her there, no matter how hard she tried to cling to me.

"I see," she said in the end. "Relatives, huh? Yeah, right."

I didn't want to upset the young woman, so I used my relaxation magic on her. Let her get a good night's sleep. I needed her bright-eyed and bushy-tailed at the office the next day.

* * *

Emre Demir's morning began with the long-awaited report from Ali. He had even canceled an important meeting when he had found out that Ali was finally ready to tell him something. "Well? What did you find out?" he hurried him anxiously.

"Not much," came the disappointing answer. "It's not clear yet where he came from. Right now, he's living in the house of healer Olga Richter."

"Continue," said Emre. "Or is that all?"

"No, my guys noticed something else strange. There are two Velasco clan cars parked outside their house. I didn't inquire from the Velascos themselves, naturally."

"That's good," the head of the Demir clan approved. "No reason to give them an excuse to stick their noses into our affairs."

"There's something else, a lot more alarming. Last night, Herman Hoffman and three of his friends left a nightclub and all drowned themselves together. Immediately. For no apparent reason."

"Details?" Emre lifted his eyebrow.

"They were seen leaving the club and walking to the sea. They looked drunk, but they did not appear to be under duress."

"What about Richter?" the senior Demir inquired. "Let me guess, was he at that club, too?"

"Exactly," Ali confirmed. "But, as far as I know, they didn't interact. I couldn't get the surveillance camera footage, though. The club belongs to the Kramers, so..."

Emre waved his hand in a dismissive gesture. He had never gotten along with the Kramers. They were his constant competitors in the entertainment and sales business. He needed no other explanation.

"So, this is his work," he concluded.

Ali registered surprise. "Who the hell is he?"

Emre thought for a few seconds, then sighed heavily, and answered: "Alright, for your own safety, I'll explain who Max Richter is."

EMRE GOT UP, PACED UP AND DOWN his office, and stopped in front of the panoramic windows looking out over the city. This view from his office window in the penthouse of a skyscraper always calmed him, reminding him of how high he had climbed.

"Ali, you know I've been around the block a few times," he began weightily. "Five hundred and forty-four years, in fact. I've seen and heard a lot of things. And you're not exactly wet behind the ears, either — you're almost three hundred! To a lot of our younger relatives, you're an old man. After all, only ten percent of all gifted live to see two hundred."

Ali nodded, but said nothing. He had endless respect for his great-great-grandfather, the head of the House of Demir, and wasn't about to butt in with his own comments. He just listened.

Emre continued, "My great-grandfather was a powerful gifted, and he was able to live almost seven hundred years. But even he wasn't as strong as the grand dukes. And they, well, once upon a time, they, too, were dwarfed by a real monster named Max Richter." Emre came back to his desk, and sat back down in his desk chair, stretching out his legs. "Hasan Demir was a very smart man. I learned a lot from him. He taught me to keep my mouth shut and my eyes and ears wide open, to memorize every single thing that may be useful one day. He turned a tiny pawn shop into a huge chain with branches in every large city. And I continued his business. My great-grandfather chose me as his heir."

Ali listened patiently. He had heard this story about how Emre had enriched and grown the clan to its present point, many times before. Their chief was by no means devoid of vanity, and was quite fond of telling stories about his various successes on the path to raising the clan's status.

Luckily, this time he didn't linger long on Memory Lane, but got back to the point: "One very wise thing my great-grandfather taught me sounded something like, 'Even when the antelope is grazing peacefully in the field, it must have its eye on the lion.' As you know, our clan is not exactly chock full of powerful battle magicians. Of course, we have a whole army, but that's through money, not through magic powers. We've always been pawn brokers, traders, and alchemists. The fact that the warlike dynasties haven't been able to consume us completely is due only to our wiliness and luck, and it's not clear which played the bigger role."

Emre's smartphone interrupted his speech. He frowned and declined the call. He continued, "I haven't forgotten a word of my great-granddad's parable about the 'lions'. And I remember everything he told me about Max Richter, too. Especially since he was the strongest predator on our 'savanna.' He passed the archmage exams at sixteen — that's the highest level of mastery, as you'll remember. At twenty-two, Max took his father's place as the head of the clan after his father was killed in a clan war. Over the next century, Richter destroyed all who had been involved in his father's death, along with their entire clans. Didn't leave a single one alive."

Emre drummed on his desk with his fingers for a second, as though he was gathering his thoughts. Then, he continued: "Soon after that, Richter consolidated all the necromancy clans under his power. Most of them came to him themselves, appreciating full-well that they wouldn't be able to compete with him. Besides, as my great-granddad said, they were too afraid to compete with him. When his grandfather reincarnated as a lich and turned the entirety of northern Gaul into an uninhabited desert, Max was the only one able to pacify him. After that, there was no further question of who was the leader. And that's only the tip of the iceberg of the things he's done — the ones that are known, that is."

"Known?" Ali raised his eyebrow. "But then why don't I know anything about him? Or about necromancers? Isn't that just an old wives' tale?"

"Because all of that happened a thousand years ago," Emre replied to part of the question. It seemed they were now in territory where the head of the clan wasn't keen to share too many details.

Ali decided to ask one more thing: "Are you sure all of this is true? I don't at all doubt the honesty of my distant ancestor, but elders who have lived a long time are sometimes themselves a little confused as to what actually happened and what didn't."

Contrary to Ali's expectation, Emre was not triggered by this question. He nodded, agreeing that Ali had a point. He explained, "Among my great-grandfather's things, there was an old portrait of an aristocrat. Hasan claimed it was the great necromancer of antiquity. And his face was exactly the face of the Max Richter I saw on the security cameras."

"Can I see the portrait?"

"Unfortunately, my great-granddad sold it to someone for an enormous amount of money. And he wouldn't say who had bought it. To this day, I can't understand who could have wanted it so badly."

Emre's answers explained a lot. But there remained one more mystery: "Where has Max Richter been all these years? A thousand years — that's nothing to sneeze at."

The head of the Demir clan shuddered. Then, as if trying to chase away the bad thoughts, hurried to say, "That's not so important. What I want to know is, what's he going to do now?"

*   *   *

Eventful night. I tried absorbing energy in its pure form for the first time. To be able to do that, I had kept two gemstones from the focus fatties, and a few small bead-sized ones from the jumpers.

Once I was sure Olga was asleep, I lay down on the couch in the part of the stable she called the "living room," and tightly squeezed a gemstone in my hand. A fire wave rolled through my channels, contorting my body in pain. Damned millennial nap! The foreign energy, hostile to our world, was trying to change my organism, or destroy it. The ungifted couldn't handle it, they just died. Magicians would mutate to adapt. Only necromancers could combat it.

Before, I wouldn't even have noticed such a small amount of abomination, but right now it was literally burning me from inside. The gemstone, which was none other than a foreign magical focus created by the body for storing abomination, fell apart in my hand, and the tiny shards got absorbed by my skin. I listened carefully to my organism and did not feel any negative effects, aside from the pain. But I had learned a long time ago to ignore pain.

So, I crushed another gemstone in my hand, and all the tiny shards went into me. Then, I fell asleep. Not for a thousand years, just for a couple of hours.

In the morning, Olga found me, as usual, in the armchair with a magazine and a cup of coffee. Fred was at the stove, wearing her favorite apron with the cat on it. Later, she would admit that when she had seen him wearing it for the first time, she was outraged, but that now all she could do was smile blissfully as she watched the wraith fuss over her, putting hot, aromatic pancakes on her plate and pouring maple syrup over them.

After breakfast, we got right down to business. Half an hour later, we were exiting the chimeramobile outside Lara's office. She worked in the city's business district, almost in the center. There were different offices all over the place. And it was my first time seeing skyscrapers up close. In my time, even hermit magicians didn't build themselves such high towers. I have to admit, I was impressed by the monumentality of these structures. But I also couldn't help thinking that only a very small clan with not much land to spread out on would build such things. In my castle, one end of my grounds was too far from the other to see.

Lara's office was in one of these human ant farms, but only on the tenth floor. We quickly got there by elevator. The young woman's office once again made me think about land poverty, as it seemed to me she sat in a tiny hole in the wall. The only thing that redeemed it was a large window.

Lara was clearly not very happy to see me. I wasn't surprised. The night before, she had been practically jumping out of her panties to get my attention, and I hadn't succumbed to her advances, so maybe now she felt rejected. Hell hath no fury like a woman scorned. If she had known the whole truth, she would have been grateful instead. My organism was so starved for magic that if I relaxed a little in the process of making love with her, I could have easily accidentally sucked her dry of her life force. Just like the vampires in those books Olga's shelves are full of.

And if I didn't relax, then what would be the point?

In any case, she started doing the agreed upon work, while never losing her scowl. She took my photo, then she shoved a packet of paperwork into my hands. When I filled it out and returned it, the problems started. She shot me another stink eye, and said that there wasn't enough information on the form for me to be granted a personal ID card. Seems my magic level needed to be verified. "There's nothing I can do without a certificate saying you've passed the test," she threw up her hands and momentarily made a phony 'sorry' face, before the hostility returned.

"But we agreed yesterday," Olga tried to object.

"How am I supposed to know you're not lying about your level?" Lara said coldly. "I can't put it down just because you say so, that's a big risk to my reputation."

While the girls argued, I carefully studied the blonde. Her facial mimicry betrayed more than just aggravation and hostility. Had I been less experienced, I might not have noticed anything strange. But to my eye, she showed several tell-tale signs.

"Lara," I finally butted in, "how often do you have headaches like this?"

The young woman stopped talking mid-word, and there was a several-seconds-long tense silence in the tiny office. "Sorry, what?" she finally managed to say.

"I can see you're not feeling well, and it's definitely not from last night's party. You party like that frequently, right?" Last night, I had used a relaxation spell on her, which meant she would not have any hangover.

"How did you know?" she said. "And why are you so sure it's not a hangover? Yes, though, I do have frequent migraines."

I stood up, approached her, and drew my finger down her neck. She started in surprise, but I had already begun to explain: "Right here. You've fried this energy channel. Hence the headaches."

There was another pause as Lara gathered herself in her amazement. Then, she began unsteadily, "I... did fry my energy system. When I was prepping for my magister exam. But how did you... Damnit!" she suddenly became very upset, "I didn't even pass it! It was all for nothing. And now, I'm stuck here in this shitty office job." She slammed her fist down on her desk. This was obviously a pain point for her. Even Olga, who didn't like Lara at all, now looked at her with palpable empathy.

"Give me a minute," I smiled and touched her neck with my fingers again. She looked at me in surprise, but did not object.

Book One

When I took my hand away, she said, dumbfounded, "The pain is gone! I've gone to healers, and no one could do anything for me. I was hoping to save up to hire elite healers from the Villon clan, but I would have had to save for several more years for that."

"Well, congratulations! You've just saved a lot of money. And you can try the exam again in about six months. Just don't use that garbage anymore."

"Garbage?" she didn't understand.

"My uncle is referring to grace," Olga interpreted.

"I still can't believe… is it true?" There were tears in Lara's eyes. "I can feel that it is. The magic is flowing differently. My God, I'm not crippled anymore!" She covered her face with her hands, but quickly gathered herself. "I don't know how to thank you."

"Just the papers will do," I reminded her why I was there.

"Oh yes, of course!" Lara started fussing around. "And I won't take my cut, so it'll be two thirds the price. Just give me a few minutes!" She went back to work with a vivacity and enthusiasm that she had probably never had before. She even made a point of phoning her colleague to get him to approve some application or other more quickly. Everything was ready in less than ten minutes.

Now that we had the envelope containing everything I needed, it was time to move on to other important affairs. Olga and I hurriedly said our goodbyes, but Lara saw us all the way to the car, all the while erupting with gratitude. I'm sure she would have gotten into the car with us and continued if my granddaughter hadn't shot daggers at her.

Finally, the blonde retreated, happier than ever, and we drove off. "We need to buy another smartphone," I said to Olga.

"For you? Won't it break?"

"You'll do everything. Register me in that healer app. It's time we saw to those organ dealers. The chances of finding that girl Alina alive get smaller with every passing day." Olga gave a serious nod, and we drove to the nearest mobile store.

When we had finished there, Olga asked, "How are you going to catch them? You want to find that order?"

I nodded. "That's exactly right. We'll use live bait."

* * *

The Free-Roaming Wolves gang, as they proudly called themselves, were relaxing at their HQ, which is to say, one of their houses. A distant relative of his had passed away recently, and he had somehow inherited her whole estate, which he wasted no time in turning into a den for his gang.

"Hey! Someone's taken an order," the gang's communications guy, nicknamed Hacker, said. The only thing hacker-like about him was that, unlike most of the guys here, who had only graduated from high school, he had gone to computer programming college for a whole year. He was the communications guy because he was the one who made the orders in the app and monitored their status. "He'll be here in about half an hour," he added.

"Let's go then, what are we waiting for?" said their chief Merk. In his case, the nickname didn't really mean anything, but was derived from his last name. He hurried toward the exit, and the others followed — some energetically, others more reluctantly. One way or another, a minute later all seventeen of the gang members had mounted their motorcycles and started their engines. Well, almost all of them. One got behind the wheel of a small van, which was intended for transporting the victim.

The gang sped off, quickly reaching their meeting place near an abandoned building that had burned down and never been restored. They hid their motorcycles and the van in the backyard, or where it had once been. They themselves hid in the shadows of the ruins, and began waiting.

"Hey Merk," one of them suddenly called out, "I heard another gang disappeared right here the other day. One of them took an order, and then they all just disappeared off the face of the earth."

"Are you collecting urban legends now?" Merk said, and spit on the ground. "That was Kir and Rik, right? I know those wimps."

The other guy nodded.

Merk continued, "They're like floating turds. They kept trying to get some action happening, trying to get a big score. Stupid punks," he said almost paternally, "He was saving money for a trip to Los Aldos. That's probably where they are."

"I didn't know you knew him," Hacker butted

in.

"I didn't really. That dumbass tried to make friends with me in a bar, started chewing my ear off about wanting to go kidnapping with us. The fuck do we need him for? Our business is booming as it is."

"Hear, hear!" the others cried out in approval.

"Here comes our victim," the one who saw better than all the others exclaimed, pointing at the shadow approaching between the buildings.

"I think that's a guy," Hacker said.

"So?" Merk snickered. "You afraid he'll kick your ass like your pa did?" The gang all laughed. Many of them had once seen Hacker being chased down the street by his father, who had his belt in hand. That was after Hacker had been accused of petty theft for the first time. His father's disciplinary actions didn't help, however. Hacker later ran away from home.

"Alright, alright, quiet down," Merk said, after laughing heartily with the others. "Don't scare away the poor healer. He's about to feel something if he's no fool."

Everyone fell silent. When the victim came closer, the thugs all emerged and went for him. The guy was scared and started looking around for a way out, but quickly realized there was no point running, especially after some of the thugs started their bikes just in case he did.

"Please," the frightened healer addressed the gang leader who had approached him. "What do you want? I have money. I'll give you everything!"

"You'll give us even more than you think,"

<h1 style="text-align:center">Book One</h1>

Merk said, taking out his taser.

*　*　*

That was hard. Very hard. I clenched my teeth as hard as I could to keep from laughing. I have no idea how they believed me. I thought my whole plan was about to collapse there and then. But, apparently, they took my shaking because I was trying to contain my laughter, for tremors of fear. Which was fine with me. I wasn't about to try to convince them otherwise, or resist.

When a weak current went through my body, I was almost found out again. I hadn't realized right away what that thing was he was touching me with. Besides, my organism reacted to that kind of input automatically, immediately optimizing its functionality and eliminating potential consequences.

A second later, I realized it was time to pretend I had lost consciousness. I relaxed all my muscles, closed my eyes, and collapsed. Luckily, that didn't give the kidnappers any pause. They put a bag over my head, and quickly dragged me somewhere.

THIS PLAN I HAD HATCHED involved a lot of diffi-culties for me. I couldn't laugh, I couldn't move now either. I couldn't do anything. I had to just lie there and play dead. It was as boring as actually being dead.

The interior of the van stank acridly of some sort of chemicals, cheap alcohol, and later, even puke. Luckily, the cart I had been placed on was relatively clean. As far as I could tell, I was not be-ing taken out of town as I had expected for some reason. I remembered how bad the road had been as we had approached the focus earlier, but now the ride was smooth.

My only entertainment was remotely directing the lizard and watching what was happening through its eyes. And, of course, tagging the thugs so I wouldn't have to look for them later. My shadow scout had learned to do that, as well. These cutthroats were never going to be normal people, but at least, after death, they could be useful as my servants. I never even remotely felt an ounce of pity for these animals. Those who sell other people for their organs to be harvested simply do not have the right to complain when a larger predator comes and tears them to pieces.

At one point, my 'unconscious' body was moved from one van into another. This one was clean and neat, but they immediately shoved a hardcore dose of tranquilizers in my vein, and stuck a mask on my face that supplied more oxygen than normal air. Any doubts that might have lingered as to the intention behind the kidnappings were gone: I was to be used as a donor.

The van turned out to be a medical automobile like the ones I'd seen in the city, all colored the same way. The people in it were wearing white lab coats, which did nothing at all to justify what they were doing; on the contrary, in fact.

"He's not gonna croak, is he?" one of them — the one sitting next to the driver — asked.

"Nah," the one next to me shook his head. "These guys are careful. They just tased him. Not like those assholes yesterday."

"Right," the other one agreed. "Right on the head with a club like that! We had to compensate him for the medical bills with his cranio-cerebral injury, or we wouldn't have made it."

"They're not gonna need their brains

anymore," the one next to me snickered.

These guys definitely deserved to be tagged, too. I would deal with them later.

Finally, the van stopped. I was wheeled outside and taken right to the back entrance of a pretty impressive building. The interior didn't seem like a gang hideout at all, but more like an expensive private clinic, like the ones I had seen in my magazines. At least a quarter of all the advertisements in the magazines were for various medical services. The descendants all seemed to have some serious health problems.

I was wheeled down a long hallway and placed in one of the small private rooms. They put me on the hospital bed and connected me to a bunch of devices. I figured these were for monitoring my condition at a distance.

The door to the room was metal, and locked, so the room was not only a hospital room, but also a prison cell. The ventilation shafts in the building were wide, though, so the lizard very quickly explored the whole place, and soon I had a full understanding of the layout. I had raised the lizard's level before beginning this plan, so it could now store and transmit a lot more information than before.

The neighboring rooms contained three other people, all unconscious. One of them fit the description of Alina, the girl we were looking for. I had hoped to find her alive. Why store the organs, when you can store the donors until they're needed?

In the other rooms, about a dozen medics

were working. All of them gifted, but no higher than adept level. But then, in yet another room, there were two soldiers who seemed to be at least executor level judging by the magic radiation coming from them. They were going to be fun.

Once I understood my surroundings, I proceeded to the next phase. Its success depended not on me, but on my new helpers. This was a good opportunity to find out whether I could truly depend on them.

* * *

"Are you sure that lizard will be able to find us?" Prokhor asked Olga.

"Of course," she confidently affirmed, "Uncle Max doesn't make mistakes."

Prokhor could only envy her confidence. He still couldn't believe he was even involved in a thing like this. But facts were facts. Right now, he and Olga were sitting inside a van he'd stolen, anxiously awaiting news.

Stealing the van had been the first unexpected assignment they'd gotten from Max. When Prokhor attempted to object, saying he didn't get involved in illegal doings, he felt the clan seal on him heat up as though hinting that the car theft was non-negotiable. Olga had to explain what it was all about. Max preferred to dole out information on a need-to-know basis, and only about battle objectives. Once Prokhor understood about the organ harvesting, he was outraged to the core. He profoundly despised fucked up lowlifes who would do literally anything for money. He no longer objected to stealing the car if it would help combat them.

He'd had no choice but to go along with the crazy Richters' plan, but that didn't mean he wasn't worried. He was sure now that the Richters were all psychos. Olga was pretty out there too, but this did nothing to decrease his attraction to her. Anyway, he was the normal one! He knew miracles didn't exist, and you couldn't come up with a good plan, and execute it, all in one day, while also single-handedly fighting all of organized crime. He was sure there was muscle behind the organ traders, most likely clan support. Before he'd met Max, he would have been sure that taking them on would be impossible. But now? Who knew? It all made him uneasy.

"That's it! Here it is!" Olga opened the van door, interrupting his stream of consciousness. The little lizard shot in through the open door. Prokhor was seeing it for the first time, and it looked to him like just any regular reptile. But then, Olga touched it and froze as though she had fallen through a portal into another dimension. It took her a couple of minutes to snap out of that trance.

She said, apologetically, "I've just started training, so I don't decipher the thought-images as easily as I'd like to, but soon I'll be able to do it faster."

Prokhor nodded, and asked impatiently, "Well? Where is he?"

"At a private clinic called 'Vitalife', I think it's

downtown."

"What? Are you sure?" Prokhor furrowed his brow.

It was one of the well-known hospitals in the city. It wasn't that he couldn't believe they could be involved in the organ trade, but they were doing it right out in the open! He had long ago concluded that the more money, power, and fame someone had, the more outrageous their behavior became.

"Of course I'm sure!" Olga huffed for some reason, taking the question as an insult. "I double-checked several times. It's cleaning day over there. There's a sign on the door."

He lifted his hands in a 'no offense intended' gesture. "Alright, alright, don't get upset. We'll go wherever you say."

* * *

My shadow scout went to transmit information to our co-conspirators. I could have watched all the surroundings through its eyes, but I didn't. When the lizard was nearby, it took almost no energy to do that kind of monitoring. But the farther it went away from me, the more energy it took to maintain a steady connection. There was no need for that right now, so I preferred to save up my power for other things.

Thanks to the energy I had absorbed that night, I was approximately at magister level. That's a step below the executors, who do nothing but wear their pants thin sitting behind their desks. In a battle of magicians, having energy stored up is not all that counts, however. As I've said, the higher your mastery, the less energy you require to perform any given spell.

Everything was going according to plan. In a little while, I felt the shadow scout approaching. At the same time, Prokhor and Olga were getting closer, too. As soon as the lizard was on clinic property, I connected to it again to see the van, with my guys in it, stopping near the back entrance, just far enough to avoid attracting the security guards' attention. The instant the driver's door opened, the lizard immediately dove out of it. Prokhor hurried to open the other doors of the van.

Time to check things over one more time, then we could begin. The shadow scout slipped inside the clinic again, and now I saw that the situation here had really changed. There was a flurry of activity outside one of the rooms where the prisoner-donors were held. The door was open and a whole squad of magicians were stationed in the hallway. These guys were battle magicians — I wouldn't mistake them for anything else. Their levels were so-so — adepts and a couple of magisters. They looked like someone's private security detail. Whom were they here to protect, and from whom?

Meanwhile, the lizard slipped into the open hospital room, where I saw several medics fussing around a young woman who was in an induced coma. I also saw the various devices all around her — the same ones I was hooked up to. I had no idea what any of these numbers, indicators, and graphs meant, but they evidently conveyed something important to the medics about the condition of the donor. To my mind, this was a sign not of progress, but of decline in the healing profession. A good healer knows perfectly well what's happening to their patient without all this tinsel and scrap metal. Even a necromancer like me could do it no problem, and it wasn't even my specialization.

More than anything, I was interested in what was happening to the young donor woman. More than likely, she was exactly the one I was looking for. Of course, I wasn't going to abandon the other prisoners here, either. But they were surrounded by a whole concilium, so I decided to wait a little while before acting.

* * *

Barbara Thorpe was born into a rich and influential family, but she still considered herself unlucky. No one in her family had a gift, and neither did she. At first, she childishly resented the fact that she would never be a magical fairy queen. But as she got older, she realized she was losing much more than that. Despite all the influence the Thorpe family wielded, the power of the clans was stronger and much more all-encompassing. Never mind that even the feeblest gifted woman, with the puniest little gift, would stay young and live much longer than she would.

Her parents had managed to explain one other thing to her, as well: though nature had not been generous to them, with enough determination and cynicism, you could accomplish anything; even outsmart fate itself.

"Money and power — that's the real magic!" her father used to say. So, she played the hand she was dealt by life. She did the bidding of the powerful, and walked all over the weak, until she had become the head of the city's Supply and Logistics Department. Now, even the clans had to take Thorpe seriously and consider her in their dealings. Not the most powerful ones, of course, but just the thought that the gifted were smiling at her flatteringly and bringing her gifts warmed her little soul.

Her bodyguards were gifted, and even her secretary was an adept. She seemed to have compensated for all the drawbacks of her background. Except one.

Now that she had turned fifty-two, Barbara was ready to give anything to bring back her waning youth and health. Naturally, she had been among the first to find out that a new technology and a new service like this was available. It wasn't cheap, of course. Not cheap at all. But it was worth it. The upcoming operation promised to give her exactly what she wanted. Finally, the ideal gifted donor had been found, and all her organs would soon be Barbara's. She greedily daydreamed about her new life.

The experiments had already been conducted, and were wildly successful. There was almost no risk, and the procedure promised a rejuvenating effect that had hitherto been only a pipe dream. The fact that someone would die for that? Not a big deal. Poor people are always dying — if it's not from one thing, it's from another. And the leech's lot in life is to serve real aristocrats and other important people like her. No, Barbara had no intention of filling her head with any superfluous worries.

When she was met by Thomas, the head of the clinic, she was literally glowing with happiness. And she didn't neglect to note his special treatment of her. They had met her in the parking lot, and led her inside, graciously answering all her questions.

At times like these, Barbara almost forgot that she hadn't been fortunate enough to be born in a clan. When she expressed her desire to see the donor, they took her to the room, no questions asked. 'She's pretty,' she thought to herself. 'Maybe those genes of hers will have an effect on me, too.'

"Ms. Thorpe," the clinic director addressed her again, in an emphatically respectful tone, "it's time for you to get ready for your operation. Please, allow me to walk you there."

* * *

Unfortunately, the medics weren't even thinking of dispersing. On the contrary, more and more people kept showing up. Finally, someone who was very clearly the head honcho appeared in the hallway, and everyone was very deferential. I had initially intended to give all the bystanders a chance to leave the clinic before starting the skirmish, but I quickly saw that wasn't about to happen. There was more and more activity going on around the woman I supposed to be Alina Aster. Only a fool would have failed to realize that she was being prepped for surgery.

My timing was perfect. I even had time for a little fun. The first thing I did was make my organism work in such a way that the devices around me went apeshit. Honestly, I didn't even expect it to go so well, but now I was happily enjoying the cacophony I had created of alarms and whistles of every sort. The equipment was demanding attention.

The medics responded quickly. Two of them appeared right away in the doorway of my room. I continued the charade, but only until the moment when one of them had bent over me, concerned, studying my face. That's when I suddenly opened my eyes, and simultaneously grabbed his chest with my hand. He yelped, and almost instantly fell to the floor, dead. I had taken his life force very quickly. But it's possible he died of fright.

Throwing his corpse aside, I hopped down off the hospital bed, at the same time tearing away all the sensors and wires hanging all over me as if I were a Christmas tree. The second adept was screaming and about to run. I grabbed him in the same way, and took his life force just as quickly. Weaklings.

* * *

"Holy shit!" yelled one of the two security guards watching the security camera monitors in a special room. "Holy fuck! What the fuckin' fuck! What the shittin' fuck is that?!"

"Huh? What?" the other one looked up from his phone.

"Look at what that prisoner is doing! We've got a dead body on our hands!"

The other guard gave a start, and looked at the screen his coworker was talking about. "So what the fuck are you yelling for? Sound the goddamn alarm! Escalate!"

"Yeah," the first guard reached for the alarm button, "and don't tell me what to do."

The argument didn't go any further than that, as the two men stared tensely at the monitor screen and watched events unfolding.

"What the hell kind of magic is that?" The second guard was dumbfounded as he stared at the shadow paws. "I thought they only took leeches for donors."

"I've got no idea," answered the first guard, just as dumbfounded. "One thing I know for sure: it's a good thing there are two executors at the clinic today. I'd hate to have to deal with him myself."

"Looks like the other one's dead, too."

"That was fast. They were adepts."

The two guards exchanged looks, and understood each other without saying a word. They were both only apprentices, which was exactly one rank below adepts. That's why all they'd been entrusted with was monitoring the cameras. Today, they did not regret this fact at all.

"Maybe we should turn on the siren, too?" the first guard asked sheepishly.

"Nah, let's wait for the executors. This guy

doesn't look like he's leaving his room yet."

"Is he waiting for something?"

"Yeah, he's waiting to die," the second guard laughed nervously. "The soldiers are gonna make mincemeat out of him. If we sow panic throughout the whole clinic, we won't get a medal for that. You know yourself, there's a lot of influential people being treated here."

"OK," the first one agreed, but still moved his hand closer to the siren button.

The two executors really were at that moment rushing to the scene of the incident. More importantly, as they focused in shock on monitoring the one camera, the guards missed the fact that another suspicious group had entered the clinic by the back door, and was moving down its hallways.

The killer donor was strangely calm. It was as though he was waiting for those who were coming to kill him. He didn't even try to hide so he could ambush them, or do anything else to increase his chances of winning in the battle that was about to ensue. He just stood in the middle of the room and stared at the door.

The door flew open, and two executors in full battle gear burst in. Each one was covered with an energy shield, and held his hand in readiness to cast an attack spell.

"Goddamnit!" the first guard suddenly exclaimed. "Hallway B6! What is this, a zombie attack?!" Like many dilettantes, the security guard didn't know his undead very well. Still, mistaking these gray figures with scythes for hands for regular zombies was an unforgivable mistake.

Book One

"We have to warn…"

"It's too late."

Max Richter's reapers had already reached his hospital room and attacked the executors from behind.

Chapter 19

THE BATTLES I HATE MOST are the ones where I have to chase my opponents around. Luckily, I had servants to do that for me. Still, I preferred to meet my enemies head-on. Especially when they were seeking me out themselves. I was sure they would come now. I didn't even need any more confirmation from the shadow scout. I ordered the reapers my guys had brought here in the stolen van to come straight to me. I was anticipating a new fight.

Since my awakening, I had only encountered weak gifted, mostly adepts. Even magister is basically only the halfway point for a magician, though far from everybody reaches even that point. Executor was the next step after magister, and meant a specialization in battle magic. So, I seriously counted on these guys — not only because I stood to get more energy out of them, but also because it was a chance to finally get some real exercise, battling opponents who can at least do something. Energy-wise, I was even weaker than they were right now. But, as I've said before, in a magicians' battle, the energy stores are not the only factor.

The door flew open, and two burst into the hospital room. They were the exact two I had been expecting, and they were ready for battle. Both were dressed in identical black clothes and masks with slits for the eyes. This clothing was not made from normal materials; I could feel magic radiating from it, very similar to that exuded by their energy shields. This fabric would not be pierced by conventional weapons, and magic attacks would not be as effective as they would otherwise be.

One of them was considerably larger than the other — he was taller, and broader in the shoulders. A real meathead. He lunged into battle first. Electric projectiles emerged from the palms of his hands and flew toward me. They were no bigger than ping pong balls, but there were about fifteen of them all at once. In a narrow space like this, it was very difficult to dodge them, as he had correctly calculated. I hadn't wanted to waste energy on a shadow dome, but the enemy left me no choice. I erected one, and now his mini-fireballs were crashing loudly against it.

The other executor wasn't in a hurry to get involved in the melée, he just stood there and watched. Which is why he was the first one to be attacked by the reapers. Two of their blades hit hard against his shield and bounced off. The magician himself immediately started evaporating into thin air, and soon disappeared. I realized the fight was going to be even more interesting than I had thought. Invisibility is a complex spell that only a few magicians with a special gift are capable of. This guy might have been almost at the next level of mastery.

The reapers switched right to the big cutthroat, hitting him on the shield several times. I didn't even expect them to be able to pierce it, but the fight drained his energy, which would provide me with an opportunity to strike the death blow. I put some extra energy into my shadow blade, and, just at a moment when the enemy was distracted by one of the reapers, I struck. My blade pierced his shield, then the fabric of his clothes, and tore into his flesh. But, when I wanted to strike him again, I felt a foreign life force right next to me. It was the invisible one! He was coming up behind my back.

I took a step forward, right into the deceptive silhouette of my shadow. I say deceptive because a necromancer's shadow is only an image of a real one. I could use it as a kind of teleportation device — I could vanish an instant before the icy dagger of the invisible executor was to strike me, leaving it to penetrate only the air in the space where I had just stood.

Now I was right behind the big guy, and could see his partner lose his concentration and become visible again. At once, one of my reapers attacked him. Meanwhile, the two others continued to come down over and over on the other one's shield. The large executor hadn't realized in the beginning what he was dealing with, and he tried to use electric attacks to drive away the chimeras, but to no avail. He shot up both hands, and materialized a weapon in them — a real chainsaw! I'd seen them in magazines, they were frightful things. He started spinning like a top with the chainsaw, threatening to turn anyone who came near him into ground meat. I reacted immediately, covering my reapers with my shadow dome, even though it cost me a ton of energy. Then, I took another step into the shadow, returning to the center of the room, where one of my servants was fighting the formerly invisible executor, who was a very good sword fighter, but could barely hold his own against the unbridled strength of the chimera. For some reason, he didn't want to use magic yet. Maybe he was saving his energy for me? That was a mistake. He got so tied up fighting the reaper that he failed to dodge my blow. I crumpled his shield with my blade. I didn't have enough strength to hit him harder than that. His suit had done its job — it had protected the asshole from being wounded.

The biggest danger was still the maniac with the chainsaw. He continued spinning around his own axis, advancing toward my chimeras. To add to that, my dome's armor was wearing thin. I had to stop this death machine at once, before it destroyed my servants.

Now, with no regard for saving energy, I

turned again to shadow magic. Catching a good moment, I tossed my blade into the wall next to him. His own shadow was my target. I hit it right in the center, turning it into a trap. The meathead slowed down considerably, and his shadow started expanding, until it enveloped him. If I had more energy, I would have made it wrap him in a cocoon in about two seconds' time; as it was, I had to content myself with making his shadow creep slowly, which gave my opponent ample opportunity to escape its grasp.

And that is what he now tried to do, but found the radius of his mayhem was strictly limited by the shadow. Meanwhile, the reapers and I were free to concentrate on the other executor. So far, he hadn't shown anything too concerning, aside from the invisibility. But he probably had other surprises in store.

As though reading my mind, he disappeared again, to reappear by the window at the other end of the room. There, he waved his arms, and spinning blades started flying at us. They covered all the levels of the room so that they couldn't be dodged: the magician intended for them to reach our heads, torsos, and legs simultaneously.

Fortunately, I could still maintain the shadow dome, so was able to repel that attack. But I had to do something about this stinker at once. The shadow had by this time chained up half of the big guy's body, so I decided to take a chance: two reapers zoomed over to him and blocked his chainsaw with their blades as best they could. One of them lost his arm, torn off at the shoulder; the other suffered a deep gash in one of his bone blades. At the same time, I came up to him from the other side and put my hand on his shoulder. This is when I realized I couldn't suck out his energy through his suit. Damn.

Happily, he was already wounded, so I put my hand on the torn flesh of his wound. I got all bloody, but I also felt a powerful stream of life force pumping into me. And it couldn't have come at a better time. The second executor had redoubled his flying blade attacks, and my dome was sustaining more and more injuries, as it also became increasingly difficult to maintain. But not anymore!

It was time to wrap things up here. The meathead was dead, and now all that was left was to catch the other one. He had seen the writing on the wall and gone invisible, probably intending to run. But that wasn't going to happen.

I clapped my hands in a picturesque move, and the hospital room was instantly submerged in impenetrable darkness. This was another shadow magic spell, which allowed a necromancer to feel the space around them. It cost a lot of energy, but it was a priceless weapon against this type of enemy. Now, I could feel everything that was happening in the dark with literally every cell in my body. I didn't need my eyes.

The invisible executor was creeping toward the door. I smiled and ordered my reapers to block his way. I thought they would just surround him and maul him to death, but he managed to surprise me. He somehow felt them coming, turned around, and bounded toward the window. Coward! A magician executor, running from some magister! It made me proud.

Naturally, the windows had bars in them. But they were no match for his power — he could knock them out in one blow, along with a piece of wall. I couldn't let that happen. I ran after him, and made it in the nick of time: he had already broken the glass, and was in the process of jumping out when I grabbed him by the collar and quickly dragged him inside.

In order to break through his shield, I had had to sprout bone claws on my hands. Now that I had gotten to a new level, I could change my body like a chimera, including growing six-inch razor-sharp blades on my hands. They looked like the reapers' scythes, but they were also full of magic. I'd had to put a ton of energy into them. But that didn't matter now. As he died, the meathead had bequeathed me a generous amount. Now, I managed to not only drag the invisible executor back into the room, but also to wound him. This meant I could take his life force, too.

Having dealt with both of them, I now had to perform the routine clearing of the other rooms, and also save the prisoners. I sent the reapers to patrol the hallway, and hurried to Alina Aster's room. I was sure now that it was her. Olga had confirmed it when she saw the thought-image, and the lizard had sent me the information.

The young woman's room was now empty. Evidently, the medics had decided to escape while they had the chance. But they wouldn't have gotten far. I could already hear their screams in the hallway. The reapers were very fast, and their opponents were weak.

I disconnected the young woman from all the machines, picked her up in my arms, and started carrying her toward the exit. I didn't bring her back to consciousness, as it was better to do that once we were in the car. She didn't need to see everything that was happening here. At the exit, I handed her off to Olga, and Prokhor and I went back inside. A clearing has to be thorough.

I didn't touch the others for now. You can't leave living witnesses, so let them remain in their comas for now. As for the fate of the other clinic workers, it was clear to me they were all complicit. My store of biomass to work with was going to receive a lot of new material today.

I didn't need Prokhor as a soldier; rather, I needed him as someone fluent in the customs and mores of modernity. He was the one who found the safe in the clinic director's office, and advised that we find out the code before killing him. That clinic director was a magister, too. The shame!

In my time, apprentices were full of fighting spirit and the will to victory. After fighting the two executors, I didn't even feel the director's power. Prokhor, on the other hand, was very impressed. "I can't believe you neutralized him so fast," he said as he rifled through the director's safe. Before his untimely demise, he had graciously shared the code with me, just as my reaper was tickling his neck with one of his scythes.

"Is there anything important in there?" I

replied with a question.

"There's no money, but there's a whole pile of papers, harddrives, and flash drives." He stuck one of these devices into his laptop, and gave a whistle. An operation could be seen on the screen — not the one from today. The man being operated on had a youngish, brazen face. "That's the vice-mayor!" Prokhor exclaimed.

The chief of medicine apparently wanted to play it safe, so he kept compromising materials on a whole bunch of people who used the illegal services of his clinic. That was a smart thing to do — that way, they wouldn't say anything — not even by accident. But now, this evidence was going to bring down everyone who was involved.

"Great," I nodded. "Let's keep that. Keep going. Faster."

In a couple of minutes, Olga would call the police, which meant we had at most seven minutes to finish everything. Unfortunately, there was no way to avoid the rush. This clinic was most likely under the protection of one clan or another, which meant their soldiers were already on their way here. And their objective would be to try to cover up the crimes committed here.

At last, we found the video surveillance monitor room. The guards that worked there had abandoned their posts, and found their deaths somewhere nearby. I was impressed by the number of screens showing every space in the building, every nook and cranny of the medical center. This was clearly a lot more convenient than keeping a whole army of shadow scouts. The scouts were way more dependable, though. I decided that, on my estate, I would combine the two approaches.

With this thought, I broke all the equipment and erased all the information recorded on it. Before leaving the building, I looked into the pre-op room, where the state official for whom Alina had almost been murdered was being prepped for her surgery. She had her own bodyguards — two adepts who nearly jumped out the window at the sight of my reapers. While I dealt with them, the lady tried everything in her power to get me on her side. She threatened me with her status and influence, and promised me mountains of gold, then she begged for mercy and lied about how she didn't know anything. To be honest, I was so sick of her screaming after just one minute, that I could have killed her just for that. But, in my eyes, she was an accomplice in everything that had gone down here. I had no qualms at all ordering a reaper to slice her head off.

Finally, we made it out of the stuffy clinic, into the fresh air. The police were almost there, I could hear their sirens. We ran to the van. The reapers obediently jumped in, and the other zombies I had harvested here also packed themselves into the van like sardines.

I lay down on the cart we had grabbed on our way out of the hospital, and Prokhor rolled me in. It wasn't too comfortable, but it was one of the few ways I could ride in the van without making contact with it, thereby breaking it.

Truth be told, that was the one weak link in my whole plan. If the gangsters had just thrown me into the trunk of a car, I don't even know what would have happened. I might have needed to look for another gang to surrender to.

* * *

Before driving Alina to her parents' place, we had to get rid of the van. We were going to dump it somewhere in the slums, and get into the chimeramobile, which would be waiting in a safe place. Luckily, Prokhor had been wrong when he'd said there are cameras everywhere in the city. There were still plenty of streets where not only were there no cameras, but no street lights either. Which came in handy.

Half an hour later, we were on our way home. Even though I had taken all the toxins out of her system, Alina felt real lousy. She had been in a coma for almost two weeks. She and Prokhor were in the back seat together, and he was able to calm her down, though not without difficulty. "It's all over," he told her. "You're going to see your parents soon."

"Only I'll treat you a little first," I added. It wouldn't do to return the young woman home in the condition she was in. After all, was I a healer, or no? I was getting more and more used to the role.

I received a thought-image from the lizard, which I had sent to accompany the zombies just in case. Unfortunately, the chimeramobile only had enough room for the reapers, so the other undead dragged themselves to our house on their own.

Some of them carried their severed limbs as they walked, and one crabby old hag carried her head in her armpit. Why waste valuable resources? I wondered if they would all fit in my lab. It might be time to move soon...

*　*　*

"Breaking news!" The TV hostess in the strict and tight-fitting suit was practically choking with excitement. "In a surprise raid, the police have liquidated an underground organ trading clinic!" The screen was flashing with police officers, many of them walking to and fro, looking busy. They were arguing, pointing at the broken walls and furniture, and writing something down in their notepads. "The kidnapping victims are already being questioned!" the journalist continued to yell. People were being brought out of the clinic, wrapped in warm blankets, helped into medical vans, and taken away. "There is evidence representatives of the city authorities on the highest levels were involved in the illegal operations. According to the Chief of Police, dozens of criminal investigations have been initiated."

Murky scenes of the operation. You couldn't see the faces, as though they'd been blotted out on purpose. A tired man with a glorious mustache promised that all the facts would be thoroughly investigated, and the guilty would be brought to justice. Judging by his signature underneath, he was the Chief of Police. He reported that all the bandits had escaped in an unknown direction, and were now declared wanted.

I snickered hearing that. Have fun finding us!

"We're already on the news! Fuck, we got out of there just in time!" Olga held up her phone so that I could see the screen. She was gesturing excitedly. Then, the news reporter said they had an urgent exclusive, and Katharine Villon herself appeared on the screen. She made her most innocent face, looking both confused and outraged at the same time.

"It's all some big mistake!" she passionately argued. "The Villon clan is being set up. Or else, they've gotten through to someone on our side. We have never been involved in anything illegal! Why would we? We have a legitimate business that's worth billions, and a reputation to uphold. The Villons have always served the people! Oh, believe me — we'll find out who did this. The guilty will be punished!" She gave a farewell flash with her eyes, and disconnected.

So that's whose feet we'd stepped on. I rolled on the floor in laughter. What a performance! The insulted innocence act, played impeccably. And I now understood who owned this clinic.

There was one thing I knew for sure: she had meant the last thing she said. What Katharine lacked in magic ability, she made up for in tenacity and vindictiveness. She was going to get to me sooner or later, it was only a matter of time.

At least one thing in this world hadn't changed. I even missed the hysterical bitch a little. Thus, one real enemy appeared on my horizon.

Chapter 20

THE EMERGENCY CLAN COMMITTEE sat around a large oval table set against the enormous fireplace in the great hall of their palace. Katharine Villon was tearing everyone a new one. Now that she no longer needed to pretend to be warm and fuzzy, she didn't hold back.

"Explain to me, Louis, when did you become such a dumbass loser?" She was addressing a guy who, despite being over two hundred years old, looked barely eighteen. He had big blue eyes, blond curls, and a babyface. There were many beautiful men and women among the Villons, but this one stood out as particularly angelic looking. That did not protect him from the ire of the clan chief, however.

"I..." he began, but was immediately interrupted by Katharine.

"You still haven't found the two missing curators who disappeared along with one of the vendor groups," she pressed him, "and not only is your pretty little head too thick to put the plan on pause, but you didn't even increase security!"

"But..." he tried to explain himself again, but he was shut down even more rudely, this time with a silence spell.

"I'm speaking!" Katharine's eyes flashed daggers. She was as mad as a fury. "You've let the clan down. Your pathetic excuses are of no interest to anyone. Furthermore, you didn't even inform anyone that anything was amiss!"

"I've always said Louis isn't fit for this job," a slim middle-aged man with a neatly trimmed goatee butted in. His facial hair made him look like the devil as depicted in medieval engravings.

The next silence spell was immediately launched, this time at him. "Shut up, Philipp. You're not going to weasel your nephew onto the committee. And the next time you attempt to use a crisis situation to your advantage, you'll be out on your ass yourself." Philipp's face instantly changed, and he guiltily bowed his head.

"Sometimes, I don't know why we even need a committee, if no one on that committee knows anything or is responsible for anything." Katharine looked at each person present. "Does anyone have any information?"

As she switched her gaze from one member to the next, each one looked down to avoid meeting her eyes. After a long silence, she spoke again: "Two of my informants are just outside this room. In the last half hour, they have found out something. How did you and your servants spend that time? Pathetic."

Katharine got up from the table, and opened the door herself. Two gifted entered the room — a young woman with a laptop, and a slightly older man, both dressed in strict suits, looking like they had just come from an important business meeting.

"Lady Katharine," they greeted the clan chieftain with a bow.

Then, the young woman placed the laptop on the table, and spoke. "First, I want to show you what the clinic looks like now." She played a video on her laptop of someone walking the hallways of the clinic, filming the surroundings. "As you see, all of our medics, guards, and other staff have disappeared. There are almost no signs of struggle. No blood, no bodies. Nothing. As if everyone just evaporated."

"No one was found at all?" one of the committee members asked.

"No one who saw anything. We don't know if they're dead, or kidnapped, but the only people we've been able to establish contact with were those who either left the clinic before the attack, or those who were in a completely different part of the medical center when it occurred."

"What about the cameras outside?"

"Yeah," Katharine said, "that whole neighborhood is under surveillance."

"Except this one block," the man shook his head. "I guess the clinic's high-profile clients didn't want to be filmed, so there was no recording there. The cameras there are dummies."

"Zoe, have you tried searching for them using their smartphone tags?" Katharine asked the young woman gravely.

"Naturally," she said. "No signals. We found a few discarded phones in the clinic itself, but the rest have disappeared along with their owners. There are no leads. All our tags must be broken."

At that moment, the video showed one of the hospital rooms, and focused in on the window. Since prisoners had been kept here, there were supposed to be bars on it, but they had been torn out along with pieces of concrete, and the glass was broken.

"I guess there was at least one fight, after all," Katharine commented.

"Yes. That much is clear. But we have been unable to get any biomaterials from the scene. Our people have not found a single hair or drop of blood — nothing that could give us any idea of who had been there."

"Was it treated with some sort of disinfectant or something?"

"Out of the question. The clan soldiers arrived five minutes after receiving the alarm signal, the police were already inside."

"So it's a spell?"

"But who is capable of working with living matter like that? Except us Villons, that is!"

There were a multitude of questions, and a

scarcity of answers. The camera continued to show the destruction in the clinic. The furniture and expensive equipment had been chopped to shreds by some sort of giant blades. Katharine furrowed her brow. This reminded her of something. Something from a very long time ago. It was just below the surface of her memory.

Then, suddenly, it surfaced: she had seen this before in the castle of Gaultier Salazar. Gaultier was the favorite grandson of Armand, the head of the Salazar clan. His ego ran off with him a little bit at one point. Once, during a party at his castle, he had been disrespectful with a female necromancer. Maybe he tried to hold her by force, and maybe he was even able to. The head of her clan at the time, Max Richter, destroyed the estate completely, and left no trace of himself in the process. It was a thing he used to do. Katharine even remembered what spell he used for that — the decay spell. Armand Salazar pretended the castle had gone empty all by itself. He thought his clan had gotten off easy.

Katharine didn't want to think about this stuff too much. Happily, the Richters had been gone for centuries. It was no time for hunting ghosts, she preferred to focus on the present. "No leads at all, huh?" she asked Zoe again.

"Well, there is one, my lady," the young woman respectfully answered. "We checked all the cameras that *were* working, and saw a very suspicious van that departed from the medical center right around the time of the attack. We soon lost track of it in the projects. Our people are combing the area as we speak."

"Great," Katharine nodded, satisfied. "Keep me apprised of the investigation in real time. The Villon clan will not leave this brazenness unanswered!"

* * *

When we got home, the two cars with the Velasco crest on them that were parked next to our house again made me think of my grandfather and his sage pronouncements. If he were here now, he would definitely be clapping his hands gleefully, and ordering us to move the cars closer to the van we had used for our attack on the Villons' clinic. Granddad was a real provocateur, and he would not have missed out on such a great chance to make the two clans butt heads.

As for me, I always found this approach unsportsmanlike. What if they kill each other off, and I don't get a chance to participate? Then what was it all for? I definitely did not feel at home in the role of spectator. So, let granddad's advice wait for now.

We did need to move the cars somewhere, though. Our house wasn't a private parking lot for Velascos, or a junkyard. And junk is exactly what they were about to become. Before hiding them, I decided to suck the abomination out of them. It would come in handy. I wasn't about to put the wraiths behind the wheel, they could just push the cars there.

But that would be later, under cover of night. Now, it was time to see to Alina. Olga helped her out of the chimeramobile. The young woman was still very weak, she swayed to and fro, and didn't make much sense when she talked. She kept complaining about being in a fog. No wonder — two weeks in a coma is nothing to sneeze at! But I expected to bring her about quickly. I needed several minutes just to clear her organism of chemicals, and restore her energy channels, which had suffered pretty bad damage. What Lara had experienced was nothing compared to the minced meat Alina's energy system resembled. I suspect something they were injecting her with was designed to suppress her magic reserves, just in case she tried to resist.

No sooner had I restored a small part of the young woman's potential, than her organism started actively healing itself. Such is the nature of our gift. It works even if you don't develop it.

Meanwhile, Olga looked around for something to change our guest into. We had saved her from the hospital, and all she had on was a hospital gown. But finding appropriate clothing, even in a large wardrobe like my granddaughter's, was not an easy task. Olga was tall and very thin, while Alina was much shorter, and more stout. Not fat, just curvy. The blouses Olga offered for her to try on could not be zipped up on Alina's chest, which made the young woman blush terribly. Finally, Olga found an outsized garment she referred to as a "hoodie," and big stretch pants.

"Sorry it's not a super hot look," Olga said, evaluating the results.

Alina started rapidly shaking her head. "Don't

say that! This is much better than anything I could have hoped for! Thank you both so much! Now my parents won't see me in that awful gown, and with my mind in a haze."

From the moment she had come to, Alina kept constantly thanking us. I even wanted to put her back to sleep so she would be quiet. But Olga liked it, and she had earned her triumph today, having conducted the function allocated to her in our operation impeccably.

"Shall we go then?" Olga asked, smiling. Alina emphatically nodded again, and we got back in the chimeramobile. This time, without Prokhor. We didn't need him, so he had gone home.

We got to the Asters' house pretty quickly. There, as was to be expected, we witnessed a very warm family reunion with tears, embraces, and kisses. Once everyone had calmed down, the hosts sat us down at the table, but realized they had nothing to feed us, and started fussing around. Linda chided herself for being a bad hostess, unable to even feed the people who had saved her daughter. Ignatius immediately ran out to the store and came back with a huge cake. We assured Linda we were happy with tea and dessert.

In actual fact, I had not decided to linger here merely to celebrate Alina being saved and our operation's success. Ignatius had sworn to serve me, and I wasn't about to let him off the hook. I told him so as I enjoyed the sponge cake he had bought. I expected him to be surprised, not thinking he had taken what I had said seriously. But Ignatius pleasantly surprised me. He stood up, put his hand on his heart, and loudly announced, "I saw what really happened there on television today. I don't know how you were able to make that happen, but there's one thing I do know for sure," his voice quivered, "You saved my daughter. My life is yours. I have no intention of going back on my oath."

"Dad," Alina began, uncertain, "you don't have to do that. I can pay my own debt. I'm the one he saved."

"I swore an oath," he answered brusquely. Then, a few seconds later, he added, "Besides, how can the person who saved my daughter be a bad person? Anyway, even if he is, I'm still prepared to give my life just so you and Linda will be alright."

"Don't worry," I spoke up, "you won't have to give your life. I value my servants. But we do need to take care of a couple of formalities." Then, I told them about the seal. "I recommend that Linda get one, too, and serve me, as well. The Richter clan seal has such a good effect on those who wear it that the abomination won't affect your organism practically at all."

"Can I think about it?" she asked.

"Of course."

"Then, would you mind if we conferred in the other room?" She made a guilty face. "I'm very sorry! You saved our daughter, and here I am, hesitating. It's just that it's all so unexpected..."

She was going to continue apologizing and explaining, but I didn't want to waste time, so I interrupted her. "Of course you can discuss it amongst yourselves as a family. Ignatius is the only one who gave the oath, and I will not demand anything more."

In a sense, my offer was a gift from fate itself for the Asters. As a healer, Alina could have gotten admitted to a clan in the status of a servant, but her parents did not have this prospect. Who needs aging ungifted servants, when the best of the best compete with each other for opportunities to serve aristocrats? Clan servants get access to benefits that regular people have never even dreamed of: high salaries, a special legal status, protection by the clan guard, and immunity from essentially all prosecution.

It was true that my clan didn't really exist yet, and they were going to be linking their lives with the Richters to emerge from all battles victorious, or die trying, together. It sounds trite, but it's a big decision. They had a lot to think about.

The Asters gave out another shower of gratitude, and went into the other room. I could have eavesdropped using the lizard, but I didn't really care that much what they were saying. I concentrated on the tasty sponge cake.

Our hosts returned after five minutes. "I will accept the seal and serve you, like my husband," Linda said decisively.

"Me too," Alina supported her mother.

Then, Ignatius spoke: "We've decided that's the right thing. Our family owes you a lot. You saved Alina and helped Linda. We trust you, and we want to pay you back however we can."

I nodded. "Then, let's proceed."

About five minutes later, the ritual was

completed. Now, I was ready to tell them the truth about myself, so Olga and I stayed at the Asters' house for another half an hour. Servants' loyalty and hard work depends on how much they know about whom they are serving, and for the sake of what. In the past, the Richters' fame was ubiquitous, and no explanations were needed. But now, we had to prep each person individually.

My new subjects were struggling to wrap their minds around the fact that I was a thousand years old. And the fact that I'm a necromancer also didn't register without surprise. "I definitely believe you," Ignatius said after I was done with my spiel, "but this is hard information to get your mind around. It'll sink in with time."

"You have until tomorrow," I nodded. "I'll be expecting you at noon, at my residence." It was weird to call the stable that, but these were the times we were living in. "There, we will discuss your new responsibilities and how your work will be remunerated."

"Yes, of course. Tomorrow it is, then," Ignatius said without hesitation.

With that, we finally said our goodbyes. It had gotten dark outside. The first time we had been caught in the darkness with the chimeramobile, I realized there was something I had missed in its design: there were headlights on the car, but they didn't work. At the time, I didn't yet fully understand what they were for. By the next night, however, I had corrected that oversight, and we could see the road perfectly.

If we looked at it, that is. I had recently

become concerned about how dependent Olga was on her smartphone. She was never without it, even for a minute. Even when she went to shower. I wasn't about to interrogate her about this. It didn't affect our business together, so let her do what she wanted. But right now was one of those rare moments when she had put her hands on the wheel, pretending to be driving the car herself. I suspect this was because, after that incident with the policeman who had stopped us, she had studied every place in the city where they might be stationed. In this way, she hoped to avoid attracting unwanted attention.

And that is why Olga noticed the small dog standing by the side of the road, waiting for a chance to cross. It was obviously not a pure breed. White, with orange spots, it looked at the same time like a terrier, a spaniel, and maybe something else — I couldn't tell what. It was a mutt.

At the same time, a sports car was speeding down the second lane. It didn't really threaten anyone, and the dog didn't try to run across in front of it. But, when the lowlife had come to where the dog was on the curb, he swerved sharply to the side, as if on purpose to hit the animal. With a loud yelp, the dog flew two yards back from the road.

I memorized the license plate number. I now knew this was important if you wanted to find the owner of a car.

Olga screamed and stopped the chimeramobile at once. There wasn't much traffic in our lane, so she was able to do this without fear that someone would hit us from behind. Swearing in a way I hadn't yet heard my granddaughter swear, she jumped out of the car, and I got out after her. After letting a couple of cars go by in the other lane, we ran across the road.

"Max, you can help the dog, right?" Olga pleaded.

The dog looked totally normal, like it was asleep. I bent down over the animal and put my hand on its side. It didn't have any visible damage, but it was unconscious. And now, I realized why.

"I won't lie, this dog is in bad shape," I said. "Many internal injuries."

"Isn't there anything you can do?" my granddaughter asked, worried. "You're so good at healing." She was scratching her fingers nervously and looking at me in hope.

"There is," I said, "but we only have a few minutes."

Chapter 21

I FELT SORRY FOR THE PUP. Practically any dog deserves to live much more than most humans do. Olga, too, kept looking to me in hope of a miracle. The miracle would indeed take place, but not here.

This incident was a clear challenge from fate. I acted immediately. I scooped up the pup and headed to the car. "Let's go, quickly," I said to Olga. She didn't need to be told twice. She got into the chimeramobile before me and we drove on. In just a few minutes, we were home.

Losing no time, we descended into my subterranean laboratory. Everything now depended on Olga. I had realized even initially that it would be impossible to save the dog in the full sense of the word. But there are certain nuances to our gift.

Book One

Take, for example, the lizard. Its reptilian nervous system is so simple that it had hardly even realized its existence had changed in any way. In fact, it became more intelligent than before. People, on the contrary, are too complex. It's almost impossible to preserve their brain in functioning order. There's time to salvage some reflexes — the wraith can respond to its own name, and retains some skills from its former life even without additional energy infusions, but that's as much as you can expect. Of course, creating wraiths isn't the only thing necromancers do. But all the other variants demand special rituals and enormous energetic expense.

A dog's brain is not that simple, but it's not nearly as complex as a human's. And they have extremely strong reflexes that are literally hard-wired into their brain structure. So, I knew if I acted swiftly and precisely, I could preserve all the dog's reactions, its personality, and even its memory. Basically, prevent brain death. Outsmart death, in a sense.

I didn't explain all of this to Olga yet. She would understand everything once she conducted the necessary procedure. Her passionate desire to save the dog was going to be useful to us now. I had intended to teach her to raise the dead in the nearest future anyway. I had planned to begin with wraiths, naturally, and I anticipated encountering the usual psychological and moral barriers all newbies experience — fear of dead bodies, squeamishness, and more. Once, I had taught dozens of apprentices from among the most gifted and potentially useful to the clan, so I was very familiar with all the challenges novices face. Now, I was hoping that the dog could help us skip ahead through hours, or even days of training. It was uniquely suited to the result we needed. The main thing now was to make it in time. As we drove, I did everything I could to keep the pup alive as long as possible. I almost completely controlled the beating of its heart myself. I'm afraid even the greatest of the Villons wouldn't have been able to do more for it.

In the lab at last, I laid the pup on the table, but didn't take my hands off it. From this position, as I continued to keep the dog alive, I began to instruct Olga: "Right now, you need to concentrate all your focus on the dog. But not in the way you're used to. Usually, you have to suck out abomination. But now, you need to do the opposite — pour your own life force into the dog."

"Me? But I thought… you would do it."

"No," I answered firmly. "It is your task to help this dog. I won't intervene."

"But why?!" she cried out, hurt. "I don't know how!"

"This is your chance to learn. Begin. You don't have much time."

Yes, it was baptism by fire. Sometimes, that's the only way to awaken a necromancer's gift. This was a rare chance I didn't want to miss. Seeing that I was serious and would not budge, Olga stopped arguing and concentrated on doing everything I said. I directed her, making suggestions along the way on how to correctly distribute the energy flow, and what doses of energy to give the dog. I also taught her a few other simple but important hacks to help her avoid making all the usual rookie mistakes and learn properly right away. The main thing was moderation and consistency. As you have to fan a campfire gradually and softly so you don't blow out the fledgling flame, so in necromancy you have to be careful not to burn out your own energy channels right from the beginning so you can remain able to give sufficient energy later in the process.

Finally, when I saw she was ready, I let go of the pup, releasing him from his perch on the precipice of life. And Olga caught him. The transition was very smooth, almost seamless. The dog sighed and opened its eyes. We had succeeded in preserving its brain without damage. An additional piece of luck was that the collision with the car had also not damaged it much. Most of the impact had been on its back and stomach. If that had not been the case, I wouldn't have fanned my granddaughter's false hopes in the first place.

"We did it!" Olga exclaimed. "Right, Max? We did it!" She began petting the dog on the head, then froze. "But... it's not breathing." Just then, the dog lifted itself up a little, butted its head into the palm of her hand, and started joyfully wagging its tail. "It's so... cute," she added, confused, but still petting the undead dog.

"Congratulations, Olga. You have created your first revenant." Before she had a chance to be upset that the dog was in fact dead after all, I explained that we had saved all the important parts.

"Even though the pup isn't breathing anymore and its heart is not pumping blood, you did everything right. And you have gifted it a new life."

"It's really weird. I can see that it's just like a living one. He's not like your zombie people at all. Even his eyes are sparkling! Ah!" she jerked her hand away as the pup licked it.

"A revenant is its own kind of undead," I explained. "Its skills depend on its level, like those of a wraith. Right now, the dog's skills are dormant. But as it develops, the revenant will sort of remember them."

"So it'll be just like a living dog?" Olga asked.

"It's important for you to understand that it will now live off your life force," I told her. "You'll be able to develop it further. With each new level, the dog will become smarter and more receptive. And you yourself will now need to train a lot more, as well."

"I understand," my granddaughter nodded seriously. "That means I need to develop my own power, too, right?"

"Naturally," I confirmed. "It's more important than ever now for you to take your training seriously. Keep practicing relaxation every chance you get. Not just before bed. You can control the spell's influence."

"Yeah, I've already felt that. Maybe there's something else I can do?" Olga's eyes were on fire. She was rearing to charge into battle. This was fantastic. That was the exact reaction I had hoped for.

"You need to train more in processing

abomination. Right now, your organism isn't able yet to quickly process the amount of that nasty stuff you can get from overdosing magicians. You are, however, ready to work with poisoned un-gifted."

"Then, starting tomorrow morning, I'll go back to volunteering at the clinic, and I'll do some training before bed tonight." She snatched up the pup and hurried toward the exit from the cellar. Right near the staircase, she stopped and turned to me. "I'll call him Archie," she said. She looked so happy that I couldn't resist smiling. I pointed upstairs, and she ran up the steps, glowing even more.

I stayed down in the lab for a while. Despite the fact that there were three rooms here, I was rapidly running out of free space. The battle with the gang and the clearing of the focus had already given me a lot of bodies to work with, and I planned on finding another gang. And that didn't even take into account the likelihood of raids by the Velascos, and even the Villons. In other words, I was facing an acute need — I had to urgently build a second laboratory. Or at least a warehouse.

With these thoughts, I went upstairs and walked around for a while near the house, study-ing everything on the street. To the left of the sta-ble, almost flush against its wall, was a five-floor building. Olga called it a dormitory, but to me it looked like a mix of boarding house, homeless shelter, and hideout. When I had shared that im-pression with Olga, she had confirmed that indeed such a description was more accurate. Our neighbors were noisy and were always having a problem or yelling. Even now, I could hear someone fighting in one of the apartments on the first floor, and the sounds of a mad boozy party coming from the top floor. I expected to be able to buy out the land soon on which that building stood. But for now, I noticed the abandoned construction site to the right of the stable-house. I had already asked Olga about it, and she had said they had stopped building there five or six years ago. It was now an empty lot with garbage and a half-ruined skeleton of a building. I figured I had an assignment for my wraiths tonight.

I raised several corpses, and sent them to clean up the empty lot. I wasn't too worried about whether its owner would be found or not. I was planning on solving that issue in the near future, as well.

Fred had a special assignment in store for him tonight. I gave him three wraiths from the latest harvest as assistants, and sent them to move the Velasco cars away from the house.

* * *

"You've done two kilometers," Hans's fitness trainer app encouraged him, "keep going!" He and Phil had undertaken to get truly physically fit. If their first encounter with zombies could be attributed to a fluke, the second one had convinced them that something truly horrible was happening. An inevitable zombie apocalypse. And what was the most important thing in fighting zombies?

$\mathcal{B}$ook $\mathcal{O}$ne

The ability to run away in time, of course. That's why, in addition to chin-ups and bench presses, they had now also begun jogging.

It was a moonlit night, and the weather was beautiful. The two friends were enjoying their jog, when they saw four men in front of them, pushing a car. In the past, they would have gotten in the men's faces, and maybe even taken their smartphones and their car radio. But now, they had been so transformed by their new knowledge, that they could think of nothing else but to offer to help the poor people with the broken-down car. After all, in the future, humanity would have to stick together to fight off the armies of zombies.

Without saying a word, the two of them stopped in front of the people pushing the car, and Phil asked in a friendly voice, "Need help, guys?"

The 'guys' continued their work, oblivious.

Hans asked, surprised, "Why don't you guys take the handbrake off? If the wheels can spin, it'll be a lot easier."

Again, no answer.

Phil put his hand on one of their shoulders, just as it dawned on him just how motley this crew was. Only one of them was dressed normally, like Hans and him. Another one was wearing a black suit and white shirt and tie, he looked exactly like a secret service bodyguard. He even seemed to have a badge. Two others had crumpled white lab coats on.

"Hey, guys!" Phil said. "Not too friendly, are you? I'm offering to help you."

"Yeah, fuckin' friendly and congenial," Hans

added, a little emotional.

Finally, one of the car pushers turned toward them — the one who had seemed like the most normal one, but bald. His face turned out to be very strange, with pale, glassy eyes — just like those others...

Phil and Hans exchanged frightened glances. The bald one opened his mouth and tried to say something to them. Probably, "Thanks." They didn't hear him because, without saying another word, the two bros had made a one-eighty, and sprinted back in the other direction. They kept running until they heard the friendly voice of the fitness app again: "Congratulations! You've run another kilometer and set a new world record!" Their hard work was paying off.

* * *

The Aster family arrived at our place even earlier than we had agreed. First, however, they had confirmed with Olga that I could see them. Had Hugo had the courtesy to do this, I wouldn't have to be running around with scythes for hands.

I have a real sense for people. My new servants were polite and tactful. I likewise expressed congeniality, and gave them some coffee. With Fred's help, of course. At first, they were very suspicious of him, especially once I explained what he was. But it was one thing to hear it explained, it was another to see it with their own eyes. However, Fred was gallant, and the coffee was tasty. In general, he was an exemplary wraith — I could easily receive a prize for him "for excellence in necromancy."

Olga and Archie's arrival completely broke the ice. Alina asked if she could pet the dog, and I didn't object. The girls sat to one side, and were now playing with the revenant together. Alina's parents, on the contrary, were very serious. As was I. Servants must, first and foremost, be useful to the clan. That is their calling. Since I didn't have many people, I needed to use the resources I had with maximum efficiency.

"How can we be of help?" asked Ignatius, openly concerned to be useful.

I was glad his heart was in the right place, but I spoke to his wife first. "Linda, when we first met, you said you used to work as a jurist before you got sick?"

"Yes, that's right," she confirmed readily.

"Then I already have an assignment for you. I want you to go to the city archive, the municipality, or wherever you need to, and find out the information I need. I want to know who owns each plot of land in this neighborhood. Some of them are maybe already for sale, others are not. But I want the full information on each of them, and about the owners of each of them. Do you understand?"

Linda nodded, and asked, "How much time do I have?"

"The faster, the better. Today is Wednesday? I expect to have all the information by the end of the week."

"I won't let you down," she respectfully

nodded her head and smiled gratefully. "And, to be honest, I haven't felt this good in a long time. I never thought I would say this, but I really miss work. So, if you don't mind, I'll start right away." With that, she got up from the table, we said our goodbyes, and she ran off.

Then, I turned to her husband. "Ignatius," I began, "can you drive a car?" To be honest, I didn't know yet how to make use of Ignatius Aster. He had worked as a garbage man all his life, processing magical waste. According to him, he had "grown up the ladder" to become assistant to the head technologist. He didn't become a technologist himself, because they wanted gifted that were stronger than he was. Well, I didn't have any need for that kind of 'specialist' either. Loyal people are always useful, though. I knew the right assignment for him would emerge in time.

"Yes, of course," he replied. "I have a CE category license, so I can even drive large trucks with eighteen-wheel trailers," he explained, realizing I may not be familiar with all the categories of vehicles.

"Great," I gave him a back slap, "then drive me to Purgatory, and we'll drop off the girls at the clinic."

"Wait a minute," Alina asked, tearing herself away from Archie, "what about me? What should I do?"

"Your main task right now is to develop your gift. As I've said, you'll go to the clinic with Olga, and she'll teach you a very important spell, which you'll have to practice every free minute you have."

"Is it relaxation?" the young woman guessed.

"Exactly," I confirmed, adding, "so let's not waste time. Let's go."

Then, we went outside and got into the chimeramobile. I had to explain to Ignatius how it worked. "Really?" he asked, "You drive it with the power of your mind?"

"Try it!" Olga jollily answered. "It's an incredible feeling!"

Ignatius gingerly got into the driver's seat and ordered the chimeramobile to start moving. For some reason, out loud. Olga laughed and explained again that you don't have to say the orders to the car out loud. Ignatius took a while to learn to trust the car.

A few minutes later, he felt more acclimated and agreed that it really was a very convenient thing. Though he still kept turning the steering wheel and pressing the pedals, I guess by force of habit. Fine with me, we'd have fewer problems with law enforcement that way.

Soon, we dropped off the young women at the clinic, and went on to Purgatory.

I had big plans for that organization. I wanted to evaluate the prospects of profits from the foci. I was going to need a lot of money soon. I was sure the land would not be cheap, even in a bad neighborhood like ours. Never mind that I had to legalize the clan as soon as possible, which would also cost a lot.

That meant Prokhor and I needed to put together a plan of clearings, so we wouldn't waste time. I planned to clear between seven and ten foci per week, but I needed to understand whether Purgatory's license would allow us to do that, or if we had to raise our level to perform such mass clearings. If we did need to raise our level, this, too, would mean more expenses.

At last, we reached our destination. Leaving Ignatius to wait in the car, I went into the building, and headed straight for Prokhor's office. The young woman at the counter tried to stop me: "Stop! Where are you going? Director Kalinin is very busy right now. Please wait here." I just waved her away. I was going to have to have a talk with Prokhor for not having explained yet to his employees that they were not to get in my way. She wouldn't leave off, and tried to physically block my path by standing in the middle of the hallway.

You shouldn't hit women under any circumstances. If she's an enemy, it's better to kill her right away. But using brute force on a woman is out of the question. I had to press lightly on the nerve node near her shoulder, which made her completely paralyzed. She could only move her eyeballs. I picked her up, moved her to one side, and continued on my way.

Having reached the hallway where Prokhor's office was, I realized why the young woman had so insistently tried to keep me from going in there. From behind the door, I could hear a discussion taking place in raised voices and emotional tones. Occasionally, the two interlocutors would yell. But I couldn't tell yet what the issue was. The men were accusing each other of something, but I couldn't hear anything specific. Only when I was right by the door was I able to make out what they were saying: "Prokhor, you have to accept this offer. Or else, you'll go bankrupt, and you'll take all of us down with you!"

Chapter 22

I SHRUGGED AND WALKED into the office. I certainly wasn't going to stand around outside the door, eavesdropping — if the argument concerned me, I would find out directly — and I wasn't planning on waiting for them to finish, either.

I used to have an aunt named Lucilia, who loved to argue. Once she was embroiled in a verbal dispute, horses couldn't drag her away. She could spend all day arguing with someone. One time, she got so riled up fighting with a tax inspector from the prince's treasury, that the poor guy died of a heart attack. Aunt Lucilia raised him again as a revenant, "because I wasn't finished giving him a piece of my mind yet," as she said. By the way, she was such a talented necromancer that it was a whole month before the inspector's colleagues realized there was anything wrong with him.

I wasn't interested in finding out whether Prokhor and his interlocutor were like her in this respect. If they wanted to continue fighting, they could do so after I left.

Inside Prokhor's office, in addition to him, I found a middle-aged man I didn't know. It was clear he wasn't one of Prokhor's soldiers. He was so fat and pudgy, a mid-sized dog could knock him off his feet, never mind a focus monster.

As soon as he saw me, he screamed, "Who are you and how did you get in here? Can't you see we're busy?!"

I raised my eyebrow, and Prokhor intervened. "He's here to see me," he said, gently guiding the fat guy toward the door. "He's a VIP guest. Let's talk later." The yappy fat guy tried to keep fighting for a while, but Prokhor got him out the door.

"Sorry about that," Prokhor said to me. "That was my CFO. CFOs are rarely pleased." He was trying to joke, but his smile was not a very happy one. I could see he was worried about something. The fragment of their conversation I had overheard hinted directly at this, too. But I wasn't in a hurry to pry. It was none of my business. If he couldn't handle the problem himself, and came to the leader of his clan — me — for help, that would be another thing. Then, I would get involved.

I cut right to the chase. I wanted to know more about Purgatory and its capabilities: the number of people serving, and the property the organization owned. I had very serious plans for

Prokhor's company.

"Follow me, I'll show you everything," Prokhor answered readily. It seemed he welcomed giving me a tour as it would take his mind off of some dark things.

We exited his office, and went back down the hallway the same way I had come.

"We only have a few offices here," he told me. "We don't need many employees here — just the finance department, basically. The soldiers don't hang out here. And then there's..." he suddenly stopped speaking, and I caught his eyes. The annoying young woman from the entrance was still standing there, where I had put her. To my mind, she was much more useful as a statue. "Ellie?" Prokhor said, dumbfounded. "What's wrong with you?"

She couldn't answer, so I answered for her: "She's fine. The young woman was acting very aggressively, so I decided to give her a time-out to calm down and think about her behavior."

Prokhor's face displayed a mix of surprise and embarrassment. "Can you bring her back?" he asked. "Like she was before?"

"Are you sure?" I said. "She wasn't that great to begin with. You want her to start attacking people again? What if she bites someone?"

"No," he shook his head, "she won't. Bite anyone, I mean. I'll talk to her."

She would have come back to herself in a couple of hours as it was, but since he was asking... I touched the young woman, and she immediately started yelling at me in outrage. "You!" But, catching my gaze, she quickly stopped herself, and instead turned to Prokhor. "I've had enough! I quit!"

Prokhor took this pretty calmly, just making a "so be it" gesture with his hands. After she ran away, he explained: "She's the CFO's niece. I took her in out of friendship. But this isn't the first complaint we've had about her. I've wanted to fire her for a long time, I just didn't have a reason."

I shrugged, thinking that being uppity must run in her and the CFO's family.

We came outside, and quickly found ourselves in the backyard. There were several other structures back there. The first one Prokhor took me to turned out to be an arms warehouse. It wasn't too big, but I could see that Prokhor was proud of it.

"We've got the best armaments of all the clearing companies at our level," he said proudly. "My old army buddy went on to continue his military career, and I was able to get a full-grade military stockpile through him. Weapons, armor, ammo — everything." He made an "all this" gesture with his arms.

I took a walk around the room, studying each item with curiosity. So far, I had only held handguns, but I had seen other firearms, including in the hands of Prokhor and his guys.

"These aren't the latest models, of course," Prokhor added, "but they're tested and true — reliable machines from long-term storage warehouses. We got them brand new."

I nodded and continued the inspection.

Some of the weapons here looked very menacing indeed. I became interested in one of the cannons — it was almost as tall as me, and its barrel was obviously over six feet long. In my time, only catapults could be this big. And, like a catapult, this weapon had to be dragged along the ground, so it was affixed to a heavy-duty cart with large wheels.

"That's a Manticore — a stationary machine gun," Prokhor explained. "Sixteen millimeter caliber. There's no point taking it along to clear foci below beta level, but it tears fatties and larger monsters to pieces."

"Caliber — that's the size of the ammunition?" I asked.

"Yes. Look," he opened a box next to the machine gun, and took out an oblong metal thing the size of the palm of my hand, which positively reeked of abomination. "This is a cartridge. A magazine contains twenty of these." He showed me the magazine, too, and also explained the general principle of how the weapon worked.

The fact that the ungifted had raised themselves to this level of fire power was truly impressive. Truth be told, just the handguns alone were enough to wreak havoc on your average weak magician. And these things here, well, they truly commanded respect.

A thing like this could overload and break even an executor magician's shield. If you could find an executor stupid enough to stand there and not move as you shot him, that is.

I was interested in the weapons of the

ungifted, not only in order to find a way of combating them, but also to figure out how to use them for my own purposes. A regular wraith could operate one of these things — stand there and load it over and over. And if I had a whole army of those?

I also examined some other weapons, non-stationary this time. Prokhor kept firing off different terms: rifles, shotguns, semi-automatic, machine guns, grenade launchers, automatic handguns, revolvers... He was a real gun nut.

Humanity really had come a long way in developing ways to kill each other. The more I learned, the more convinced I was that I needed to make these advances of science work for me.

"You said this was a machine gun, too," I nodded toward one of the weapons, "but a handheld one. Is there a place here where I can try it out?"

"Of course," Prokhor smiled widely. "It's a Gryphon handheld nine-millimeter machine gun. It carries a round magazine with fifty cartridges." He took the gun off the wall, and brought me into the adjacent room — a long hall with a wide partition right near the entrance, and various targets at the other end. Prokhor retrieved some headphones from a locker hanging on the wall nearby, and tossed one of them to me. "That's so you don't go deaf," he said.

That was interesting. I hadn't thought handguns were that loud, but I guessed larger weapons had certain disadvantages. Indeed, when I shot a few rounds at one of the targets, I could hear the din of the machine gun even through my headphones.

It was not difficult at all to hit the target. I never had any problems with accuracy of aim. All my bullets hit the head of one of the target monsters directly. Prokhor gave a whistle. "Is this really your first time shooting?"

"From a machine gun, yes," I responded, "but I've shot a handgun once."

"So this is your second try?"

"Yup."

He snorted. "Is there anything you're not this good at? I thought at least in shooting I would have an edge on you."

"Don't even try to compete with me," I said. I wasn't bragging, I was just stating a fact. "It'll only make you upset for nothing. You'd do much better to concentrate on what's really important. Besides, I was planning in any case to take a few lessons from you. I want to understand better how modern weapons work. How to reload them, and other specifics."

Of course, I could do just fine without knowing these things. But I've always been naturally curious. And besides, I was determined to arm at least one battalion of wraiths with firearms, which meant I would need to understand how they worked.

Just out of curiosity, I tried a few more types of weapons. I was especially interested in the sniper rifle, but just the firing range alone didn't have enough space to properly evaluate it. This weapon was supposed to be able to hit a target at a truly impressive distance. Not every battle magician was capable of such accuracy.

After we were done with the arsenal and shooting range, we went back outside, and this time, Prokhor took me into the garage. It was pretty spacious, by the way.

And very clean. As were the cars housed in it. There were three of them — two all-terrain vehicles, and one big truck.

"That's the Wild Boar," Prokhor said, putting his hand on one of the jeeps. "It's absolutely essential for traversing uncharted territory. You can even drive it through quicksand without getting stuck."

"I remember that one, you drove it to my focus."

"Yes," he said, moving to the second off-roader. "And this is the Buffalo," he said proudly. "I had to fight tooth and nail to snag it at an army surplus auction. It's a reinforced all-terrain minibus, unique in its class. It can carry up to forty soldiers, it's fully armored, and has reinforced engine protection. Prokhor walked around to the side of it and called me over, pointing out the openings right under the windows, which were closed now. "Those," he thought for a second, "are sort of like arrow slits — I figure you're familiar with those. The barrels of weapons come out of here — machine guns, for example — and the soldiers can shoot right from the bus."

"Convenient," I affirmed.

Prokhor affectionately patted the vehicle's hood, and moved on to the powerful automobile with a booth behind the cab. "And this is the cornerstone of our whole operation. You've seen this one, too — we used it to bring the equipment to the focus. It has a very powerful battery, which powers our air cleansing machine, and the refrigerators for perishable ingredients."

"All of that is inside?"

"Yeah. Want to see?"

I did want to see, but I could not yet be sure I wouldn't break it by instantaneously sucking the abomination out of it, so I decided not to risk it.

Prokhor suddenly appeared downtrodden. "Too bad it's all leased, and soon the bank will impound all the equipment. We met at a bad time," he sighed. "You must have expected to clear foci together. I did, too. Just yesterday, I still thought we would make it, but it looks like it's not going to happen. I'm bankrupt."

That didn't sound very good to me. Then again, people often exaggerate their problems, especially when they fail to account for me in their calculations. "Let's go have some coffee," I said to him in a tone that would abide no protest, "and you'll tell me everything."

Five minutes later, we were at a coffeehouse I had noticed on the opposite side of the street. I asked them to seat us at the most remote table, where no one would interfere with our conversation.

Prokhor began the story from afar. "Before I talk about my problem, I need to explain to you how the system of clearing foci works in general."

"Of course," I agreed, enjoying a huge cup of cappuccino with frothy foam. It even had a little flower drawn on it, can you imagine! For me, coffee was, without a doubt, the saving grace of modernity.

"Most foci are distributed among the clans," Prokhor explained, smelling his cup. It seemed to me he would have very much enjoyed a large glass of whisky right about now. "But the weak ones, or ones that the clans didn't like for one reason or another, are auctioned off to private proprietors."

"Auction?" I asked in surprise. "You pay to clear foci?"

"Exactly," Prokhor nodded. "Cleansers make bids for an 'assurance fee.' Whoever offers the biggest one gets the rights to clear the focus. So, you can't just go to any focus you want whenever you feel like it. You'll get caught right away, and be lucky if you get away with just a fine."

I nodded. It was an obvious thing — in the modern world, where a whole lot of stuff was powered by abomination, it was natural for the clans to want to keep the best pieces for themselves.

Prokhor continued, "After clearing a focus, cleanser companies have to forfeit the insurance fee to the treasury, and they keep the rest. Well..." he drummed on the desk with his fingers, "minus salaries, equipment maintenance, ammo, and so on. People often think we're rolling in dough here because gemstones are very expensive. But the truth is, about a third of the time, we barely break even. Half the time, we make a tiny profit. Only five percent or so of cases brings us any kind of real income." He sipped his coffee, then added, "And sometimes, a company will go into the red on an outing. For example, say a company pledges a large assurance fee, and the focus turns out to be a dud. Or, suppose you aren't able to clear the focus in the allotted time. No one gives a shit — you have exactly a month, no more, no less. If you don't make it, you have to pay the assurance fee in full, out-of-pocket, and the focus goes back on sale."

"So your problem arises out of this structure you're explaining to me?" I asked.

Prokhor sighed heavily. "Yes, I really got in deep. It all began with a lot of promise. We won the tender to clear a gamma-class focus. This was a big contract for us, but at the same time it was the last level we are capable of clearing. After this level, it immediately gets much harder, and Purgatory doesn't have enough people, equipment, or skills for that."

"And something went wrong," I was pulling teeth with this guy.

"Exactly," he hung his head. "The focus was in the process of transitioning to delta-level. We didn't know that till we were already there. Even though we used literally every bit of fire power Purgatory had... I told you we had two battalions of soldiers — the operative word being 'had,' with twenty people in each." Prokhor gave another heavy sigh and took another sip. "Damn, I should have ordered something stronger," he shook his head. "Basically, we failed. That focus wiped the floor with us, and we lost four guys. Seven others were hospitalized, and I don't know if they'll recover. Naturally, giving it another try is out of the question."

"So you decided to recoup the assurance fee by taking a bunch of small foci?"

Prokhor nodded. "I knew we'd have to pay a huge fee no matter what at this point, but we still had enough strength to try to minimize the damage. We even managed to clear a few alpha-class foci and made a small profit. Then, you cleared one more by yourself." He fell silent.

"But?"

"But, our credit rating with the bank fell because of the failure in the large focus, and they demanded that we pay for the equipment early." Prokhor was staring at the table, forcing himself to continue the story. "Then, this morning, several soldiers quit Purgatory. They said they no longer trusted a commander who had put people in harm's way. They believe I move too fast and clear alphas without appropriate preparation. I can't blame them, but now I stand no chance of getting out of this debt at all."

"When is the deadline to clear the gamma?"

"Tomorrow," he said darkly.

"So you still have the right to hunt there?"

"Yeah, but what can be done in one day?"

These descendants and their defeatist attitude. I wasn't accustomed to throwing away assets through simple negligence like they apparently were. And I naturally thought of Purgatory, which belonged to my servant, as clan property.

"We still have plenty of time," I said, calling over a pretty waitress. The coffee here was absolutely excellent, and I definitely needed more than one cup.

"What do you mean?" Prokhor asked, confused.

"Call your technicians, and all the others," I said. "We're going to clear that focus today."

end of Book One

Want to be the first to know about our latest LitRPG, sci fi and fantasy titles from your favorite authors?

Subscribe to our **New Releases** newsletter:
http://eepurl.com/b7niIL

Thank you for reading *The Dark Healer!*
If you like what you've read, check out other sci-fi, fantasy and LitRPG novels published by Magic Dome Books:

NEW RELEASES!

Crossroads of Oblivion
a portal progression fantasy adventure series
by Dem Mikhailov

Gakko Academy
a portal progression fantasy adventure series
by Evgeny Alexeev

War Eternal
a military space adventure LitRPG series
by Yuri Vinokuroff

The Hunter's Code
a LitRPG series by Yuri Vinokuroff & Oleg Sapphire

The Order of Architects
a portal progression series
by Yuri Vinokuroff & Oleg Sapphire

I Will Be Emperor
a space adventure progression fantasy series
by Yuri Vinokuroff

An Ideal World for a Sociopath
a LitRPG series by Oleg Sapphire

The Healer's Way
a LitRPG series by Oleg Sapphire & Alexey Kovtunov

A Shelter in Spacetime
a LitRPG series by Dmitry Dornichev

The Village
a LitRPG progression fantasy series
by Dmitry Dornichev & Alexey Kovtunov

The Dark Healer
a historical progression fantasy series
by Alex Toxic & Nadya Lee

Ghost in the System
An apocalypse LitRPG series by Alexey Kovtunov

The Last Portal Jumper
a LitRPG series by Konstantin Zubov

Lord of the System
a LitRPG progression fantasy series by
Alex Toxic and Furious Miki

Kill to Live
a LitRPG progression fantasy adventure series
by George Bor and Yuri Vinokuroff

Kill or Die
a LitRPG series by Alex Toxic

The Strongest Student
a portal progression action fantasy series
by Andrei Tkachev

Living Ice
a portal progression alternative history series
by Dmitry Sheleg

Law of the Jungle
a Wuxia Progression Fantasy Adventure Series
By Vasily Mahanenko

Reality Benders
a LitRPG series by Michael Atamanov

The Dark Herbalist
a LitRPG series by Michael Atamanov

Perimeter Defense
a LitRPG series by Michael Atamanov

League of Losers
a LitRPG series by Michael Atamanov

Chaos' Game
a LitRPG series by Alexey Svadkovsky

The Way of the Shaman
a LitRPG series by Vasily Mahanenko

Level Up
a LitRPG series by Dan Sugralinov

Level Up: The Knockout
a LitRPG series by Dan Sugralinov and Max Lagno

Adam Online
a LitRPG Series by Max Lagno

World 99
a LitRPG series by Dan Sugralinov

Disgardium
a LitRPG series by Dan Sugralinov

Nullform
a RealRPG Series by Dem Mikhailov

Clan Dominance: The Sleepless Ones
a LitRPG series by Dem Mikhailov

Heroes of the Final Frontier
a LitRPG series by Dem Mikhailov

The Crow Cycle
a LitRPG series by Dem Mikhailov

Interworld Network
a LitRPG series by Dmitry Bilik

Rogue Merchant
a LitRPG series by Roman Prokofiev

Project Stellar
a LitRPG series by Roman Prokofiev

In the System
a LitRPG series by Petr Zhgulyov

The Crow Cycle
a LitRPG series by Dem Mikhailov

Unfrozen
a LitRPG series by Anton Tekshin

The Neuro
a LitRPG series by Andrei Livadny

Phantom Server
a LitRPG series by Andrei Livadny

Respawn Trials
a LitRPG series by Andrei Livadny

The Expansion (The History of the Galaxy)
a Space Exploration Saga by A. Livadny

The Range
a LitRPG series by Yuri Ulengov

Point Apocalypse
a near-future action thriller by Alex Bobl

Moskau
a dystopian thriller by G. Zotov

El Diablo
a supernatural thriller by G.Zotov

Mirror World
a LitRPG series by Alexey Osadchuk

Underdog
a LitRPG series by Alexey Osadchuk

Last Life
a Progression Fantasy series by Alexey Osadchuk

Alpha Rome
a LitRPG series by Ros Per

An NPC's Path
a LitRPG series by Pavel Kornev

Fantasia
a LitRPG series by Simon Vale

The Sublime Electricity
a steampunk series by Pavel Kornev

Small Unit Tactics
a LitRPG series by Alexander Romanov

Black Centurion
a LitRPG standalone by Alexander Romanov

Rorkh
A LitRPG Series by Vova Bo

Thunder Rumbles Twice
A Wuxia Series by V. Kriptonov & M. Bachurova

Citadel World
a sci fi series by Kir Lukovkin

You're in Game!
LitRPG Stories from Our Bestselling Authors

You're in Game-2!
More LitRPG stories set in your favorite worlds

The Fairy Code
a Romantic Fantasy series by Kaitlyn Weiss

The Charmed Fjords
a Romantic Fantasy series by Marina Surzhevskaya

More books and series are coming out soon!

In order to have new books of the series translated faster, we need your help and support! Please consider leaving a review or spread the word by recommending *The Dark Healer* to your friends and posting the link on social media. The more people buy the book, the sooner we'll be able to make new translations available.

Thank you!

Till next time!